The Opposite of Romantic

The Opposite of Romantic

A Belle Époque Novel

MELINDA COPP

TINY PIANO
PRESS

Book Cover Design and Illustration by LA Villavicencio

FIC027200   FICTION / Romance / Historical / 20th Century
FIC027460   FICTION / Romance / Historical / Gilded Age

First edition: August 2025

ISBN: 978-1-964546-04-9

LCCN: 2025916471

For Matthew.

Love is an incurable malady.

Marcel Proust

Chapter One

July 1901

They say Paris is a romantic city, but I wouldn't have noticed. I was determined to make something of myself. Not a wife. Not a mistress. But a professional, serious woman. A respected journalist. That's all I thought about. Work. Getting better at it. Achieving more as a result. I must have been born this way. Even as a child, I was always keeping a journal filled with notes and observations. A record of days passed in our house. Commentaries. Stories I'd heard at school or from friends. Gossip. Then, not long after I arrived at the Saint Genevieve Maison des Filles Immaculeés, I unearthed that dusty printing machine from the storage room. A tabletop hand press; fully functional, it turned out, and capable of printing ten lines of text on a quarter of a sheet of letter paper. Someone had donated it to the orphanage, and even though I was supposed to be cleaning the store room as punishment for slapping one of the other girls, Sister Clothilde said I was welcome to the machine. Perhaps that was when my fate was sealed. I was founding editor and lead reporter of the orphanage's premier news pamphlet in less than a week. Most of the other girls were more interested in mending and baking, but they enjoyed reading my publication. When I left years later, Sister Clothilde said I could take the printing press with me. But I declined; it could spark something in another girl someday. Sister Clothilde, working some connection or other within the world of Catholicism, secured me a job in the administrative pool at *L'Entreprise* newspaper. My career in the booming field of French journalism had been on an upward trajectory ever since. Romance—especially the kind that involved men—was the furthest thing from my mind.

The day everything changed began like any other. I was living at a women's pension on Rue de Fortuny owned by a stern but fair widow named Madame Tremblay. After waking at six, some reading in bed, and my morning toilette, I ate a breakfast of berries and baguette with my housemates and Madame. Then headed out for work. My blue bicycle—my transportation, my freedom—stood waiting in the little yard behind the house like a trusty steed, only better because I didn't have to clean up after it. Granted, horses, I'm told, have personalities that make them fun. I was more of a cat person. But that bicycle, purchased with my first paycheck, was my most cherished possession. I tucked my skirt in the elaborate way necessary to ride, took off pedaling, and felt, for those few minutes it took to get to the newspaper, like I could do anything. Anything!

The offices of *L'Entreprise* resided in an old bank building on Boulevard Haussman. It had an imposing facade and dominant half pillars, like an institution. There was a sense of mission and duty, particularly in the departments that covered the government and financial news. Our culture and lifestyle section took great pride in our rigorous critique and wise commentary. I rode past the front entrance, down the side street, and parked my bike next to the delivery bay, concerned only with the story I'd been working through in my head all morning.

I entered the building through the staff entrance in the back, greeting the doorman as I passed. My heels clicked with each step across the polished lobby floor, past the stately reception desk, and up the curved green marble staircase to the newsroom. The outer edges of the vast upstairs were lined with offices, and the center of the room, where I and the other reporters and assistants worked, was the pen—not the kind that's mightier than the sword, but the kind where animals are kept. Most of us preferred to think of our collective efforts as the former. I, for one, behaved that way.

My career was my life raft out of the precarity that had characterized most of my twenty-four years. Losing both parents made me acutely aware of the need to be my own stability; career was a huge part of that. Security, but also respect. I was on a mission to prove myself with my compelling words and stellar reporting. I wanted to be taken seriously.

I nodded and greeted my coworkers as I passed them, smiling with pride. I had been here four years already. I spent six months as an assistant to the culture editor, but after proving my worth as a writer, he agreed to let me work as a reporter. The only woman reporter at the paper. I wasn't just making my way to the desk I'd use to type my story, I was taking my place within the institution.

I removed my jacket, hung it from the back of my chair, and sat down to work. I had been pulling together the threads of a trend piece on summer theater and planned to spend a few hours drafting up everything I had. The typewriter in front of me sat quiet on the scuffed wooden desk. I breathed in deep. The louvered windows along the top of the exterior walls had been tilted open to keep the warm, summer air moving through the massive room. The faint, sour aroma of the city and the commotion of carriage traffic on the street below carried with it. I removed a stack of pocket notebooks from my black leather work bag. I untied the grosgrain ribbon I'd fastened them with that morning, and spread them out of the desk in a satisfying row. Five little notebooks, bound in thread and covered with kraft cardstock, all filled with my careful notes. I delighted in the tactile pleasure of my work for a quick moment before restacking the notebooks into a neat pile save for one, which I opened to the first page and propped open with the stapler. Then I settled my hands over the typewriter keys and began.

But before I could finish my first sentence, the doors to the large conference room on the other side of the pen opened and all the important newspaper people—the editors and managers and board members—emerged. The way they blustered out of the room, clearly this wasn't an ordinary meeting. Red faces and glistening, creased brows. In general, I had little use for men's bluster. I tried to continue working, but the flutter of discontent spread through the newsroom. The murmured stirrings of drama moved from desk to desk. Someone gasped. What had they been meeting about?

My editor, Monsieur Olivier Paquin, his face drawn and grave, came stalking out of the conference room and crossed the pen, heading for his office. He wouldn't meet my eye, not even as he passed right by my desk. Without slowing his determined pace, he opened the door to his office, stepped through it, and closed it tight behind him. Then a bang came from behind Paquin's door. Followed shortly by a shattering crash that immediately brought to mind the gorgeous blue glass vase that sat on his bookshelf. His assistant, Marie, always made sure it was filled with flowers. Daffodils in spring and evergreen branches in winter. Just yesterday she'd come in with a lush bundle of white irises. If Paquin had broken that vase, those flowers would be scattered all over the floor. Poor Marie would probably have to clean them up.

Then the managing editor—Monsieur Lapin, my boss's boss —called for attention from the far side of the pen. I turned in my swivel chair. A few of the other reporters got up and moved closer. Monsieur Lapin cleared his throat and swept the crowd with his gaze.

"There's no easy way to say it." As he spoke, his brow furrowed. Whatever news he had to deliver was clearly troubling him. "The paper has been purchased by *L'Etoile*. Effective immediately, we are merging *L'Entreprise* and *L'Etoile* into one publication."

Swears erupted, followed by utterances about them eating us alive and the ridiculousness of the notion.

"Their newsroom is smaller than ours, and so they're moving in with us. They've got movers starting today on the other office." Lapin shrugged, the words as baffling to him as they were to us. "But the full transition will likely take weeks to sort out."

Several of my coworkers shouted questions. What did this mean for our paper? What about our jobs? Lapin repeated several times that he knew little, only having just learned himself. There would be more information to come, but changes were imminent.

Paquin considered *L'Etoile* our direct competitor, and so I read it every day. It was one of those papers that some rich financier started to serve as a mouthpiece for touting his own interests. But it had grown from that into something credible enough. They had admirable writers. Unfortunately, they also had a culture and lifestyle section made up of my professional foes. They were the ones I'd been implored day after day to beat, to scoop, to outsell. There was no way I could work with those people. Never.

"They have a sports reporter," the sports and leisure writer said, echoing my thoughts.

"Yes. A real star," Lapin said without malice or appreciation. "They have a managing editor too. They already have a full staff."

"So everyone's on the chopping block is what you're saying?" Someone shouted from the other side of the pen.

Lapin raised his hands in surrender. "This isn't the best of news for any of us. But yes. I'm not exactly sure what will happen. The plan is to combine the two publications so that the paper will be bigger. We will have a bigger readership. But perhaps not big enough that everyone keeps his job."

We stayed gathered there for over an hour. Talking through our questions, considering our options, standing in solidarity together.

The news was bewildering. The life I'd spent years building now hung in peril. I'd worked so hard for so long in an institution that I assumed would stay the same and continue to reward me for my dedication. I never imagined that a change so dramatic and potentially life-altering could sneak up on me like this, nowhere in sight one day and then crashing through the door the next. It wasn't fair. One paper couldn't just buy another and dismantle it for parts. Could it? It didn't seem like that should be allowed.

When we'd all said everything we could, we made our way back to our desks and got on with the work of the day. I typed up my notes, and made a half-hearted list of places I needed to stop and people I needed to talk to for this and other stories I was working on. Then I bundled up my notebooks and my fresh draft, and I left my desk, heading back down the staircase.

As I crossed the lobby, a group of determined and sure men were coming in through the front doors. They all looked vaguely familiar, though none were from *L'Entreprise*. Vaguely familiar because most of my coworkers were men just like these ones. Hired into the same position as me without having to prove themselves serving coffee. They usually had an uncle in an office somewhere, pulling strings on their behalf. Or they were sleeping with someone whose husband was unwittingly helping him along under his wife's sly influence. Arrogant in writing and in person. Smart, but not smarter than me.

Then there he was: Benoit Levin. All of those clichés about men in the news business combined. The man whose job title at *L'Etoile* was senior culture reporter, the same as mine. Seeing his name in the newspaper every week never prepared me for seeing him in person, which thankfully had only happened a few times. He was tall, taller than me, with neatly trimmed light brown hair and a thin mustache that punctuated his perfect mouth. He was probably in his mid-thirties. And he had these inquisitive, mocking blue eyes like he was a step ahead of me. He was always plainly and impeccably dressed, and he moved easily in the company of all the right people. Handsome in a sophisticated, mildly rugged way. I knew him all right.

The first time we met, I was backstage at the Comédie Française in the flurry of activity that happened after the show. Nadine, one of my housemates at the women's pension, had just signed her contract with them to be an understudy. I was also a relatively new reporter then, and I needed connections in the business. Nadine was thrilled to introduce me around. She helped me secure press credentials. One of her contractual duties was attending the afterparties and mingling with the important theater investors and distinguished guests. If I could make friends with these people, they'd talk to me and tell me things they perhaps shouldn't. Building relationships like this took time, and I was so grateful to Nadine for helping me even though she was new at Comédie Française too.

Although I liked writing and researching and asking questions, I lacked an outgoing nature. I much preferred to observe rather than mingle. Nadine had no problem with this; she was like a magnet for attention. She introduced me to the theater promoter, who took my card and promised to add me to his list of press contacts. She introduced me to several of her fellow understudy performers, who were happy to talk about themselves. And she pointed out the wealthy patrons, who were mingling in close company with the biggest stars. I remember being dazzled by the atmosphere. Comédie Française was a state theater and the fanciest place that I'd ever seen behind the scenes. But by far, the most memorable person I met that night was Benoit Levin.

Even in a room with all those big personalities, he drew my awareness. A wide, full smile that he suspiciously offered to everyone. I noticed him because he was noticing me in a way that made me uneasy. I didn't know who he was. The woman he was standing next to—one of the actresses—was gazing up at him dreamily and twirling a lock of her blonde hair. All evening, I ignored his glances. And then, toward the end of the reception, they were there in front of Nadine and me.

"Mademoiselle Nadine Duval," the pretty blonde actress said, "I want to introduce you to Monsieur Benoit Levin. He writes for *L'Etoile*."

"Oh, do you?" Nadine said while he kissed her hand. "Enchanté. I'm the newest understudy actress."

My gut sank while they spoke. I knew that name. Rather, I knew that byline. I had read his work, and Benoit Levin also had a reputation. *L'Etoile* had made a big fuss over hiring him—the esteemed, traveling correspondent whose work had thrilled readers in many prestigious publications was making *L'Etoile* and Paris his permanent home. Needless to say, *L'Entreprise* didn't make any sort of announcement when they moved me up to the culture pages. They'd lectured me on the importance of a woman having a pseudonym to protect her propriety and reputation, which was dumb. But Benoit Levin was reason for a headline. I hated him immediately. His handsome face and charming presence I found most repellant.

"And this is my housemate, Vanessa Marnet." Nadine smiled, unaware. "She's a reporter too."

"You are?" He turned his attention to me, extending a hand and holding it aloft while waiting for me to give him mine. I did not.

"I'm Vanessa Marnet. I write for *L'Entreprise*."

"Really?" He reappraised me. "Are you V. Marnet?"

"I am."

"I recognize your name. It's a pleasure to meet you."

This satisfied me greatly. I still didn't give him my hand. "Is it always a pleasure to meet your competition?"

"Not always." He surveyed me from head to toe in that way some men felt they had the right to do. "But this time it is."

I rolled my eyes. "A pleasure that is now coming to an end. Au revoir."

I turned away from him, touching Nadine's shoulder to get her attention. She was chatting with the blonde actress now. But we'd agreed to leave the theater together and share a carriage back to the house. "Are you ready?"

"I am. Give me a minute to say goodbye to the director?"

"Okay." As she walked away, I was left alone with Monsieur Levin, who was still standing there, watching me. I needed to find somewhere else to wait. Before he could speak, I said, "Please excuse me."

"I liked your story about cabaret culture."

"You read it?" Because I'm cursed with vanity, I took his obvious conversational bait. Instead of twirling a finger in my hair like a mindless girl, I crossed my arms over my chest.

"I always read all the papers. Keeping an eye on my colleagues, or competition, as you call it."

"What did you like about it?" I asked only because I thought I could catch him fibbing.

"The article? I liked the way you set the scene. You have a knack for using detail to paint the picture." He didn't even have to think about his answer. "Like the one you did a few weeks ago about the art dealer. I felt like I was standing in his drawing room with you."

I admit I was flattered—anything for a little validation. "You always read my work?"

"Don't you read mine?"

"Of course." I wanted to lie, to deny him the satisfaction. But that would have made me look like an uninformed person who didn't read the papers, like I wasn't keeping up. My pulse quickened. And I was strangely no longer in such a hurry to get away.

"It is truly a thrill to meet you. I don't know many reporters from other papers outside of their work." He didn't take his eyes away from my face. "You're not what I expected from V. Marnet."

"Oh no? You're exactly what I expected," I said, summoning my bitchiness to reestablish a distance between us.

"Ha. You're beautiful and a challenge. I like that."

I gave him a bored smile. "Au revoir, monsieur."

"Wait. Do you really have to go?" There was a hint of something in his voice, a faltering of some kind. "There's a café near here; we could go have a drink and talk."

The idea struck me as ludicrous. "And then what?"

"I don't know, darling. Get to know each other. See what happens."

"Now you're being funny. You and I will never, ever see what happens in any respect." I walked away before he could tempt me with any more compliments. My skin felt hot and clammy. Very tempting indeed, that one. A woman could completely lose her head over a man like that, which was exactly why I hated him. Then and now.

If he was in this crowd swaggering into the *L'Entreprise* headquarters, then they all probably worked for *L'Etoile*, the new owner. This was when it all truly sank in for me. Everything I'd worked so hard for was now at risk. The hostile takeover was beginning.

I turned instinctively to avoid them, as if they were a pack of wolves. But as I moved away, his gaze caught mine. He lifted a perfectly arched eyebrow and smiled devilishly. I scowled and stalked off.

A buyout of my workplace would have been bad enough. But certainly whatever came of this merger would not be big enough for two senior culture reporters. Him and me. There was no way.

Him of all people! To be honest, I knew little about Benoit Levin outside of his work. Aside from that first interaction, I'd only seen him around a few times. We'd acknowledged each other in passing. But he was still the object of my professional rivalry. I read all his stories, skin prickling with a desirous disgust. His attractiveness only made him worse, more of a force to be reckoned with. Something about him—many things —stoked a rivalry that, for all I knew, didn't exist in his life. He probably didn't think about me at all.

Perhaps most infuriating was that his work was so well-liked. He'd traveled to the Far East and published stunning and well-respected stories about the people he met and the food he ate. He probably lived on some generous inheritance that allowed him a lavish life of travel and intrigue. It had caused a big stir in our newsroom when he started at *L'Etoile*. People speculated about why he'd take a job that kept him in Paris. Why he'd settle for a less exciting subject matter and lifestyle. How long he'd last. And everybody loved his stories. His smart takes and keen eye for emerging trends. Other writers talked about whatever he wrote about. Everybody cared about what he had to say. Everyone raved about his talent. I got raves too, but not like he did.

And now here he was, walking into my place, merging. This was not a reality I was prepared to face.

I had never been so grateful for the ability to pedal off tension. I rode as fast as I could across the ninth, up Rue de Rome, passing the tall wooden fence separating the road from the subway construction, and then left on the tree-lined Boulevard des Batignolles. I pumped my legs and wove through traffic like I was being chased. By the time I was home, the realization had fully settled over me: everything was going to change and there was no way to tell how.

I parked my bike under the ledge and clicked my tongue a few times to see if the tuxedo cat that hung around the carriage house would come say bonjour. We had cats come and go from time to time, most of them just passing through. This little beauty, with big green eyes and white mittens on her paws, had been here for weeks. She came around the corner then, rubbing her chin on the door frame because, while she was curious, she was not usually eager.

"There you are, pretty kitty." We had cats at the orphanage, long elegant things that grew fat and lazy off our food scraps. They kept the rats at bay and all had little personalities. Some were so scared they'd never let us close; others, like this one, could be friendly. When she'd had enough coaxing, she trotted up and extended her nose to my skirt. I bent down to rub her behind her velvety ear, and she cocked her head and pressed into my hand. She meowed and purred and let me scratch her shoulders and run my hand down her back to the tip of her tail.

She dropped then and rolled onto her side, gazing up at me. While tempted to bury my fingers in her soft belly fur, I knew better than to push my luck. She could turn from sweet and inviting to ready to kill in an instant. Every time I tried to pick her up, she turned into a furious ball of fluff and claws that didn't stop swiping at me until I put her down again. She followed me to the door, and I let her into the kitchen. Soft heart that she was, Cook had started keeping a bowl for kitchen scraps just for the kitty, who was less and less of a stray every day.

"Bonjour, Cook."

"Bonjour, dear." She was stirring something on the stove that smelled herby and divine. The cat whizzed past her skirt. "Ah. There she is. I saved you some chicken, kitty."

The cat trotted straight for her bowl like she owned the place, while I stole a berry from a colander on the counter and headed upstairs.

Madame Tremblay inherited the house from her husband when he died, and having no children, she opened the place up to renters. There were five of us—respectable, professional women.

I passed the first floor, where there was a wide hallway, the dining room where we all ate, and the drawing room with the arched set of glass doors that connected the pension side of the house with Madame Tremblay's personal quarters. The next floor up was where the American sisters Diane and Catherine lived. Across from that was a small parlor where we often gathered in the evenings, especially after Madame had gone to bed. I continued up to the top floor where my room was one of three. Nadine had lived here longer than anyone else; her room was next door to mine. She was practically a daughter to Madame, though we were all practically that to some degree. Charlotte, the up and coming literary writer, was on the other side. I didn't know her well, as she'd only just moved in two months before. No one seemed to be around.

In my room, I slipped off my shoes, removed my hat, and then let down my hair. The latest copy of *L'Etoile* was on the edge of my desk where I'd set it that morning. The culture section was always the first page I checked, and of course there was Benoit Levin's story, right on top. It was regrettably a good profile of Anatole France and his new novel *Monsieur Bergeret*. I'd hung on every word and then set about finding or inventing flaws so I wouldn't feel inferior. Now, I unfolded the paper and flipped back to the interior of the first page, where the masthead took up the bottom third. This was basically a list of my future coworkers. They were probably moving into the building right then, shifting things around, planning what to wreck.

L'Entreprise was a Paris fixture. An institution of France. An arm of the country's identity, the one holding the mirror. How could something like that even be sold? And what would become of it? What would become of everything I'd built for myself there? They'd bought it right out from under me.

Chapter Two

"I know him," Nadine said, pointing at me slyly.

She, Charlotte, and I were having whiskey in the small parlor after dinner that night. Diane and Catherine had family in the city and were at the Grand Hôtel with them. We were rarely all present in the evenings because of work and active social lives. But we all chipped in to keep a bottle of American whiskey on hand for whoever was here and in need of company. I sat in one of the two Louis XIV chairs and gulped down a mouthful of the fiery brown liquor. The cleansing burn left a warm calm in its wake.

Nadine was sitting in the other chair, dressed in a nightgown and silk kimono with her red hair piled on her head. "He's quite the charmer."

"He's worse than a charmer. He's a legitimate threat. He's got more experience than me. It's his bosses in charge now. And I can't see them keeping both of us."

"Are you sure? Culture pages are popular. And maybe it's too early to tell." Charlotte was perched on the settee. She was more reserved than the rest of the housemates, but she was cute also. Her prim manner and the way she'd added whiskey to her cup of tea. She was a working-class girl from the provinces who happened to get lucky and get a story published in *Le Figaro*. It wasn't even a true story. But it was one of those career-making publications that had all of Paris talking even before she got to town. It was hard not to like her, even though I was a little jealous of what looked like good fortune instead of hard work or earning it.

"I don't know anything for sure," I said. "But it feels naive to believe it's not my job or his."

"He's handsome, too," Nadine said breathily.

I took another satisfying gulp of my drink. "Oh, he's handsome all right. In a dirty, villainous sort of way. Like it should be criminal to be that good-looking and that despicable at the same time. It shouldn't be allowed. And there's a smugness to his face that I both can't stand and can't help but look at. Do you know what I mean?"

"Oh, for sure."

"And he's such a good writer that I can't stand it. I'm jealous; I know that's all it is. But it's all-consuming. Sometimes, when I read his stories, I can't get the words out of my head. Like his little turns of phrase keep coming back to my mind, pestering me constantly. When I see him, like today outside work, my skin literally burns. Like his presence stirs me in this sickening way. I absolutely can't stand him. It's like he's so perfect I want to kill him."

"Oh, that sounds quite terrible," Charlotte said in a sarcastic tone. "It sounds like you don't really want to kill him, but something else.

"What could it be?" Nadine tapped her chin mischievously.

"Well," I said, shocked when I realized what they were suggesting. It was unthinkable to consider Benoit Levin in a romantic or even friendly way. "This is not like that at all.

You've misunderstood me. I actually hate him. With a deep passion."

"Yes, I can see it's all very passionate."

"Stop, Nadine, or I might lose my dinner."

"I can't help it, Vanessa, darling." Nadine raised her glass with a kimono-fluttering flourish. "It sounds a lot like attraction to me."

The idea made me want to burst into flames. It was uncomfortable. But what was even more uncomfortable was that they'd suggest such a bizarre idea in the first place. How outrageous! There was no way the intense reaction and swirl of feelings I had about Benoit Levin were anything but negative. Very negative. The very opposite of romantic. Existing on a completely different emotional planet. "It's not funny at all. I could lose my job to him. My job that I love. He makes me redundant."

"Ooh la la," cooed Nadine. "Redundant and aroused."

She cackled with glee, and I threw one of Madame's embroidered pillows at her. "It's not funny."

It would have been funny if we'd been talking about anyone but Benoit Levin.

"I know, dear. I'm sorry. It's the booze." Nadine straightened up, thankfully. "You have to be vigilant in a situation like that. You never know what will happen. You have to fight until the battle's truly lost because he might break his leg in the next practice. Or whatever the journalist equivalent is of a career-ending injury."

"Oh!" Charlotte raised a finger. "He could sprain his wrist and not be able to type."

"Or maybe suffer a brain-wiping fever."

"Many handsome and popular men do have syphilis, you know." Charlotte delivered this suggestion with such seriousness that both Nadine's and my mouths dropped open.

Then we looked at each other and said at the same time, "He's probably got it."

I laughed so hard that my eyes filled with tears. All three of us did. By the time I was pulling myself together, my ribs ached.

"I desperately needed that laugh," I said.

"Oh, me too," Charlotte said.

"Is someone coming?" Nadine cocked her head toward the door. There were footfalls on the stairs. I was wiping my tears when Diane came in.

"Bonsoir, mademoiselle," Nadine said to her, blotting her eyes with a corner of her silky sleeve.

"I've had a horrible evening, ladies." Diane sprawled on the open half of the settee and sighed. "You have no idea how glad I am to see you."

"Tell us all about it. We're always up for a tale of woe." Charlotte raised the bottle in Diane's direction. "Care for a drink?"

"That does sound good," Diane said. She and her sister Catherine were wealthy Americans who'd come to Paris for a season and then decided not to leave. They sent their maid back home to tell their father, who promptly cut off all their money. Now both Catherine and Diane had jobs. The sisters shared that very American wild-at-heart quality, but Diane was the more flamboyant of the two.

I passed an empty tumbler from the hutch behind me. Charlotte poured two fingers and then passed the drink. She splashed some into her tea cup before setting the bottle down.

"And did you lose your sister along the way?" Charlotte asked.

"I'm starting to wonder if that wouldn't be a bad thing," Diane said. "Can you ladies keep a secret?"

We all three spoke at once.

"No!"

"Absolutely not."

"Are you crazy?"

"Well," Diane laughed. "Try this time."

Then she explained this complicated story about pretending to be engaged to one of Charlotte's aristocrat's friends that culminated in an explosive dinner at the Grand Hôtel where her family revealed that she was engaged to a boy back at home.

When Diane finished, she sighed again. "I don't know what to do now."

Charlotte, whose mouth had dropped open and hung there through the duration of Diane's story, held up her hand as soon as Diane stopped talking. "I have so many questions, Diane, about all of this. But the most pressing one is: does Madame Tremblay know you had a man in the house?"

"Not that I know of." Diane's eyes went wide in amazement at her own brazenness. "And I walked him out in broad daylight."

Madame had a strict policy against overnight guests in the pension. Definitely no men. Sneaking a man into the house undetected was remarkable, considering it sounded like she was quite drunk at the time. Diane was stupid for even risking it. But I squealed along with everyone, and briefly felt the mild sense of relief that comes from sharing our trials and tribulations with friends.

Charlotte was right. I needed to focus on my work, not the possibility of losing my job. I was used to hard work and struggle. I could be ruthless when I needed to be. I was an excellent reporter. Culture was one of our most popular sections, and I had earned my place. No need to panic yet.

When I arrived at the *L'Entreprise* building the next day, the changes had already begun. The vast bank building felt fuller and less spacious than it had always been. There were filing cabinets and desks haphazardly set in places where they didn't belong. Unfamiliar faces mixed uncomfortably with the familiar ones. Usually I was the first reporter to arrive. The others—all men, though that would change now too—didn't show up until three or four. Some of them had typewriters at home. Others had wives who did their writing for them or with them, and so they did it discreetly before coming in. Now there were new people everywhere.

In particular, the desk where I always sat was occupied. I walked towards it, gut sinking with every step as the realization dawned. Broad shoulders in shirtsleeves, a dark blue jacket slung over the back of the chair. Hair short and tidy and smoothed into place. Neck I wanted to wring. It was him. Sitting in my desk, typing away. It wasn't really my desk; the pen was a shared space. Anyone who had work to do and needed somewhere to do it could grab any open seat. But we always had enough desks that no one else ever sat in the place

I liked. Now here he was, moving in on my position and my desk. I couldn't let him get away with this.

A dangerously handsome sort. That was exactly what I thought as I crossed the room to him. Dangerously handsome. I ignored the frisson of pleasure at knowing his backside was in the chair mine knew so well. That tickling fizz of seeing his hands on my typewriter keys, which was ridiculous of me. He was invading my space even if he was lovely. So if there were any flutters, I crumpled them up and stuffed them into the fire of my contempt. I marched to the front of the desk to face him, crossing my arms and squaring my stance.

"What are you doing at my desk?" I demanded, purposefully rude. Confrontation heated me from within.

He looked up, smiling with surprise and something like delight. Then he stood, presumably because it was the mannerly thing to do when in the presence of a woman. Or perhaps, extending to his full size to make me small. "Pardon me, mademoiselle. I was told the desks are shared."

"They are. But that's where I always sit and work."

"Can you choose another one?" He looked around at the many empty desks around us, his face drawn with innocence.

"Can you?"

He smiled again, devilishly, rolling his shoulders back. And then he gestured at the room with both hands. "I work here now, you know."

"You may work here." I copied his gesture, and then placed my hands on the desk. "But I work here."

His smile faltered, and something I couldn't read passed over his face. And for a flicker of a second, I felt bad for being so mean to him.

"I'm almost done." He sat back down and returned to his work. A flush of red had risen from under his collar. "It's nice to meet you, by the way. New colleague."

"We've met, unfortunately." My heart thudded in my chest, like a quickening drum.

He looked up at me again, catching me with his eyes and raising a brow. His mustache twitched. "I know that. Just using my manners."

Now I faltered. My face and every centimeter of my skin tingled. What was it about him that flustered me like this? I was no longer clear on what I had hoped to accomplish by confronting him in this way. It was unprofessional. But I'd done it anyway because it was the only real claim I could stake here. My usual seat. And if nothing else, there would be no question about the dynamic between us. I would not be simpering or batting my eyelashes. I would not smile or concede to him. I was in this for the fight.

I turned on my heel and walked, head as high as it would go, to the furthest away open desk. I sat in a huff and then took a deep breath to collect myself.

Of course, I had anticipated that there would be confrontations like this now that my work was being taken over by an outside entity. But I certainly hadn't expect to find that Benoit Levin had beaten me to the office and my spot. I would have guessed him for the sort who never rose before noon, tumbling from this or that mistress's bed for a burning piss and drink to soften the edges. There were plenty of men in the office exactly like that. But, at least for his first morning of this collective nightmare, he seemed to have himself together. This would make him more difficult to beat, unfortunately.

I got to work, untying the ribbon on my notebooks and arranging them on the unfamiliar desk in front of me. Then I tried to pretend like he didn't exist. I ignored the hard clacks of his fingers on the typewriter keys, stifled the urge to tell him that he was hitting them too hard. Banging wasn't necessary; a light touch was sufficient. But I kept that to myself. I ignored his loud yawns. The noisy way he seemed to do everything. Even as more coworkers—familiar and not—filtered in and started making noise, Benoit Levin was the only other person in the room. More than once, I had to stop myself from staring at him as he typed away and wiggled in my seat, distracting me from what had always been a solid and productive work time. The managing editor's words from the previous day echoed through my mind: not all of us would get to keep our jobs. Determination hardened in me like a sharp stone.

The lay of the land changed dramatically over the next few days. I was no longer the only woman reporter. The new culture section editor or co-editor or whatever was a woman. But she treated Benoit Levin like the star of the show, so I wasn't sure I could trust her. And there were now two more women reporters in the newsroom. One wrote the gardening column and lifestyle pieces that usually centered on gardening or flowers. Madame Tremblay read her every week. The other woman was Algerian and probably in her thirties. She wrote international news and political commentary that was just as serious as any man's. She was truly impressive even though I'd only seen her from a distance. I was both excited about more women in the building and wary of them. We were all wary of each other. And as silly as it was, as treacherous as it made me,

I was secretly a little mad about being rendered less special now that I wasn't the only woman.

Even though *L'Etoile* took us over, they wanted to keep the name *L'Entreprise* because we'd been in print longer and held more prestige. This was satisfying, because of course we were better than them. But it was also frustrating because they had ultimately been able to buy us anyway. The newspaper itself expanded, was thicker and heavier in the hand. I didn't hate it. But every day was unpredictable.

Soon, and perhaps this was by design, people started leaving. Some were let go, and others jumped ship, finding positions at other papers or making life changes that they'd been putting off or avoiding. The politics editor was going home to Rouen to work in the family business. Two senior reporters and an assistant got jobs at *Le Figaro*. The first week, while the physical merging was taking place and their office was brought into ours, I never knew what to expect when I walked into the building. Aside from wolves circling.

The culture and lifestyle section hadn't lost anyone yet, but the two editors were sharing one office. There was a general understanding that changes were forthcoming, and they couldn't afford to keep everyone. These dramas were playing out in every department at the paper. It was a complete upheaval, and it was, frankly, miraculous that we managed to produce papers in this environment.

The tension was never more palpable than when we all crowded into the editors' office on the day of our regular section meeting. Like the rest of the old bank building, the office was spacious and grand with a substantial fireplace, bookcases, and a big couch, in addition to Paquin's wide desk.

The vase that his secretary had kept filled with flowers was now gone. And there was an extra desk set up where a small conference table used to sit.

Sharing an office had to be a nightmare, and I felt for my boss. I got mad about someone sitting in my spot; I couldn't imagine suddenly having to share an office with someone who wanted my job. Except they looked awfully cozy, standing close and talking to each other in whispers. Paquin closed the door when we were all inside, and I perched on the arm of the couch.

For a minute, everyone chattered, primarily sticking to our home camps. Even with the two teams combined, we were a small mix of news assistants and journalists. One of many smaller teams on the staff of the paper. The other paper's culture staff was smaller than ours. Without even trying, they were on one side of the room and we were on the other. But with all of us assembled, it was obvious there was overlap in coverage on many topics. And there were, even more glaringly, two bosses. It was clear that, if the new owners and whoever was making decisions these days wanted to run this business efficiently, there was room for cuts in the culture department.

And the restructuring was the primary concern.

"They let go half of sports this morning," our literary critic said to another reporter.

Across the room, someone said, "Three courts reporters left yesterday."

My coworkers were as nervous about this as I was. There was an air of suspicion in the room, in the guarded looks and lack of friendly chatter between the two groups. None of us could look each other in the eyes. When Paquin tried to draw our attention to him, he became the object of our collective uncertainty.

"So do we know who gets to stay?"

"Have they decided anything?"

The new boss—Eloise Vartre—raised her hands in a pacifying gesture. "I know you're all nervous about this. I know half of you don't trust me or know me at all. But I'm nervous too. All week, we've been watching our colleagues lose their jobs. The fact is, nothing has been decided yet for our section."

"Why not?" the literary critic said.

"Culture is our most popular section, and both publications have exceptional teams. I mean, I am thrilled to be working at the place that publishes 'Potins Culturels' every week. It's a phenomenon in itself," Vartre said. She wasn't wrong. The culture gossip column was so popular with readers that all the culture reporters loved contributing to it. "And so the owners aren't rushing to make changes here. It's the same in government. They want to combine and strengthen what both publications bring to our new *L'Entreprise*. We don't want to risk losing readers from either publication by changing up their favorite thing to read."

"They want to build upon what we collectively have," Paquin added. "And they're taking their time to make decisions it seems. As inconvenient as that is for all of us."

"So when will we know?"

"Well, they're watching, for sure. They're reading your work with great interest. And they're trying to decide what the future of the publication should look like. We're meeting with them again in a week, so I know I'm going to work very hard until then."

One of the *L'Etoile* reporters asked, "Should we start looking for other jobs?"

"Well, that's your decision, isn't it?" Paquin shrugged. He was in his shirtsleeves and looked as tired as ever.

"I, for one, am looking," Vartre said. Her dark hair, which she wore in a low bun, had come loose around her face. "Everything right now is uncertain. We're all in different positions with different demands and needs. There's no reason not to hedge your bets in a situation like this."

Hedge our bets? I rolled my eyes. Lots of eyes were rolling around that room. But Vartre wasn't exactly being unreasonable. Some people had children and families relying on them. Any gap in income could be quite troubling. Finding a new job would eliminate some of the risk.

I wasn't going to look for something else. In the worst case, I could weather the financial setback of losing my job because my father hadn't left me with nothing when he died. I had a small inheritance in investments that I tried not to touch. This was what kept me at the orphanage while other girls from poor families were usually placed with farm families who needed help with labor. Now I lived primarily off of my income as a reporter. I was paid a modest weekly salary, plus a little more per every line of text I wrote and published. But I could live without it if I lost my job. It wasn't about the money.

I had worked hard and been promoted twice—from secretary to reporter and then again to senior reporter. I had written more "Potins Culturels" than anyone besides Paquin. I had proven my worth already. Everyone had encouraged me and told me I could have an editor position if I kept at it. I had a future at *L'Entreprise*. Going to another publication, being new somewhere, especially as a woman, would likely mean starting over. I was determined to stay and fight for my rightful spot.

Leaving would make it all so much easier for the decision-makers, whoever they were. But this was another problem. A week ago, and throughout my tenure at the paper thus far, I always knew who was in charge. I knew exactly whom I had to please to get my paycheck, and I knew whom he had to please as well. Now that wasn't so clear. Not knowing whom to please made doing so all that much harder.

Across from me, Benoit Levin shifted and stretched his not unattractive arms over his head. The way his large, ink stained hand gripped his other wrist and pulled into the stretch compelled me to look away. So what if his arms were long and strong and shaped in that perfectly manly way? This made his presence all the more maddening. Of course a pompous, infuriating man like him would also be the most attractive in the whole building. I would say maybe even the whole world if I didn't dislike him so much. I had to cling to the hope that more beautiful men existed and weren't annoying.

There was some more huffing and puffing from my frustrated colleagues, and the editors continued to assuage their concerns. Then, finally, Paquin started on the regular business of what we were working on.

As reporters, we didn't bother ourselves too much with what our colleagues were working on except when we discussed our stories in these editorial meetings. It was all very perfunctory, with each person talking about what they were working on for a minute or two, taking questions and comments from the editor—two editors, now—and anyone else who had a source or insight to share in the spirit of helpfulness.

About halfway through it was my turn. Sharing my story ideas and reporting in front of all my coworkers had been intimidating at first. But I'd gotten used to it and earned the respect of everyone. Now there were more people, and some were likely judging me harshly. But my idea was solid, and I'd already started reporting it. There was no need for this meeting to be any different from the one we'd had last week just because the room was more crowded. I put the part about our jobs being at stake out of my mind.

I took a breath. "I am working on a piece about the new art charity that Marquess Montmorency and Madame Leclaire are founding. I heard from a source that the society ladies are falling all over themselves to be involved, so there's a hook for readers who like that sort of gossip, and then of course the charity aspect."

Benoit Levin's hand rose sheepishly before I'd even finished. He hadn't shared yet and had been mostly quiet throughout the meeting. So of course he'd have something to say about my idea.

As soon as I finished talking, Vartre nodded at Benoit.

He cleared his throat. "Sorry, but I am actually working on the same story."

My mouth fell open. "I've already interviewed Madame Leclaire."

Vartre looked at Paquin and then asked Benoit what he had so far.

"I've interviewed Madame Leclaire and two other women involved. I've got a draft right here." He held a sheaf of papers aloft and gave them a little shake.

"Well, since you seem to be a step ahead on this one, Levin, Marnet can give you her notes."

I knew better than to protest, but I wanted to. My jaw clenched. I had chased that interview with Madame Leclaire for three days. She'd given me names of other people to talk to. I could have done the story. But I was truly a step behind if he had a draft already. The bastard.

"What else do you have, Marnet?"

I couldn't say "nothing," but that wasn't far from the truth. "I've spent the past three days looking into the charity. So I will have to go through my notes, but I should be able to come up with something."

"Good. Just follow up with me. And meet with Levin to give him everything you've got."

I nodded and pulled my mouth into something that could, hopefully, be interpreted as a submissive smile. Benoit Levin looked at me with his eyebrows raised. He shrugged. And then he winked at me, like I was a little girl he was teasing. I looked down at my shoes peeking out from the hem of my pale gray suit. At least I was wearing my favorite suit through this utter humiliation because otherwise I was miserable. My face was so hot it had to be red. Winking, of all things, at work. I wanted to slap him. If we weren't in that stupid meeting, I would have done it.

Chapter Three

I was the first one out the door when the meeting ended. As I headed for the stairs, someone called my name. It was Benoit Levin. Of course it was. Who else would interrupt my swift getaway from the worst meeting ever.

"Wait. You forgot to give me your notes." There was sincerity in his tone, which only offended me more.

"Did I?" I didn't stop walking away, but I did slow down when I reached the grand staircase.

Regretfully, he fell into step with me. "You did."

"I have them here." I held up my black leather bag, still walking. "I'm not just going to give you my notebooks. I'll have to go through them. I can give you the notes tomorrow."

Crossing the lobby now, I headed toward the staff entrance. When I pushed open the heavy door, the dim, narrow service yard was busy with a paper delivery. Men were unloading giant rolls of newsprint from the back of a wagon. My bicycle stood against the wall behind them, waiting to carry me home.

But before I could reach it, Levin touched my arm. "You don't have to do all that work. Let me buy you a drink next door. I'll copy what you have in my own notebook."

The warmth from the touch penetrated my linen sleeve, making my blood rush. Not because I was thinking about that hand touching me in other places, but because it was the hottest part of the summer day. Regardless, it nearly caused me to spontaneously combust. I would rather burn than go anywhere with him.

At the same time, I could get this transfer of the damn notes over with. The restaurant he suggested next door was a popular place where many of my coworkers went for lunch or meetings or drinks because it was so close. The food was consistently delicious. It catered to a professional clientele. And it had ceiling fans. Electric ones that spun so fast you couldn't see the blades. I shrugged, relenting.

He removed his hand from my arm, finally, and clapped. "Good. It will be my pleasure."

"I'm sure it will."

He gestured toward the exit, and I started walking that way. The gate was open because trucks had been coming and going, so we passed through it and onto the sidewalk.

"So was that your blue bicycle back there?"

"It was." We crossed the street and headed toward the front of the restaurant.

"Do you ride to work every day?"

"I do."

"That seems like a fun way to get around."

"It's nice not to have to rely on cabs. And I don't live far. Not that it's any of your business where I live."

"I would never presume that it was." He held the door open for me, and I passed reluctantly through.

Inside, though, the fans didn't disappoint. The breeze licked at my face so pleasingly. The dining room was nearly empty at this hour. It was too early for dinner but after lunch. The host sat us at a small table near the bar. As soon as I settled into my seat across from him, that wink in the meeting flashed in my mind and stoked my fury. This was a mistake. No matter how good the fans felt, I was too mad to be civil to him, even just for a drink.

I unfolded the flap of my bag and took out the little notebook where I'd written everything Madame Leclaire said about her charitable efforts. Not once had she mentioned being approached by another reporter, but that was no longer important. I didn't want to give him my whole notebook, but now perhaps I was willing to sacrifice it to not have to sit with him. I'd only written on two pages before the notes he needed. And so I tore out those and slid the notebook across the table.

"Just take the notes, so you don't have to buy me that drink after all." I started to stand.

"Oh, come on. Stay." He put a hand across the table. Perhaps in that moment he realized just how upset I was with him, because something humble passed across his face. "I didn't mean to swoop in like that."

"And yet you did it." I was poised on the end of my chair, ready like a runner at a starting line.

"I'm sorry."

The server arrived then, greeted us and told us about the soup du jour.

"I think we're just here for drinks," Benoit said.

The server turned to me. "I'm fine. Thank you. I'm not staying."

"Get her a glass of wine, s'il vous plait. A white. If she doesn't drink it, I will."

"Two then?"

He nodded. When the server left, to show him just how serious I was about not keeping him company, I stood to leave too.

"You really won't stay?" He put his hand on his chest like I'd wounded him. "I'll have questions about the notes. Talking to me now almost assures you won't have to talk to me at all tomorrow."

He was kind of right about that. I did want to get this little collaboration over with.

"S'il vous plait."

"Fine." I fell back into the bar-height chair and hung my bag on the arm. "Look at the notes and ask me whatever you like."

He smiled victoriously, which sent up a flare of rage within me.

"But if you ever wink at me again, I'll slap you as hard as I can."

He laughed. "Is that why you're so upset?"

"I'm not a child."

He surveyed me like I was a full patisserie case and said, "I never doubted you were anything but a woman."

"I mean it."

"Okay. I'll never wink at you again." Benoit's face had flushed a rosy pink. It could have been from the heat, but it gave me some satisfaction knowing that I'd perhaps riled something in him.

The server returned then with two glasses of pale golden wine on a tray. I sipped at the cool, refreshing wine as he dutifully opened my notebook and started reading. I'd written in pencil, and I always went back over my interview notes right away to clarify and correct and fill in everything while it was still fresh in my mind. He spread the pages with one hand and held his wine glass in the other. His thick fingers on the delicate stem. My pulse throbbed, particularly between my legs. As he raised the glass to his lips, his eyes caught mine watching.

"Are you hungry?" His eyebrow arched with interest.

"Not for anything here." My words were cold, but another rush of warmth swept through me. Damn it. I dropped my gaze to my own glass of wine, of which I took a big drink.

"Ha. Mademoiselle, you are too much fun."

"Stop it. You… flirt."

He set his glass on the table and leveled his eyes on mine. "What if I told you I can't help myself because I like you."

"Oh, please. You're doing it intentionally to fluster me. You want my job and nothing else."

"Actually, I want my job."

"But I thought your job was high seas adventures and filing stories from abroad. Don't you have somewhere exotic you can go and write?"

"That was my job. But I have obligations in the city. This is my job now."

"How did you get the job in the first place? An uncle in the boardroom or something?"

"No. I worked for it, just like you. I spent two years in the Far East, working for the public relations office during my military service. I'm trained and experienced."

"I'm sure you are." I swallowed the last of my wine. Military service was admirable, of course. I would never not be grateful on some level to a man who'd served France. But getting those cushy jobs in the press office meant knowing someone, whether he acknowledged his privilege or not. It existed, like a bubble that allowed men like him to float along a little above everyone else. He had every advantage against me—more experience and connections within the new leadership. He didn't lack talent. He was a man. Everyone would always pick him over me. And here I was, helping him write the story that I should have been writing to secure my career. "Do you have any questions about my notes, or not?"

He closed the notebook. "I guess not. Thank you. And I'm sorry again."

"Enjoy the rest of your day, monsieur."

"You as well." He rose when I did, but sat when I walked away. As I made my way through the dining room, his gaze, or at least the potential of it, burned in my back. I didn't dare turn to see. Then, as I reached the door, he called out to me. "I'll see you tomorrow, Marnet."

I pushed open the door and walked outside without acknowledging his parting words, friendly as they sounded.

The next few days, competition with Benoit consumed far too many of my thoughts. The inconvenient fact that all of my story ideas seemed to be falling apart didn't help. I checked in with sources, followed up leads, read other papers for scraps. Nothing was coming together. I wrote a small item about the new entertainment director at one of the big cabarets. And another about an exhibit at a gallery. But I needed a feature story or fresh gossip for "Potins Culturels," something that would impress Vartre and Paquin. Something juicy that no one else had.

One morning, after tossing and turning through much of the night, I came downstairs early to see if Cook had coffee ready yet. It was before seven, but Cook would be up. She always was.

Cook was pouring a kettle of water into the top of the percolator when I came downstairs.

"You're up early, mademoiselle."

"I am."

"It won't take long for coffee."

"Merci." I sat on the stool where Cook would be working later in the day, stringing beans or peeling potatoes or one of those other laborious kitchen chores. The kitchen was dim and cozy with high walls made of grand-looking stone. Being in there with Cook reminded me of life at the orphanage. We had a big kitchen there too, and the nuns were wise, practical fixtures who fed us whenever we came around. Cook had worked at 77 Rue de Fortuny since before Madame married into the Tremblay family. She was a wide, plain woman with salt and pepper hair. She prepared all of our meals, which were included with room and board. Nothing fancy, but always delicious. "Any sign of our kitty this morning?"

"Not yet." Once the coffee was going, Cook went to her lists. She often said that her lists were part of her brain. She kept a stack of papers in the same place on the counter. Then when she left the kitchen, even for a quick errand, she rolled the papers up and tucked them in her apron pocket. Now she smoothed out the curled edges and ran her finger down the paper.

I was going to talk more about the cat, one of our favorite topics, when the door opened and Charlotte walked in. Her dark hair was loose, and she looked as guilty as sin with a cheap sweater on over her evening gown. There was a price tag dangling from the back of her collar.

"Bonjour," Charlotte cheered. She had shopping bags in her hand. "I couldn't sleep, so I went out nearly an hour ago for a walk. I wanted to see the city wake up, I suppose. Plus, I needed to experience it for a story. Or, at least I thought it might help."

All of these words that sweet, innocent Charlotte strung together added up to nonsense. I was awake too. I would have heard her. "Did you get a new sweater?"

"No. I've had it for some time." She pulled a pastry box from her bag and put it on the table. Inside were ten golden, flaky pastries that smelled like browned butter. "I've brought croissants. Help yourselves."

Maybe she'd had the sweater. But it held a freshness that sure looked new. Plus the price tag. Why would she lie?

"I'll just go up now and see if I can get some work done." Charlotte hitched up her skirts, took the steps two at a time, and was gone.

Cook raised her bushy gray eyebrows. "Seems she had fun at the fancy people's ball last night."

"What do you mean?"

"You don't believe that she got up this morning, put on her party dress, and went out for a walk, do you? That girl didn't leave an hour ago. She left last night."

"Interesting." I poured each of us a cup of coffee from the percolator.

"I'll say. They're always a little silly about the parties when they first arrive in the city. And someone's been sending her all those gifts and letters." Charlotte was new to the city. And I didn't need to see her hometown back in the provinces to know how different—how provincial—it was in comparison. Cook put a spoonful of sugar in her coffee and continued, "Now if she's spending the night with him, it's only a matter of time before she ends up like that last one."

"Fleur?"

"That's the one. Those girls from up north have it the worst. A man gives them an expensive little something and they lose their heads."

Charlotte had been in Paris for less than a month when a vicomte—one of the last real ones that went back to the early Bourbons—sent her a very expensive typewriter "in support of her work." There was a letter from him in the post almost every day. And Charlotte was no aristocrat; quite the opposite. This didn't seem to deter Charlotte, and I couldn't blame her for that. If a wealthy man were so interested in sending gifts in support of my work, I might have kept up the letters too. But she seemed too naive to realize that she was practically in the lion's den if she was on that man's arm.

I sipped my coffee while Cook offered a series of familiar anecdotes on women who'd come to the pension respectable and fallen out as courtesans. Madame and Cook took a practical stance on women climbing the social ladder through affairs with men. Madame was strict about who she let move in. This was a place for professional women of good reputation. There were laws about prostitution and brothels. With a house full of women, Madame's place couldn't be mistaken for that. She was always going on about the women in the house next door, who seemed to always have male visitors. Madame had an upstanding reputation to maintain. No boyfriends or overnight guests. And men weren't to be coming to the door or hanging about in any other way unless his intentions were a respectable marriage. Madame Tremblay didn't always know what went on in her house, but when she found out about it, she tended to take swift action. I had no trouble keeping these rules, though I'd seen many a housemate succumb.

Outside of the legal concerns about housing prostitutes, I suspected the house rules were also a reflection of Madame Tremblay's moral stance. But it was hard to tell with her. When she did talk about it, her concerns were always about our future and our ability to live independently. She insisted that relying on a man could be precarious. The concerning part was that the man supporting the woman could change his mind on a whim and have her on the street with nothing but the gifts he'd bestowed on her. These women could be reduced to nothing if he lost interest or found someone else. Fleur, who I still kept in touch with, started with a nice apartment and all the dresses and earrings she could wear. But the last time we spoke, she'd been selling all her jewelry because she had to part ways with her vieux protecteur.

I had recently learned how a livelihood could become vulnerable to the whims of others. I didn't look down on women who relied on men. How could I when so many did it? There were worse ways to survive. And it didn't seem any more or less precarious than any other way of life. Charlotte wouldn't be stupid for tucking under the wing of the future vicomte Antoine de Larminet.

I didn't care where Charlotte spent the night, at least not personally. Professionally, however, it was as if I'd struck gold.

"Potins Culturels" was a crowning jewel of our newspaper. It was a gossip column that focused on the artistic and literary sets. The byline on it was a vague H. De la Maison. The H stood for homme, and so the column was signed by the man of the house. But in reality, there was no man of the house. There never had been. The column was a catch-all for all the juicy bits that the reporters picked up as they were working on other things. The insider gossip that made all the literary men and art snobs and tastemakers feel like they knew the artists in real life. Usually Paquin wrote it. Sometimes, one of the reporters had something big enough for a full write-up. Other times it was a group effort to smooth smaller pieces into something to get the salons and drawing rooms talking. Even people from other departments sometimes threw in bits of gossip they came across. Although there was no real recognition in the form of a byline, there was newsroom clout in getting something good. My own work in this column helped get me promoted to senior culture reporter.

Charlotte, the up and coming writer, seeing the city's favorite aristocratic son? That was perfect "Potins Culturels" column fodder. It was much better than the arts charity idea that Benoit Levin scooped me on. It could save my career.

When you work as a journalist, your livelihood depends on your sense for story. It's an ability, a curiosity, an inkling. And the more you do the work, the sharper your senses become. I hate to admit it, but my senses were lighting up like fireworks. The vicomte's son was a gossip column darling. All the aristocrats were. A person like Antoine de Larminet couldn't spend time with any woman in public without attracting attention. Especially Charlotte, whose stories were popular and widely discussed. I warned her once that people in the press were noticing. And up until now, the association between her and Larminet was loose. Or at least as far as the press was concerned.

I refilled my coffee and then went up to my room, leaving Cook to the business of breakfast. I kept a stack of newspaper and magazine back issues. It came in handy when I was looking for ideas or pulling together background. I put my coffee cup on my nightstand and went straight to my stack. There had been the first mention of Charlotte and Antoine together several weeks ago. I'd given that paper to Charlotte when I showed it to her. But there had been more mentions since, and so I started flipping through my old papers and setting them aside. In no time, I had several small mentions that, when grouped together, added up to a story. Most were simple—Antoine de Larminet chatting with Charlotte Devereaux at this party, Antoine and Charlotte dancing together twice at this ball, that sort of thing. Nothing with any real meat. But I had real meat.

I'd used my housemates as sources for gossip and information, but I had never actually written about any of them. I'd never had a housemate who was semi-famous the way Charlotte was. Nadine was hopefully getting there, but no one so far had a life worthy of reporting in the paper.

People recognized Charlotte's name, society people perhaps more than others, because of her stories. Charlotte wrote fiction about aristocrats and rich people being foolish, and so her work was both controversial and quite popular among them. Her stories showed them exactly as they were in the most compelling way. That she was involved with an aristocrat was simply good gossip. It wasn't exactly salacious. He was unmarried, though there had been rumors about a forthcoming engagement to Louise Montmorency, another society type with a title in the family—a marquis, in her case. Coincidentally, her mother was involved with the arts charity I'd been writing about before Benoit Levin stole the story. Charlotte had never been romantically linked to anyone. She was new in Paris, just making a name for herself. All of this made it the perfect topic for a gossip column.

If I hurried, then I could break it first, before any other journalists who may have seen Charlotte and Antoine together last night could get the story together. This was even better than the charity story. It was fresher, the kind of thing everyone would be talking about in their drawing rooms all day. Just the sort of job-saving story I needed. I would have been a complete fool not to write it.

So that's what I did. I sat down at my little desk and wrote through breakfast. I didn't go down because I'd already had some coffee, and though I didn't acknowledge it at the time, I was afraid of encountering Charlotte, afraid of facing her. I might lose my nerve.

Life as an orphan forced me to make selfish decisions. I had to take care of myself; I had no one else. And I didn't have time to write anything else before deadline at the end of the week. I needed to prove myself over and over again because every issue that didn't have my mark on it was a mark against me. I needed a story, and Charlotte had practically handed me one.

When it was done, I tucked the pages into my bag and dressed for work in a gray suit, like it was any other day. Like a criminal, I checked to make sure the hallway was clear and then tiptoed past Charlotte's room. She was inside tapping away at her typewriter as I crept down the stairs. The foyer was empty, but I paused before going down and out through the kitchen. Cook would be in there, not that this had anything to do with her. But she'd unwittingly become a source of information for my story. I went out the front door.

I didn't hesitate or let myself think about this as anything more than a professional victory. I put the story in my editor's hands and stood there smiling while he read it. It was a quick read, so it didn't take him long.

"Good work. Here," Paquin said, holding the papers out to me. "Pass it over to Vartre."

I did as I was told and waited for her to read the story too.

"This is good, Marnet. It connects the dots and suspicions that were already swirling around them. I think they were even mentioned in one of your pieces, right Paquin? This is exactly the kind of thing we want. It's perfect for the 'Potins Culturels' column." She nodded approvingly, and the careerist in me swelled with confidence. "We can run it tomorrow."

At first I was relieved. My editors were impressed. I had proven my worth. But the rest of the day, a low-grade dread settled inside me, deep in my gut. Sitting there at my desk in the pen was like sitting outside Sister Clothilde's office door to await punishment. I knew it was coming, but I didn't know what it would be. Career-wise, everything was great, as long as no one scooped me on the story. I scoured the morning papers, but found nothing. As the afternoon issues came out, I checked those too. Nothing. No one had the story of the writer and the aristocrat but me, which made it both more professionally exhilarating and personally risky. Once the chance of getting scooped disappeared, I was faced only with what I'd done and what it would do to my living situation. Everyone at my house would know I wrote the column or at least supplied the information. This professional victory would have some personal consequences.

I liked Charlotte. I had to live with her. I was a little jealous of her, perhaps, but who wouldn't be? She was quite talented and pretty and smart—all the things one would want in a friend. I was not the first journalist to write about someone without permission. Doing it to a friend was different; I could have warned her. What I'd done was sneaky, if not unethical. I didn't like the idea of myself as someone who would sabotage a friend out of jealousy.

Ungenerously, I tried to dismiss my guilt by downplaying what I'd done. I hadn't known Charlotte all that long, so our relationship wasn't that important. Cook was right that she'd probably be moving on soon. My writing about her private relationship might actually benefit her personally and professionally, and no one knew for sure what the future could hold. But, no surprise, thinking ungenerous thoughts didn't make me feel any less villainous.

There was a chance Madame Tremblay would kick her out of the pension, though I didn't think so. The only reasons Madame ever tossed a woman out were the inability to pay rent and keeping inappropriate male company. Charlotte had been walking a fine line with the vicomte's son, but he hadn't been coming around the house. Staying out all night was hardly an offense on Madame's territory.

Unfortunately, Charlotte's involvement with the vicomte's son was not going to end in marriage. A man of his stature would only be interested in a woman of hers for one reason: sex outside of marriage. There was so little chance that the fancy man would make Charlotte an honest woman. She was obviously brilliant and lovely, but the aristocracy never cared about that. They only cared about lineage. So this situation would either unfold with Charlotte becoming his mistress or refusing him. Charlotte was perhaps learning firsthand that there's no such thing as fairy tales. I didn't like playing a role in that sort of lesson for anyone, let alone a housemate.

And further troubling: would my housemates understand? Was what I'd done even defensible? Charlotte probably wouldn't, but what about the others? Some dumb part of me considered maybe they wouldn't even see it, but that was impossible. The paper was delivered to the house every morning; we passed it around at breakfast. There was no way they wouldn't see it. And even without my byline on it, there was no way they wouldn't attribute the information in the story to me.

I lingered in the office for far longer than necessary. And instead of riding straight home, I stopped in shops and took detours and delayed so long that, by the time I made it back to the pension, I had missed dinner. In the kitchen, Cook fixed me a plate, which I took up to my room and ate with my door closed. I could hear my housemates through the walls, Charlotte typing away. Catherine and Diane laughing. Nadine was at work, as she often was in the evenings.

I loved living at Madame's, and I didn't want to make enemies of my housemates. I cared what they thought of me. The weight of this had never been more significant, now that it was all on the verge of dramatic upheaval. All my life, I struggled to make friends—surprise, surprise—and so I liked to keep the ones I managed to make.

For hours that night I lay awake, thinking through all the possible scenarios of the how the following day might unfold. I couldn't get my brain to stop spinning. Unable to settle myself, I got out of bed and got dressed. Not even Cook was up yet. Then I left the house long before dawn.

The only place I had to go was the newspaper, and so I went there. I rode my bike. It was so early not even the bakeries were open. And I took several deep breaths when I passed the newspaper truck delivering stacks to the newsstands. The paper was officially out. Within a few hours, the tied bundles would be distributed across the city. There was no going back now.

The newspaper building never truly closed. The front lobby was dark and locked up, but the staff entrance had a doorman there around the clock. News happened at all hours, and so there was almost always someone around. This morning, there was no one in the building except for the doorman at his counter and the remains of the printing crew, who were heading out.

Upstairs, I had the place to myself. The pen was dark and shadowy. I had no reason to be there, at least not any professional reason. I didn't have any real work to do, nothing that couldn't wait. So I went to the editors' office. It was empty and open, thankfully, because there was a couch. And maybe my restless nights caught up with me, because without even really deciding to do so, I lay down. Within minutes, the sleep that had been evading me all night finally came.

Chapter Four

I awoke with a start to a sound—something like a door slamming—and promptly sat up. I wiped a little stream of drool that had made its way along my cheek. Daylight was pouring in the windows; according to the clock on the mantle, I'd slept for nearly five hours. And I no longer had the office to myself. Benoit Levin was standing there, leaning against the doorway, with a poison scowl on his face.

"What?" I said, smoothing my hair. Waking up was a disorienting, embarrassing endeavor. "I fell asleep."

"That's obvious." His words were tight and venomous. "One question: are you sleeping with him?"

"What? No! Who?"

"Is that your plan?" His eyebrows were tightly furrowed and his arms were crossed.

"Eww, no." I had never been more offended by a suggestion. "What plan?"

"For keeping your job."

"Excuse me?"

"Well, you are waiting here for Paquin, aren't you?" His face reddened. He was mad. Why in the world did he care where I slept?

"I'm not waiting here for anyone. I came in early and got tired. I didn't sleep last night—and not because I was with

Paquin or anyone else." I stood up and shook out my skirts. My actions were quick and self-righteous, even though I was deeply embarrassed about sleeping at work. I should have had myself better together, not that I would ever admit it to him.

I charged toward the door. He was still standing there, effectively blocking my exit. When I ducked to squeeze around him, he moved to stop me. I took a step back and stood tall, facing off with him. My shame at having been caught asleep by the least sympathetic person in the world burned on my skin. And the way he was standing there, like he'd caught me in some unseemly act. Sleeping on my boss's couch was, arguably, unseemly. At least unprofessional. But if I were a man, he'd think nothing of this.

I wanted to push him out of the way, all the way out of the building. Forever.

I swallowed hard. And then I drew back my right hand to smack him. I wasn't fast enough because he caught my wrist and held it—not hard but firm.

Oh, to be denied the sensation of my hand hitting his smug face! It was agony. Our eyes met in a fiery stare down.

Well, my end was fiery. His stare was more amused. One of his eyebrows quirked. "That's cheating, you know. Sleeping with the boss."

"I could say the same to you. Maybe that's why you're so suspicious of me. You're doing it yourself. Are you sleeping with Vartre? Maybe that's how you got your job." I pulled my arm free and fisted my hands at my sides. "Please move out of my way."

"I'm not sleeping with anyone."

"I don't care." I didn't. But I can't lie: my first reaction to this unsought admission was relief. He was close enough that I could smell the cedar in his cologne. It was earthy and vaguely floral and appealing in the most unwelcome way. This was the man I hated; not the man who smelled good. "Now I'd like to end this unpleasant little exchange and get to work."

He narrowed his striking blue eyes at me, and then moved aside. But when I stepped into the hallway, Paquin and Vartre were heading toward their office. They were smiling and walking close. Why were these two always together now? Shared office aside, they came and went together. They both referred to themselves collectively. We. A real team, suddenly. It occurred to me that I had perhaps been sleeping on the surface of their sensual encounters, but I quickly pushed that out of my mind. I could only hold so much rage at a time.

Benoit and I stood frozen there in front of the door. Paquin's eyes brightened when he saw us. "Just the two people we need to see today. Please, come in for a minute."

"Bonjour," said Vartre as she filed past.

"Bonjour." I shot Benoit a questioning look. What could they possibly want?

Benoit shrugged. He had no idea either.

Back in their office, the scene of my petty crime, I avoided the couch, choosing to lean against the bookshelf instead.

"First of all, this isn't going to be easy," Vartre said. She wore a linen skirt and a bright red blouse that was ruffled and frilly; a contrast to her cool personality. She settled into her desk chair and looked at Paquin, as if she were sending the ball his way.

"Some additional changes are coming on the horizon, as we've all expected. One of them will be in this office."

My mind raced to fill in the gaps of their diplomatic opening. So one of them was leaving? Her, most likely. She'd said from the beginning that she was looking for something else. Paquin and Vartre were gazing at each other with such open admiration, like they were about to break into song and dance. Then Paquin reached out and touched Vartre's arm so tenderly and with such familiarity that it was obvious they were sleeping together. A chill ran up my spine.

"We've grown quite close over the past week or so," Vartre said carefully.

"And worked so well together."

"So well." She beamed at him. They were going back and forth with their mutual affection like Levin and I weren't even in the room.

"But we're doing what's right for the paper."

"And what's right for us."

A vomitous feeling rose in my throat. Were they announcing their engagement or getting ready to fire one of us?

"I'm stepping down as editor," Paquin said, snapping the tension in the room.

"You?" This was doubly bad for me. He was the one who'd hired me and taught me half of my best tricks. If he left, then that increased the likelihood I'd be eliminated too.

"I'm leaving the paper. I'm done at the end of the week. Vartre is now the one and only editor of the culture pages."

"What are you going to do?"

"I'm taking a few weeks in Italy. Then I'll be launching a garden and lifestyle section for *Le Nouveau Français*."

"This is news," Benoit said. "Definitely news. But what does it mean for us?"

"Nothing. No one is getting fired, if that's what you're worried about. We're keeping you both."

"I'm keeping you both," Vartre corrected, shooting Paquin a look that was definitely sultry. She looked back at us. "And I want you to work as a team."

I gasped, then tried to cover it by clearing my throat.

"Work as a team how?" Benoit asked tentatively.

"I'm sending you both to the beach for three weeks. I want you to cover all the Paris beau monde who are flocking there for the summer."

"Three weeks?" Benoit Levin spoke directly to Vartre. "You know how difficult it is for me to travel."

"Yes. But you said things have stabilized," Vartre said with a flick of her wrist. "I promise it will be the last time. We'll put you up. Don't worry about that. And there's a new casino opening that I want you to focus on first."

"The two of us?" He seemed as frightened by this proposition as I was.

"Yes. And Apolline Trouvé. She's going to do the sketches and photography."

Vartre looked at me, ready for my arguments. I didn't object to going to the beach, especially if the paper was paying for it. But traveling with Benoit Levin, being part of the team with him, would be disastrous. I might end up quitting in a fit of rage, and then all of my work would have been for nothing. And this felt suspiciously like another case of my not being taken seriously because I was a woman. As a woman editor, the only one in the building, she should have understood. "I can do it by myself. Apolline and I can do it. We won't need him."

Vartre examined me, reassessing. I could never tell what she thought of me. I'd even hoped that, being a woman, she'd be even more helpful than Paquin had been. She pursed her lips. "I disagree. If it were just the casino opening, then maybe. But everyone in Paris is going to be there. We all know nothing happens in the city from July to September. So this is what we're doing. We're sending a team to where the people are. Making it a whole thing."

"The focus feature." Paquin gazed at her admiringly.

"Is this another delayed decision about which one of us gets to stay, or does it mean we both get to keep our jobs?"

They exchanged looks and shrugs.

"Listen. You can't repeat this, at least not yet," Paquin said conspiratorially. "But if things go well for me at *Le Nouveau Francis*, then I'll be stealing Vartre away at my first chance."

Vartre smiled and nodded. "Everything is temporary. And you two will be the only ones left who could potentially step into the section editor position."

"Just something to keep in mind."

"When do we leave?" Levin said.

"Monday. Marie is making the arrangements now."

I had not been to the beach in many years, and perhaps I should have been excited by the opportunity. The paper had never sent me anywhere outside the city for an assignment. But this particular assignment did not make me happy.

I had potentially wrecked my home life to prove myself at work, and now I had to work on a team. With Benoit Levin. The man who found me sleeping on a couch in the office, for goodness sakes. It was like nothing in the world made sense anymore. Nothing was happening the way it was supposed to. And now our bosses were sleeping together. This was too many revelations for so early in the day.

"Oh, don't look so glum," Vartre said. "This is a tremendous opportunity to prove your ability to work as a team. And it's the beach!"

"Thank you," Paquin said, dismissing us. I scowled at Benoit as I left the office.

When I got back to my desk, I wrote to Nadine asking if she could meet me, and sent one of the newspaper's messenger boys to take the note to her. To my relief, he returned with her response: *Yes, of course. Bouillon Juillet at 6.*

Nadine chose Bouillon Juillet because Diane was working there now, and Nadine liked to be supportive. This made the lump of guilt in my throat grow slightly bigger.

"There she is." Diane greeted me when I pushed through the door at the restaurant. She was standing behind the host podium, dressed in her crisp white shirt and black tie. I assumed she'd read the gossip column, but her face revealed nothing. She gestured toward the tables by the bar. "Nadine is already here."

"Merci." At least she didn't seem too mad.

Nadine was tucked into the corner table with a glass of red wine. She was dressed in a ruffled blue and green blouse. In my rumpled, slept-in pale, gray suit, I looked like a pigeon landing next to a parrot. When her eyes rose to meet mine, there was disappointment in them. It stung so much I had to avert my gaze.

"Bonjour." I sat across from her, arranging my skirts instead of looking at her.

"Bonjour, Vanessa. Our busy, busy Vanessa."

I cringed. "I assume you read the 'Potins Culturels' column."

"Oh, I read it, all right. At least you're not denying it. And to be honest, Vanessa, I was pretty surprised that you would be so cruel as to write something like that."

"I didn't mean it as cruel, truly."

"Then how did you mean it?"

I sighed. "You don't understand the pressure I'm under at work. I was desperate. And she's carrying on with him like she doesn't even care about getting caught. If I hadn't written about it, someone else would have."

Nadine's frowned. "I'm sorry to hear that, Vanessa. But none of that adds up to a good excuse."

I groaned. "I know that."

A waiter came to see if I needed anything, and I asked for a glass of wine.

"Charlotte's a mess," Nadine said. "Her gentleman asked to see her; his messenger arrived even earlier than yours. Apparently, his mother's in a fit about the marriage she's arranged for him to Louise Montmorency—I'm sure you know of her."

I nodded.

"Anyway, I guess he's still going to marry her. Charlotte was coming in as I was leaving the house. He asked her to be his mistress, and she was furious. Bright red."

"Oh, god."

"Oh, god, is right. You must hate her to do something like this."

"I don't. It wasn't supposed to be personal. But it was selfish." Neither one of us spoke for a few minutes. I drank my wine. Nadine was mad at me, and I knew I was wrong for not speaking to Charlotte about the story. So I didn't argue that this would have happened between Charlotte and Antoine eventually, whether I wrote about them or not. "Do you think she'll forgive me?"

"You should talk to Charlotte. She might understand. Though you might want to wait a few days to see how things unfold."

"What do you mean?"

"Well, he'll either come to his senses and ask Charlotte to marry him. Or he'll marry this other bird, and Charlotte will have to come to terms with the fact that she's fallen for a foolish man. It's an honest mistake. One we're all bound to make at some point. But right now, I bet she's ready to kill you."

"Do you think he'll change his mind?" It seemed unlikely.

"Probably not."

"I thought I might write to her."

Nadine furrowed her brow disapprovingly. "I understand that's you're primary mode of communication. It's hers too. And you should write to her. But I think this will require face-to-face interaction. You need to look her in the eyes and explain yourself. Preferably after the dust settles."

"How long will that take?"

"I think Charlotte gets to decide that."

"I'm supposed to leave town in a few days. A work trip."

"Oh, how convenient." Nadine cocked her head to the side; she was not letting me off easy. "Is that what you outed our housemate for? Travel opportunities?"

"No. It's actually a disaster. A whole other disaster. I'll be gone for three weeks."

"Well, maybe it's for the best." Nadine sniffed coldly. "That will give Charlotte some space. And in the meantime, you can enjoy all the professional benefits you've reaped from this."

I hated to tell her that my treachery was motivated by preservation and not some astronomical launch into something better. I was merely clinging on to my job. And now I'd thrown my home life into disarray as well. I already suspected that my betrayal probably hadn't been worth it. Even Nadine was eyeing me warily, as if she might not trust me ever again. I could practically see her imagining me doing the same thing to her one day.

"Is Charlotte at home?"

"She was when I left. Door closed, screaming into her pillow."

I let my head fall onto the table and groaned again. "I feel terrible."

"I hate to say it, but if you feel terrible about this, it's because you deserve to."

She was obviously upset. My mess was proving to be quite messy. "I appreciate you coming to see me."

"Of course. But now I have to get to work. I have to rehearse in costume and the wig takes forever." She swallowed the last of her wine. Then she said, "Everyone is disappointed by what's transpired."

"That's very clear. Yes."

We said au revoir and à bientôt, and Nadine got up and left. I finished my wine and got up to go as well. On my way out, I looked for Diane, but she was busy with guests in another part of the dining room. I waved, but she didn't wave back.

I was used to being alone. Being an orphan, I couldn't avoid it. I had some friends at Saint Genevieve's, and I also had some enemies there. And some of the people had been like family. But friendships were not easy for people who've lost everyone and been left to the whims of an imperfect system. We were all alone together at the Saint Genevieve's. And so we were all a little selfish, all a little ruthless. We had to be, even with our friends. This sometimes served me in adulthood, but this time it had led me astray.

I went back to the office and kept busy reading everything I could find about Cabourg, the beach town where they were sending me. Anything to avoid going home. Despite Nadine's admonishment, I tried to comfort myself by thinking of all the good things that could possibly happen for Charlotte in all of this. Her career wouldn't suffer. Her popularity could grow from getting her name in the paper in connection with a man with such high social capital. Ultimately, she would be fine. I told myself this over and over again. And then I spent another night at the office on my bosses' couch.

The next morning, it was early when I opened my eyes. Not early enough, it seemed, because Benoit was already there, standing before me. He was dressed smartly as usual, another blue suit and the black cravat this time. And he had a cup of coffee in each hand.

"What are you doing?"

"That's my question." He set one of the coffees down on the table where I could reach it.

"What?"

"I was going to ask the same of you. Because here we are again, meeting under these suspicious and deeply unprofessional circumstances." He perched on the edge of Vartre's desk, facing me and my makeshift bed. "That coffee is for you, by the way."

"Merci, and go to hell. I was working late and got tired. I took a break."

"Yes, because the cultural commentary can't wait," he said facetiously.

"You write about the same things as I do."

"Yes, and that's how I know it's not important enough to spend the night in the office."

I was sitting up now, and I reached for the coffee. It was in one of the cups from the kitchen downstairs.

"Where did you get this?"

"There's a kitchen here, you know."

"I do know. I've just never seen a man use it before. Most wait until someone else makes the coffee."

"I—a true renaissance man—can make coffee."

"Is it poisoned?"

"No, but that's not a bad idea." He watched me as I sipped the deliciously hot liquid. I only achieved my human form after having coffee. Perhaps he understood this because he let me take a few drinks before asking, "Are you vagrant, Vanessa?"

"What? No."

"Then why have you been sleeping at the office?"

"It's none of your concern." I scowled at him.

"Yes, but I want to know. And if you don't tell me, then I'll be forced to ask one of our superiors."

"You wouldn't."

"I might. This is your chance to control the story."

"Oh, stop it," I said exasperated. "I'm not vagrant. I just can't go home right now. Or I don't want to. Everyone is mad at me there."

"Why? Did maman and papa catch you with the butcher's son?"

"You're despicable, you know that? A truly devious mind. No. I live in a women's pension. My housemates are mad at me. One in particular. Charlotte Deveraux." I stopped confessing to see if he'd add it all up on his own. I could practically see his mind whirling. And then his eyes widened with realization dawning.

"You mean the Charlotte Deveraux from your column? She's your housemate?"

"She is. And before you ask for all the salacious details, she didn't know that I was going to write about her affair with Larminet. I did that all on my own, and of course she's furious."

"Why? You made it up?" He sipped his coffee, and I forced myself to look away from his mouth. His mustache was so neat and tidy.

"No. I wrote about it when they would have preferred to keep it a secret, I suppose. They are involved, I'm sure. I just didn't talk to her about it. Now everyone at my house is mad at me, and I'm spending as little time there as possible." I don't know why it felt good to tell him all of this, but it was momentarily cathartic. "So here I am, sleeping on the couch at work. Again. Are you happy now? I've destroyed my life to keep you from scooping up my job."

"I never would have guessed that, Vanessa." He eyed me thoughtfully, like he was seeing just how treacherous I was for the first time. "You must really want this job."

"I do. More than you."

"I'm not so sure of that. But I did underestimate you. And I won't do it again."

"You won't tell anyone, will you, about finding me here on the couch?"

"No, Vanessa, I won't tell anyone. I—for one—have some boundaries. But I will make you a deal."

"That sounds like a terrible idea."

"Maybe. But hear me out." He stood up and started pacing between the two desks. "Only one of us can get the editor position, right? Most importantly, we both feel certain that we could never work for the other. So, let's say whoever gets the job stays, and the other one will go."

"So if I don't get the editor position, I have to quit the paper."

"That's right. And if I don't get it, then I'll move on. It's a gentlemen's agreement. Winner takes all, if you will. That will prevent bad blood and further competition or sabotage."

"A gentlemen's agreement?"

"Yes. All or nothing. This is how men do things."

"Fine. It's a deal. When I get the editor position, you'll leave." I said this believing with my full being that I wouldn't have to go. I'd get the editor's position. And if I didn't, I'd never want to see his face again. So either way the situation went, the deal would hold. "But if you tell anyone you saw me anywhere near this couch, the deal is off."

"I admire your complete dedication to self-preservation. I don't think I could tell my friend's secrets to keep my job."

"Well, if you hadn't taken my story out from under me, then I wouldn't have had to."

"You're still on about that? You have to learn to let things go, Vanessa."

"I can't let it go when it put me in such a difficult position. A position where I had to betray a friend."

His shoulders fell. "So why didn't you say anything? I would have given you a story, you know."

"I wouldn't have taken it."

That night, I didn't stay at the office again. I went home. Late. So late that everyone had gone to bed. I wouldn't say I was ready to face the consequences of my actions, but I was also desperately tired of being at work.

The following day, I was in my room, hatefully re-reading one of Benoit Levin's stories, when I heard Charlotte's door open. I didn't think the dust had settled yet, but I also knew that continuing to hide and avoid her would make it worse. Without thinking too much, I took a deep, strengthening breath, and went out to catch her.

"Charlotte?" Her eyes were damp, and she was carrying a valise. "Do you have a minute to talk?"

Her look was so sharp, it could have cut me. Her brow crumpled painfully. "No Vanessa. No. He's marrying her. It's in the paper. And you're the last person I want to talk to right now."

Charlotte rushed down the stairs and was gone before I could ask where she was going. I went to my room and checked the paper. Sure enough, there was Antoine de Larminet's engagement announcement. He was marrying Louise Montmorency, the marquis's daughter, which was the most expected outcome to everyone except Charlotte, the poor thing. A little while later, Madame found a note that Charlotte left to explain her hasty departure. She'd gone back to Vernon, her hometown, which made me feel quite rotten. Of all the possible outcomes of my writing her gossip, I never considered it might drive her out of the city. All this trouble over a man!

This wasn't the end of it, however. Antoine de Larminet didn't stop sending messengers to the house. Then finally, a few days after Charlotte's departure, he showed up himself. I heard someone at the door when I was passing through the hallway upstairs. I could only make out every few words, but then I heard Charlotte's name and something about the tone of the man's voice made me want to go down and be nosy. And there he was, at the front door, arguing with Madame and Nadine.

"That's not what it said in the paper," Nadine said.

"The paper is wrong. Rather, it's no longer accurate. I am not engaged to anyone and only want to be engaged to Charlotte Deveraux. Is she still in the city?" I'd only seen him a handful of times, usually from a distance and in some fancy setting. He was well dressed as always, but disheveled in a very un-aristocratic way. His face was unshaven. There was a glint of desperation in his eyes. His mustache quivered when he spoke her name.

Whatever was going on between him and Charlotte—and I still didn't even know all the details—it was ruining him inside.

I had never seen anything like it. Something made me want to put him out of his misery. I stepped forward between Nadine and Madame. "She's gone home to Vernon."

"Vanessa," Nadine hissed. "I wasn't going to tell him."

I shrugged. "I can't keep my mouth shut apparently."

Nadine laughed wickedly. "You're terrible."

"And you," I said, pointing over the threshold at Antoine. "You are terrible too, from what we've heard."

"I am aware of my flaws, mademoiselles, merci beaucoup. But I have to go. I have to get to Vernon." His relief livened him up. Then he took off in his gilded carriage, leaving Nadine, Madame, and me standing there at the door.

"I can't believe he's thrown off the marquis's daughter," Madame said, pushing the door closed.

"Do you think he'll really go to Vernon?"

"I'd be surprised if he didn't," Madame said. "He was a mess."

"You know what surprises me," Nadine said slyly, nudging Madame with her elbow.

"What's that?"

"This one telling the lovesick aristocrat where to find his darling," she said, tipping her head in my direction. "It turns out Vanessa's a romantic."

I scoffed at the suggestion. "I have no idea what you mean."

Chapter Five

The morning I was to leave for Cabourg, the paper sent a carriage to pick me up. I hadn't considered that I would be sharing the same ride with my coworkers until the driver and I had to make room on the luggage rack for my valise among several other trunks and what appeared to be a tripod. I opened the door and saw Apolline Trouvé, the illustrator, sitting inside. She was dressed in a linen suit and floral print blouse. Her graying hair was braided and twisted into a low bun.

"Bonjour." She smiled benignly.

"Bonjour." I stepped in and sat opposite her on the bench. We'd gone on assignments together before, meaning little more than we'd been in the same place at the same time, but never anything like this. I had never traveled outside the city for work. I had rarely traveled outside the city at all. As silly as it made me, I was nervous. But it was a perfect distraction from the havoc I'd created at home. With Charlotte gone, everyone seemed to be a little less mad at me. I'd tried but failed to write to Charlotte and explain myself because I still wasn't sure what to say. All I could think about was the cutting way she'd looked at me as she left. I was hopeful that getting away would somehow make everything better.

"Do you live nearby?"

"Not too far. I'm in Clichy."

"So then are we meeting Monsieur Levin at the station?"

"I believe we're picking him up too."

"Oh. That's unfortunate."

She raised her eyebrows but didn't comment.

"To be honest, I'm not even sure why they're sending him at all. Maybe we could just go on ahead without him! Ha."

Apolline regarded me sympathetically. "Everything's a mess since *L'Etoile* took us over."

"Has it made much trouble for you in the art department?"

"It's not terrible." She shrugged. "We needed more people, and now we have them. But we're starting over in many ways. And this trip wasn't my choice of assignments. No offense if it was yours."

The trip, yes, but Benoit Levin as company, no. "Not exactly. Do you have family at home?"

"A husband and our daughter, though she's grown. They're quite jealous of my trip to the beach, I have to say."

"Have you been to the seaside?"

"A few times, here and there. Though not Cabourg. What about you?"

"Only once, as a little girl. My father took me to Nice. But I hardly remember it." It wasn't long after my mother died, and he'd been convinced a change of scenery would help ease the pain. It didn't work.

"The ocean is so vast; that's what gets me. Makes me feel small, like touching an unknown world. Makes me want to read Jules Verne." Apolline's eyes sparkled behind her wire-rimmed glassed. "And what do you know about this other one who's coming along? He's a *L'Etoile* person?"

"He is. I don't like him all that much, to be honest. I don't like anything at work since we've been acquired. And Paquin is leaving, which doesn't bode well for me, I'm afraid."

"Is he? Oh, you'll be all right. Even if you do end up leaving. Lots of people will. We might get back from this trip and not recognize the place."

The carriage drew up between a café and a market. There was some commotion on the street, and our driver shouted at someone to watch where they were going.

I imagined Benoit Levin living in some stately place his rich parents owned, or maybe even a filthy hovel on a side street somewhere in Montmartre. But aside from the traffic, this was a clean, respectable-looking middle-class neighborhood with apartments above the storefronts. Maybe he had a generous benefactress?

The driver thumped on the side of the carriage to get our attention. "Can one of you ladies go knock on the door of number sixty-eight? I can't park the carriage here at this hour."

"So much for chivalry," Apolline said. She looked at me primly. "Go ahead, honey. I've got a bad knee; you'll be faster."

I shrugged and disembarked the carriage. The day was heating up. There were delivery trucks on either side of our carriage with another one that appeared to want our spot on the narrow street. Sixty-eight was an ornate metal door between the two establishments. I pushed it open and followed the stairs up to another door on a narrow landing.

When I knocked, there was a commotion on the other side and maybe a child screaming. Something thumped, and another shriek penetrated the walls. There were definitely kids here. Was I in the right place? Then the door swung open and

Benoit Levin was standing on the other side. He looked perfectly pulled together—hair neat, dark blue suit as usual—despite the commotion.

"Oh," he said, obviously surprised to find me. "Bonjour."

"Are you ready? The carriage is waiting."

"Yes. Just let me grab my things. Come in for a moment."

"You could have been waiting outside, you know." I followed him into the cozy foyer. The walls were papered in a blue pagoda print, and there was a lush green fern on a stand. "It would have made everything a lot easier."

"You're early."

I didn't think so, but I conceded the point when a toddler came tearing through, followed by a pretty young woman with a baby on her hip. The woman had dark hair that had escaped from a braid and pink cheeks flushed from exertion. God, was this his wife and children? A vague recollection of him mentioning obligations to someone at work came to me. Had this poor woman procreated with my nemesis? It was like I'd stepped into a troubling dreamland where everything was distorted. I hadn't anticipated or prepared for this situation at all. Something inside of me seized in those moments before introductions were made.

"My sister, Rachelle, and my niece and nephew, Brigitte and Claude."

"Oh, really? Wow." Thank goodness. A laugh came bubbling out of me. How silly of me to think he was married. "I'm sorry. That's wonderful. Enchanté."

"Enchanté," Rachelle said.

Benoit Levin was watching me with an odd look on his face. Perhaps he hadn't prepared for this moment either. Then he raised his eyebrows. "We should go before I have to introduce you to my mother."

"Your mother lives here too?" This was so strange to hear. I don't know why I cared, except that, for the first time, I saw him completely detached from the world of our work. My enemy was a human being. With a family. Astounding to discover this unsettling truth.

"She's resting, thank goodness," said the sister.

I was baffled, I didn't know what to say. And so I didn't say anything more.

Levin gathered his small valise, attaché, and hat. When he was ready, he nodded toward the door. "Shall we?"

I followed him out. When we reached the carriage, the driver was still defending his parking spot. Levin opened the door and held out a hand to help me inside. His eyes sparkled with something untrustworthy, but I let him assist me anyway. After putting his bag with the others, he climbed in and sat across from me next to Apolline. Our knees bumped in the middle of the close space, and I quickly moved mine away. His thighs were broad and substantial enough to straddle, a thought that sent my eyes skipping off in the other direction with a shudder. Nothing about this man or his thighs was compelling. Nothing.

While he chatted up Apolline, I watched the city pass through the window as if Paris in the morning were the most interesting thing I'd ever seen. Anything but look at the man sitting across from me in the tiny carriage, whose presence filled the air with a clean lavender scent.

He laughed generously at something Apolline said.

"I'm serious," she said. "If you're not married, then I have a daughter who I would absolutely love for you to meet, Benoit. I think you'll like her."

"I'd love to meet her."

I shot annoyed looks at both of them. "What is this, a country dance? Maybe we can keep the conversation on professional topics. This is a work trip."

Apolline raised her eyebrows but then changed the subject to photography. The carriage had become so stuffy. I tugged at my collar and searched my bag unsuccessfully for a fan. I either forgot it or put it in my valise.

Finally, we were at the train station. As soon as the carriage stopped, I hastily alighted, eager to breathe air not tainted by him.

I took several deep breaths while he climbed down and then assisted Apolline.

"Thank you, monsieur." She tittered. "It will be nice to have a gentleman along."

While I'd been trying to keep my wits about me, he'd apparently charmed her. When I saw that he was pulling my bag down from the luggage rack, I hurried over to assist. I, for one, didn't need a gentleman along. And there was no way I was going to let him charm me.

"I can get it." I stepped in front of him and reached for my things at the same time he moved, causing us to bump into each other much too intimately.

"Pardon," he said, surprised to find me there in his way. But also seemingly delighted by it, considering the way he dragged his gaze down the front of me. I was, as always, covered from neck to toe. All of my curves smoothed and hidden behind my armor of a suit. He smiled anyway. A sultry, hungry smile that accompanied a particular gleam in his eyes, which were as blue as sapphires.

"Merci. But I can get my own bags."

He smiled. "Of course."

The station bustled with traffic. We made our way toward the ticket counter, where we'd been assured by Vartre that our tickets awaited us. Without a problem, we obtained them and found the platform where our train was scheduled to depart in thirty minutes.

We found a bench that wasn't big enough for the three of us. Placing her bags at her feet, Apolline sat, leaving enough room for one.

"Please," Levin said, gesturing at the empty space.

"You take it. I'm going to run to the newsstand quickly."

"We don't have much time," Apolline said.

"I'll walk over with you," Levin said.

"That's okay. I can go alone."

"I know that. But I usually stop on my way to work. I didn't have a chance this morning. I'd like something to read on the ride."

"Fine. We can both go."

"I don't need your permission, you know." His words were cool.

"Fine."

"Take your bags with you," Apolline said. "I don't want to watch them. And if you two keep carrying on like this, you'll miss the train."

I looked at her, aghast at her suggestion. "I'm not missing the train."

"Oh, yeah. Here it comes." A rumbling approach grew louder.

We all three looked at each other for a dumb beat, then Apolline snapped us out of it. "Go, for heaven's sake. Or you'll miss your chance."

I grabbed my bags and hurried back down the platform toward where I was sure I saw a newsstand, hoping that Levin had decided to stay behind. No luck on that. When I slowed down to reconsider where I needed to go, I glanced over my shoulder, and there he was, toting his bags a pace behind me.

"Where did you say you saw the newsstand?"

"I thought it was right here." Had I taken a wrong turn? The station seemed suddenly larger than it had been only minutes ago. "But maybe we have to go back upstairs."

"I'm not sure we have time for that." The train was sliding to a hissing stop behind us.

But it was full of people who needed to disembark. And it wasn't scheduled to pull out for at least another twenty minutes. "You can go back if you're worried. I'll meet you there."

"It's fine. I need my papers too. Let's go."

We climbed the stairs, which seemed more crowded than they'd been when we'd passed through a few minutes ago.

"Is that it over there?" He pointed into the distance. The newsstand, which I'd been so sure was close, was all the way back by the ticket counter. Swerving to avoid a woman with two small children, I took off across the crowded station. If I hurried, there was plenty of time.

But nothing from that moment went smoothly, if it ever had been. We reached the newsstand and both quickly found what we wanted. I grabbed the *Le Figaro*, *Le Point*, and *La Nation*. He picked up a *Le Petit Parisien*, *Le Matin*, and a crime novel. I noted his reading selections, refusing to feel any sort of way about his inner life. I didn't care. I swear I didn't. The line to pay was short—only one woman in front of us. But then she got into some tedious discussion with the news agent and haggled over the price of a magazine. Next was my turn. I paid, and then Levin did as well. But he paid with a large coin and the news agent had to find and open his spare cash box to make change. Everything seemed to be taking forever, but time didn't slow for us, unfortunately.

After getting what we needed, we wove our way back across the busy station and hurried down the stairs to the platform. The train was still there. We were going to make it.

Or we should have. But then a large man bumped my bag, which bumped my leg and knocked me off balance. My foot flew out and took the rest of me with it. For a brief moment, I was airborne, flying backward through space. Then I landed hard on the stairs, freeing my bag from my grip, and sending it hurdling onto the ground. When it hit, the valise bounced and twirled like a ballerina before crashing back down. The latch split open and the contents—my corsets, my stockings, my toilette, my comfy robe—exploded forth like confetti. I lay there helplessly watching as my things came to land on various public surfaces and passersby. I couldn't tell you which hurt worse, the ache in my rear and elbow where I made impact with the hard stairs or the sting of my embarrassment that the contents of my luggage were scattered all over the place. One of my best pairs of black silk stockings landed on a burly gentleman's shoulder. His face turned as red as mine felt.

The whistle of our departing train screamed at the same moment Benoit turned back and saw me on the ground.

"Oh no!" He yelled, though I could barely hear him over the commotion.

I thought—hoped?—for a second that I'd pass out or die. But then he was there, tossing his bags aside and reaching for me the way one might reach for a baby.

"Are you all right? Are you hurt?" Concern creased his forehead. Genuine concern. He lifted me as if I were weightless and righted me with the utmost care.

He tended to me for an astonishing and horrifying moment, and then the motion of the train leaving the station drew my eye.

"Are you all right?" He repeated the question when I didn't say anything. He was looking at me as if I were a fragile doll.

"No, dammit, I'm not all right. My underthings are all over the place, and we're missing the train!"

I pointed, and he looked. Panic flooded my mind. What were we going to do?

But when he turned back to me, he shrugged. "We can catch the next one."

Then he helped me down the last few stairs, made sure I was steady, and started cleaning up my clothes. The throbbing pain, compounding with my growing humiliation and the anger about missing the train squeezed me into a fury.

"Please," I begged through clenched teeth. "Don't do that."

He was picking up my things with the same enthusiasm as children searching for pretty stones. He lifted my best garter between two fingers and held it aloft. The pink lace and ribbons fluttered in the breeze of the departing train. And the look on his face was infuriating.

"Stop it!" I screamed, and he nearly dropped it. But he didn't. He simply tucked it back into my valise and hurriedly swept up the remaining garments. I have never been so mortified in my life. Never. And I wanted to kill him. I snatched the handle of my bag out of his hammy fist. "Stop touching my things. I can get them."

"I was just trying to help." He held up his hands in surrender. Then, with indignation, he said, "For god's sake."

"Excuse me?"

"I said I was trying to help, and you're angry with me? That's simply ungrateful."

"Oh yeah? Well, I'm not grateful. How about that? I would be happier if you'd have just gotten on the train and left me here."

His jaw dropped open and hurt flashed across his face. But he didn't respond. A small gaggle of onlookers had gathered, as if we were circling each other in a boxing ring, and they might place bets on the outcome.

I smoothed my hair, which had come loose during my tumble. And I swallowed hard to fight back all my emotions, conscious that people were watching, and we likely looked like idiots. I put all my focus on repacking my bag and collecting my thoughts. We'd missed the train. I wasn't even sure what happened now. I didn't want to cry, desperately didn't want to do that. But my eyes welled as I closed my bag and stood up. My backside and arm ached. And the only person with me was my primary foe. Everything was terrible, worthy of tears for sure. But I couldn't—wouldn't—dare. Not in front of him.

"It appears Apolline has gone on without us."

"Oh, well, of course. She probably would have." I nearly choked on the words. "I can't believe this is happening."

"Hey," he said softly. "It's okay. I'll call the paper and tell them what happened. Then we'll get our tickets switched. It will all be fine."

I bit my lip as the tears welled again. I would die if I cried. I sniffed, and that seemed to hold it back. He put a comforting hand on my forearm. "Are you sure you're okay?"

Hating myself, hating him for being so nice, I groaned. "I'm fine. Just stop asking. This is your fault anyway."

"My fault? I didn't push you down the stairs, darling."

"Don't darling me! If you hadn't paid for your papers and your book with a gold Napoleon, then we wouldn't have been in such a hurry."

"How was I supposed to know he wouldn't have change. What news agent doesn't have change? And it was your idea to go to the newsstand, you know. Which you—you, mademoiselle—insisted was close by. When really it was on the other side of the station."

"Well, if you'd have stayed with Apolline, you could be on your way to Cabourg right now."

"Are you serious? You know we both could have gone without the papers to read. I would have been perfectly happy making conversation the whole trip; because I am a decent human being."

"Oh?" My pulse raced and a heated fury that felt strangely sexual whipped up inside me. "And what does that make me in your estimation? Not decent?"

"How about cruel? Cold and cruel. Does that sound more like it?"

"Fine." We were standing at the base of the stairs, facing off. People were still watching, and there was no way I could count on him to be the bigger person. So I relented. Swallowing hard, I said, "Merci. Is that what you want? Merci, Benoit, for stopping to help me. I'm fine. I can take care of myself. Let's just go find out about the next train."

"Yes, let's." He sniffed, perhaps noticing our audience.

I had sacrificed friendships to keep my job, to get opportunities like this. I needed to do well. I needed to beat him. I couldn't let him distract me with charm or insincere concern for my well being. Because there was no way it was anything more than that. The stakes were high and rising. This was war. And I had to wage it carefully. Screaming at him in a train station, or letting this situation escalate any further would not benefit me in the long term.

With my things collected and in tow, we went back upstairs toward the ticket counter. But even though we were no longer locked in battle, my temper wouldn't cool. I was furious with him, furious with myself. Afraid that this would reflect poorly on me when I needed to earn Vartre's good opinion now more than ever. I tried to breathe and tell myself everything would be fine. We'd catch the next train. But it felt like this was another in a growing line of life-altering crises arising in my life. Benoit Levin, however, seemed relaxed, moving through the crowd with loose ease.

As we crossed the station, Benoit suggested we split up. "I can call the office while you see about the tickets."

"Oh, no you don't. There's no way you're calling work to tell them it's all my fault. I'll handle Vartre; you check on the tickets."

"Maybe we should just stick together, since I can't be trusted."

"Don't be ridiculous."

"I'm not the one being ridiculous."

And so I talked on the phone while he stood right next to me and listened to every word. Then we went to the ticket counter together. We explained the situation to the clerk, who clicked her tongue and searched her ledgers.

"I'm sorry, but the next train is the busiest all day, especially this time of year. The economy cabin is the best I can do."

"We don't need to sit together." I assured her. "Not even in the same car. You must have two individual seats."

"I'm sorry. The economy cabin is the only thing left. Unless you want to wait until tomorrow morning."

"There are two individual seats in the economy cabin?"

"There are two seats, yes. It's nice. Very private. You'll like it." She looked between us and smiled suggestively. "I won't tell."

"Fine. If that's all we can get," Benoit said at the same time I said, "We're not together."

"Sure." She shrugged, unconvinced and not really caring.

I resented that she assumed we were a couple. I was most certainly not part of a couple.

To be honest, I never imagined myself in any sort of coupling. I had been kissed—there was a boy in school whom I loved and who loved me back—in our childish, bumbling ways. But I'd never had a real, adult petit ami. I didn't really want one. I didn't want a girlfriend either, if that's what you're wondering. I wanted my work. I needed my work. I imagined no other future than working at my highest capacity.

It had always been that way. I was hired as a secretary because I was a woman, but I wanted to be a reporter. My first story was about an up-and-coming playwright from Montmartre whom Nadine introduced me to. I interviewed him, wrote up the story, and then I spent two days not giving it to the editor because I was so nervous that he wouldn't take me seriously. I was afraid he would dismiss me outright. But he read it while I stood there, to my utter mortification. Then he published it without changing a word. And he payed me for it. That was my first small success, which led to many more. My ambitions ran high, much higher than my experience and, frankly, my maturity level. But I wanted it, whatever was available. I had no one but myself, and so I wanted everything I could get. Every time I achieved something, the next goal always became visible. Now it was section editor. Who knew what I could be or accomplish from that higher place? Needless to say, I wasn't thinking about love or any sort of coupling, regardless of what the ticket clerk assumed. Not even when Benoit Levin stirred terribly inconvenient and most unwelcome desirous feelings in me.

Back on the train platform, there were open spots on two benches that faced each other. I sat on one side next to an older woman who smelled like lemon, and he sat on the other. We had four hours to wait. For a long while, neither of us spoke. His proximity was maddening. There was no way we'd make it five hours on a train in an economy cabin, whatever that was. I tried to put it out of my mind. That nightmare was still hours away, while my current nightmare—the one with him watching me from across the way with some unreadable, smug expression on his perfect face—was happening now.

His presence aroused something destructive in me that I struggled to control. This trip was turning into some kind of impassable test of my strength as a woman, as a human being. How not to kill a bastard who deserved it, or something like that. But I couldn't give up. We hadn't even left Paris yet.

Benoit pulled a cigarette case from an interior pocket of his jacket and held it up to offer me one. I accepted, and he stood to pass a cigarette and light it for me. I nodded in thanks.

There was just something about him that made my skin crawl so bad I wanted to rip off my clothes. Not in a sexual way. Not at all. A frustrated release, maybe? No, that didn't sound right either. Whatever it was, I needed to get it under control. So I watched the crowd. I smoked a cigarette. I read my papers. And if I didn't look at him, it was almost as if he didn't exist.

Chapter Six

My stomach started complaining of hunger about halfway through our wait for the next train. When I stood and began gathering my things, Benoit watched me questioningly.

"If I don't eat something, neither of us will make it to Cabourg."

"I'll join you."

I would have rather he didn't, though I didn't say so. Now that I'd calmed down, I could see how… maybe… I had been cruel to him. He did stop to make sure I was okay, after all. He did help me up. And although he touched my underwear in doing so, he did help me pick up my mess. I wouldn't have screamed at Apolline if she were trying to help me in the same way. When I was honest with myself, in those long hours on the hard train station bench, I could see how some of what had happened was my fault. We shared the blame.

I had to preserve my energy, and, yes, being spiteful was costly. Actively hating him would distract me from my mission, which was to get better stories than him. Crush him with my talent and capabilities. Ruin his career. I couldn't fight him the whole trip and maintain my professionalism. I had a job to do. And no matter how I felt about my colleague, he was my colleague, and we'd been tasked with working together.

Passively hating him would be more practical. So I nodded my acceptance and walked toward the café.

We sat together at a small table in the concourse where we could watch other travelers passing by. Sunlight streamed into the station through the wide skylights in the ceiling. A server came and filled two glasses with water from a large carafe. The menu was simple, and after the business of ordering lunch, we sat facing each other, our bags tucked under our seats so they were out of the way. And it occurred to me that we would, unfortunately, be sharing many meals like this in the coming days.

My next thought was that at least he was pleasant to look at. He had sparkling eyes in a shade of blue that I'd never seen on anyone else before. And his thick brown hair fell in a glossy swoop over his forehead. His jawline and cheekbones could have been carved in marble by a master. His face drew the eye. A regretful fact. Beautiful people always got away with more, made it further in life, because of their physical pleasantness. Now if only I could figure out how to get him to keep that perfect mouth shut.

"How well do you know our illustrator?" he said, breaking our silence.

"Is that why you've followed me to the café? To find out gossip about our coworker?"

"I'm just curious. And hungry."

"We've never traveled together, if that's what you mean. She's been at *L'Entreprise* longer than me. I've encountered her in various professional settings. I'm familiar with her work. What do you want to know?"

"I suppose I want a sense of what she's telling Vartre right now about why we missed our train."

"Oh. Well. I'm not sure. I hadn't considered that she'd tell her anything." Perhaps I should have, but when I'd spoken to Vartre, it didn't sound like we were in any trouble. "I think it will be fine. I fell. You were helping me. She got on the train without us."

"You're probably right."

The server returned with our soup and bread. It was hot and looked delicious with creamy white beans and rosemary. The baguette was crisp and fragrant. We ate in silence for a few blissful minutes. He had decent table manners and swept up his own crumbs when he finished his bread. Had his mother taught him to do that?

"Your family seems nice."

"Oh, did they? For having raised a villain like me, you mean?"

I laughed, despite myself. "No. I just mean they seemed so normal."

"Again. Compared to what?"

"I'm trying to be nice, you know. And I mean it." I almost told him about my own lack of family life, but I held back. There was no reason to get that comfortable.

"Well, thank you. I appreciate it. They are nice. Maybe not normal, though."

"How do you mean?"

He raised an eyebrow, perhaps surprised that I'd asked. I was a little surprised myself. "Well, my father, who never approved of me, died a few years ago. My mother is unwell. My sister's husband is a captain in the navy, and so he is rarely around. With the children and my mother when I'm at work, it's a lot for Rachelle. I have an older brother, but he's a doctor in Orléans and has three young children of his own."

"Have you left your sister in the lurch for this trip?"

"No. We've recently hired someone to help with my mother; it seems to be going well. And we have a housekeeper who has been with us for so long she's like family. They'll manage, I hope."

"It's not what I pictured of your home life."

"You pictured my home life, Marnet? Now you must elaborate."

"I guess I assumed something less wholesome."

"Why?"

"I don't know. Because it gave me another reason to dislike you, I suppose."

His blue eyes glistened. He didn't care at all that I hated him. "Well, I appreciate your honesty. Do you come from a big family?"

"Me? No." I wasn't going to say more, but when he stared at me instead of continuing on about himself, I had to fill the space. "My mother died in childbirth. My little brother's, not mine. I was eight. My brother didn't make it either. And so it was just my father and me after that."

"Oh, I'm sorry to hear that. And is your father in Paris?"

"No. He's gone as well now. Died when I was fourteen."

"Goodness, you're an orphan. I had no idea." His brow crumpled with what seemed like genuine pain over my circumstances. Most people felt bad for me, which was why I should never have brought it up.

"It's fine. It made me who I am today."

"Well, no one would envy you. But as a man who has always lived in an over-crowded house, I can see some obvious benefits to having fewer people around."

The server came with coffee and cleared our soup bowls; an interruption that allowed me to step back on what was a deepening conversation. I needed to be vigilant and careful about deepening anything with this man.

When the train rolled in, we were both waiting on the platform, ready. Puffs of steam filled the station. The arriving passengers debarked, and finally it was time for us to board. A porter directed us toward the back of the train, and as we passed other cabins, I saw roomy bench seats facing each other with little tables mounted between them. For a brief moment, I was relieved. It would be annoying to share a cabin, but they seemed roomy enough.

"Here we are," he said, opening a narrow door at the back of a train car. "Oh."

"What?"

"This can't be it. There isn't room for both of us in here."

"Let me see."

He stepped inside, struggling to turn in the tight space and face me. "It is certainly tight."

"Tight? Where am I supposed to sit? On your lap?" The cabin—if you could call it that; it looked more like a cabinet— was less than a meter wide or deep. There was one bench seat that seemed much smaller than all the others we passed. There was no table and the window was more like a peephole.

"Did we open the right door?" He stepped out again, brushing past me and craning to look at the surrounding cabin doors.

I didn't want to believe that this could be it. I checked the ticket against the plaque on the door twice, hoping my vision would miraculously clear, and we'd be in the wrong seat. But no matter how many times I blinked, the numbers didn't fail to correspond. There was not a more spacious cabin waiting for us somewhere else. And yet there had to be. My chest tightened at the thought of cramming myself in there with him. Desperate, I said, "I think we should find someone to ask. Maybe we're in the wrong car."

His pretty face betrayed no sense of humor. "I don't think so, Vanessa. I am afraid this is it."

"Well, I refuse to accept this." I shook my head like an insolent child. "This is not going to work."

"Now you're being intentionally difficult. There are two seats. Plenty of room." He stashed his bag under the bench and offered to do the same with mine.

"I can handle my own bags." I tried to step past him and put away my valise, but there wasn't enough room. My hip rubbed against his, and when I tried to move in the other direction my breasts pressed against his firm arm. My heart began to flutter in the most uncomfortable way. I had never been claustrophobic, but a panicky surge of denial hit me, standing there in that tiny space. All I could smell was him—the cologne, the floral something (a lavender soap maybe), and a hint of sweat. He was touching me even though he wasn't trying, and there was no room to share. I wanted to scream. "That treacherous ticket clerk lied to us! That's maybe one and a half seats. Two children couldn't sit here comfortably."

"It will be fine. After everything that has happened today, I'm sure we can manage. It's only for a few hours." He sounded like he was trying to convince himself as much as me. But a small, reluctant part of me appreciated his positivity.

He sat on the bench seat, taking up most of it. Then he scooted toward the wall as far as he could and looked up at me. We were still so close that my skirt was brushing his leg. He smiled when he saw my face, which had to be twisted and ugly. It felt like it might melt off. I groaned and let my shoulders fall and my head hang. Why? Why me? I had asked it a million times in my life, and I was asking it again now. The train whistle signaled departure. There was nothing to do but sit. And so I did.

Carefully, trying not to touch him, I lowered myself onto the bench. It was thinly cushioned and without a center armrest to separate the space, and despite trying to avoid it, the entire side of my body, from the peak of my shoulder to to the edge of my knee was pressed up against the corresponding parts of his body. I scooted as far as I could in the opposite direction to no avail. He was right there. His face centimeters from mine. His breath mingling with mine. Right there.

"Cozy, isn't it?"

I let out a dry sob that turned into a cackle, even though nothing about this was funny. Nothing. "Cozy is not the word I would choose."

"Some might say that train travel is romantic."

"I definitely wouldn't use that word either."

"Do I want to know what word you would choose?"

"I'm sure you can imagine."

He laughed, and so I laughed again, harder this time. It was ridiculous. Everything about this day had been so ridiculous. Laughing about it at least eased some of the tension.

He sighed and shifted. "Are you uncomfortable?"

"Wildly so, yes. Is there any way you can take up less room?"

"I'm considerably bigger than you."

"I realize that, but to be fair, the space should still be split in half."

"Oh should it?" He scoffed playfully.

"Of course, it should."

"I suppose you're right. But I can't shrink myself."

"Maybe if you didn't sit with your legs spread out like that, taking up as much space as possible." I waved my hand in the general direction of his lap.

"What, like this?" He put his knees together, but it didn't really free up any space. He was still bigger than me, and there just wasn't space to free.

"Oh, never mind."

The train rocked and jerked and left the station, slowly gaining speed as it chugged through the city. The conductor came by to check our tickets. When I asked if there happened to be any empty seats anywhere, he reiterated what the ticket clerk had explained about this being the busiest trip of the day and told us the café car would open in about an hour. Through the window, the city's behind-the-scenes views—the alleys and buildings' backsides—passed.

After a short while, crammed in there next to him, my skin stopped crawling and my blood ceased boiling. The air, somehow, was circulating and fresh instead of stuffy and unbearable. At least for now. And I found that his body, which was an admittedly perfect male form, wasn't so terrible to be pressed against. He didn't smell unappealing; quite the opposite. Definitely lavender soap. His clothes, up close, were worn but well-made and well-cared for. He obviously took pride in his appearance. I was uncomfortable with how comfortable it turned out to be next to him like that.

"Should we plan our strategy for when we arrive in Cabourg?" His voice was low and close enough to make my ear tingle.

"Our strategy? I prefer to keep our strategies separate."

"We're supposed to work together."

I sighed and closed my eyes for a second. He was right, but I wasn't ready to face that reality yet. "I know. But maybe we can just read quietly without talking to each other for a while."

I shifted and reached for my bag, which I'd stuffed under my seat. All my reading material was in there, but there was nothing left to read. "I read all my papers at the station."

"I did too. We could trade?"

"Okay."

He reached for his bag now and produced his stack of papers. Every time one of us moved, the other had to adjust position to accommodate it. We exchanged, and I leafed through the papers, considering not only the material but also him. Again. He'd chosen an interesting mix and dog-eared several pieces that he must have wanted to return to. And they weren't limited to the culture pages. He read widely. News reports and serial stories and announcements. It felt so inappropriately intimate, being that physically close to him and considering his mind. It was repulsive and compelling at the same time.

The cabin was warm, but not uncomfortably so, and if I positioned my reading in just the right way I could block most of him from my vision. The train swayed gently through the rolling hills and quaint little towns. It had been so long since I'd been out of the city, I had almost forgotten what was all around it. I read for a while, but then inadvertently drifted into a dreamless, welcoming sleep.

Some time later my eyes gently opened. There was no startle, not at first—just the peaceful, easy awakening after the most rejuvenating nap. I could have been in my own bed. But in seconds I realized I was not. I was curled up against Benoit's broad chest. My face was pressed up against the smooth fabric of his shirt. And his long arm was draped around my shoulders. This was what startled me.

I sat up fast, wiping my mouth because of course I had been drooling. There was a little wet spot on his shirt where I'd lain.

He smiled and gently retracted his arm. "Nice nap?"

"What happened?" The last thing I remembered was reading.

"You fell asleep."

"Obviously. I mean about the cuddling."

"Cuddling?" He smiled devilishly.

I was so hot with embarrassment that steam probably shot out of my mouth. "Please, just tell me how I ended up with your arm around me."

"My darling, once you lost consciousness, you transformed into the sweetest kitten. You curled in like you didn't belong anywhere else. I've never seen anything so adorable." His hat was off, and his hair was mussed. His eyes danced while he told me all of this. "And you have the most precious snore. I didn't notice it the other times I found you sleeping."

I have never wanted to kill a man more than I wanted to kill him. But it was different from the other times I imagined violence, of which there had admittedly been a few. The simple mix of hatred and professional jealousy now was complicated with embarrassment and something else very unwelcome. When I imagined putting my hands on his neck, I was as tempted to pull him closer as I was to wring it. Something was very wrong. I had felt his heart beating on the side of my face. And I had liked it. No sensation in my life that I could recall had ever felt so right. I cleared my throat. "Why didn't you wake me or move me over?"

"I assume it takes a lot of energy being so feisty all the time." He shrugged innocently. "You need your rest."

"Did you remove my hat?" It was sitting on my lap, and I had no recollection of taking it off.

"I did. I hope you don't mind. It was poking me in the face."

"I apologize." I fiddled with my hat. What was it about this man that made such a mess of me every single time?

He smiled—again!—with that smooth charm. "No need."

"There is a need. It was terribly unprofessional of me. You could call the office and complain and probably get me fired."

"For falling asleep on an extended work trip? That's hardly fireable."

"For inappropriately touching you. For revealing my underthings. For making you miss the train."

His eyes narrowed, and he reconsidered me. Or reconsidered something.

"Let's just forget about it." He looked out the window, where green countryside seemed to go on forever. Then he turned back to me. "We still have an hour or so before we're there. Should we find the café car?"

"Oui, absolutely. Anything to get out of this tiny cabin."

The café car was crowded, like every other centimeter of the train. But Benoit managed to grab a little booth where we could sit and drink our coffee with a table between us. And the coffee was surprisingly hot and delicious. It soothed many of my difficult feelings, like humiliation and confusion.

Benoit blew across the surface of his black coffee and relaxed into his seat. He seemed perfectly at peace in every situation, while I was continuously flustered. Someone left a paper that neither of us had read yet, and he wordlessly separated it and passed me the culture section. We read and sipped our coffee and watched the other people in the café car, sipping their drinks and reading their papers. And it was almost like we'd come through something, like we'd been spit out on the other side, and it wasn't so uncomfortable or infuriating to be in his presence anymore. His calm rubbed off on me.

His company wasn't as awful as I'd expected it to be. He wasn't some spoiled rich boy, and maybe he wasn't exactly a shallow womanizer. And I found myself wanting to know more about him. I was curious. I had questions. Inconveniently, the desire to curl back into his chest grew like a tightness in mine, a thirst.

Chapter Seven

The train slowed as we approached Cabourg. The town was spread out on a field of green grass like picnickers in the park, but became more crowded the closer we got to the station. Finally, after what felt like days of travel, we arrived at Gare Dives-Cabourg without further ado. I was tired and jittery after so much time on the train. Anxiety about being in an unfamiliar place trembled in my chest. And I was on the verge of a low-grade existential crisis over Benoit Levin. I could barely look him in the eye after sleeping literally in his arms. His heartbeat was still reverberating through me. I took a deep breath and pinned my hat on my head. Then I gathered my bags and didn't spare a goodbye for our tiny quarters.

We waited in the lumbering line of passengers to disembark, squeezed up against each other in collective anticipation. The station, a dignified brick building with one line of track passing alongside it, was a fraction of the size of the one we'd left in Paris. Train passengers—mostly well-dressed families visiting for vacation—flooded the little platform and dispersed.

Benoit and I peaceably hired a carriage to take us to the hotel, which was a quick trip over the Dives River toward the beach. The carriage was a spacious dream compared to our economy cabin.

All I knew about the town was that most of it was relatively new. Two Parisian financiers put a big hotel on the relatively quiet stretch of beach not far from all the other popular area beaches. Then other hotels soon followed. The sky was cloudless and scrubbed bright by the sea wind, and the air was dizzyingly clean. Vacation homes built in the timber frame style lined the residential streets. There were wide sun-drenched gardens with hydrangeas and oleanders in full, vibrant bloom. I had never felt so far from Paris in my life.

I caught a glimpse of the sea just before we passed the palatial Grand Hôtel, around which almost the whole town was oriented. Our hotel, the Hôtel de la Plage, was much smaller and less ostentatious than the Grand, and it sat among a cluster of shops and vacation homes. The carriage dropped us in the front, and as soon as I stepped onto the pavement, I could hear the delicate swish of the ocean. Inside, the lobby was decorated in pale blue and creamy white; it was simple and comfortable. The water was on full display through the windows along the back. The ocean and the sky were a picture that contained every shade of blue. Seeing it eased some of the tension that had collected in my shoulders all day.

No nightmares unfolded during the check-in process—there had been no mixups, we weren't forced to share a single room, and I didn't embarrass myself any further. Our rooms weren't even right next to each other.

Apolline found us as we were finishing at the desk.

"You made it!" She called as she crossed the lobby.

"Finally."

"I checked the train schedule when I arrived. I never doubted you." She'd changed out of her linen suit and into a comfortable-looking blue cotton dress with fluttery sleeves. She must have been waiting in the lobby for us to arrive.

"You left without us," Benoit said placidly. He put a hand on her shoulder and pulled her in for an air kiss.

"You didn't leave me much choice."

"Did we miss anything?" I asked.

"I was going to ask you two the same thing." She winked, though I wasn't sure why.

"We're reporting from the beach," I said, blinking rapidly. "Not the train."

"No. I know that. Never mind. I took a nap and then walked along the promenade. The new casino is about a block from here, right on the water."

"Did you talk to anyone?"

"No, but I drew a picture of the facade. Quite regal."

"We'll all go tomorrow," Benoit said. "They're doing a press tour and preview before opening this weekend."

"I'd like to talk to some local people for a sense of the public opinion about the opening."

"That sounds like a plan," he said.

"Should we meet down here for dinner?" I asked as a courtesy, not because I wanted us to all share a meal. The hotel had a dining room off to the side of the lobby.

"Oh, dear, I had something in my room just before coming down to meet you. I believe I'm done for the day. But you two go ahead."

Benoit looked uncertainly at me, and then he declined as well. "I don't think I will either. I'm going up to settle in."

A prickle of disappointment passed over my skin, which was silly. It was no matter. I didn't need him. I'd been squeezed up against him all day, and it would be good to be free to think and do my work for the evening. I wasn't quite sure what to expect traveling on assignment. But I needed to make the most of every moment while I was there. If he was settling in for the night, then I would have a head start.

My room was modest, smaller than what I had at the pension, but more coherently appointed. Rather than the assorted collection of furnishings, everything matched and coordinated. There was a blue and white toile armchair and bench with children and dogs in various scenes at the beach. There was a desk by the window, fully stocked with thick, embossed hotel stationery. And the full-sized bed was dressed in blue and white stripes. Through my window, the street and walled gardens of the houses across the way were visible. There were pots of red geraniums on one of the stoops. No ocean view, not that I expected the paper to pay for that. It was still a nice room, and staying there would be fine.

Being alone for the first time in hours loosened every muscle in my body. The problem of Benoit Levin was only getting stranger, but it was no longer closing in on me. He was in another room down the hall. Even though I apparently had no trouble curling right up and relaxing next to him on the train.

The problem was not so much that I'd fallen asleep on him, physically in his arms. My feelings on that, though initially revolting because of the embarrassment, had settled into something less familiar. I kept revisiting that blissful moment upon waking when I was pressed against him, the smooth, soft fabric of his shirt on my face, and the pleasant weight of his arm around me. It had been the best nap, like that of a child after a long morning. I had been engulfed in the smell of him—his body and his clothes and all the physical, aromatic elements that made him up. I wished I thought it was gross or repulsive. But I didn't. That nap had been warm and rejuvenating; waking up from it a moment of pure bliss. Fleeting, but undeniably something. I wanted to hate it, but all I could think was: how could I experience that feeling again?

I shuddered to shake off the memories of it. I did not want to be reveling in it. I did not want to return to it. It should have been unnatural to curl up with that man. No matter that my body seemed to desire it, I knew better.

How ridiculous? Craving the physical presence of my sworn enemy?! It was all very confusing.

After I unpacked and arranged all my things in their new, temporary locations, I cleaned up and dressed to go out. My work companions may have been tired, but I wasn't. Dressing for work as a reporter, I never wanted to stand out. My clothing and appearance needed to blend in rather than attract attention. Because I wanted people to talk to me about the story, not about what I was wearing. I wanted to observe things as they were happening, not intrude with any ostentatious dress. So I wore my plain gray suits every day. It was easy, and gray made my blonde hair seem brighter, icier.

But covering cultural events often meant evening attire. In Paris, one could stand out for being out of fashion or too casual. And so, I may have dressed plainly, but this didn't mean I was unfashionable. I'd built up a small collection of understated, unassuming evening wear. Nadine gave me a few things, and Catherine and Diane and I went shopping when they first moved in. The Americans embraced shopping and wardrobe building with unbridled enthusiasm. Traveling light and packing dresses meant I'd chosen every item in my valise for its versatility.

I removed my blouse and wet a towel from the pitcher of water that came with the room. I freshened up and then redressed in a gray satin bodice that coordinated with the same skirt I'd been wearing all day. No one could accuse me of being frumpy or unfashionable in that bodice. It was a staple of my wardrobe for quick changes exactly like this one. I tied my hair back in a black velvet ribbon and put a little stain on my lips. I sharpened a pencil and tucked it into my skirt pocket with one of my small notebooks. I put a few coins in my other pocket, so I could buy a drink and something to eat if I got hungry.

As I saw to my toilette, there were sounds of music and people moving around the hotel. When I heard a door open and close somewhere down the hall, I thought about Benoit. He'd said he was going to his room, but that had been nearly two hours ago. There was always a chance he'd gone out since then. And I didn't want to see him.

I opened my door and scanned the hallway. There was no one around. So I darted toward the stairs and went down. I kept my eyes focused on the exit as I crossed the lobby, so that whether he was there or not, I wouldn't see him. I went out the back and onto the wide, paved promenade that lined the beach. The breeze was salty and damp and slightly stiffer than it had been on the street side of the building. It was near dark now; a sliver of the sun's light still peeked from the edge of the horizon.

Many of the oceanfront hotels had casinos and theaters, making the promenade the center of nightlife in an otherwise sleepy coastal town. I started walking toward where Apolline had said the new casino was located, watching the passersby as I went, taking in the scene and their bits of conversation. Revelers traveled in groups and couples from one venue to the next. I thought about finding a bench somewhere and perhaps sitting and observing for a while. But observation was hard in the shadowy light, so I decided to walk until I found somewhere that looked interesting to duck inside for a drink and note taking.

Three doors down, fashionable people and lively music were spilling out from two sets of matching gatefold glass doors. I went inside, where a busy, casual dining room abutted a stage where a woman in a long sparkling dress was singing. Everything at the beach was more casual than venues in Paris. It enhanced the freewheeling vacation feeling of being out of town and closer to nature. It was more rustic. More summery. I could see why everyone wanted to come. For some people, getting out of Paris was as much a part of Parisian life as the city. Not so much for me, but for some people. Although getting here had been quite an ordeal, it was fascinating to be somewhere so different.

There was a lot of pleasure in dining out alone in a new place as well. I sat at an open seat at the bar, which was also crowded but not full. The bartender passed me a menu and glass of water, then told me about the wines. The menu was small and simple with classic rustic seafood dishes and a roasted chicken that sounded delicious. Chicken was always a safe choice, but I was feeling adventurous and decided les fruits de mer were more in the spirit of my first night at the beach.

"I'll try the steamed oysters, s'il vous plait. With the chardonnay."

He gave me a business-like nod and poured my wine, which was cool and buttery. I was smiling to myself and feeling quite smug, thinking about my coworkers snoozing in their hotel rooms, when there was Benoit, across the bar, watching me, equally as smug.

I gasped, but my heart didn't sink. It did something quite different, more fluttery and strangely joyful. He waved and then got up and started toward me. I had not been lonely or in need of company, and now suddenly I was glad to have it—for what reason I had no idea. Him of all people.

He had changed his clothes as well and was now dressed in an evening coat and bowler hat. He was smiling, and for a second, my mind—rascal that it was—went back to those moments of sleepy bliss when my cheek pressed against his chest. Again.

"I thought that was you."

"Shame. I tried to sneak in undetected."

"My dear, in that dress, everyone in the room noticed."

I smiled like a foolish girl, and then promptly caught myself and straightened out my face. "I thought I had the place to myself. You said you were staying in for the night."

"I said I was settling in and not joining you for dinner, which was nice of me."

"Underhanded, you mean?"

"No. What do you mean?"

"I mean that you tried to leave me behind so that you could gain an edge on your reporting. You know, the reporting that determines which one of us will remain at the *L'Entreprise*."

Something like pain twitched across his otherwise sly and sculpted face. "I assumed you'd had enough of my company. I was giving you your space."

"Could you do that now?"

His eyes narrowed, but his seductive smile didn't falter. "No."

Before I could protest, the bartender returned with my oysters, and Benoit seated himself on the empty stool next to me.

I thanked the bartender and turned my attention to Benoit. "So you're here for the show? Or you've come to work?"

He shrugged. "Maybe a little of both. We'll have to see where the evening leads."

"I came to work." I pulled my notebook and pencil from my pocket and held them aloft.

"And eat oysters?"

"Yes. I was hungry." Twelve steamed oysters were splayed on my plate, arranged in a circle around a pile of sliced lemons nestled in a bed of bib lettuce. It looked delicious, and he was still looking at my plate. "Do you want one?"

"Hm? Oh, no merci."

"Suit yourself." I squeezed a lemon wedge over several shells, then scooped up an oyster with the provided tiny fork. Oysters were often on restaurant menus in Paris, but they were too fancy for Cook. I'd eaten them a few times, but these were better. The bodies were delicately rubbery with pockets of seawater. These must have been so fresh compared to the ones I'd tried. It was the most delicious and potent thing I'd ever consumed.

I groaned in pleasure, and then realized he was still watching me.

"Good?"

"Oh, they're wonderful. Are you sure you don't want one?"

"I'm sure." He sipped his wine, which was red and half gone. "I ate not long ago."

"Well, pardon me." I scooped another salty oyster into my mouth. "Have you talked to anyone?"

"I did speak to a few gentlemen from Rouen who've been coming here since they were boys."

I was not happy to hear that he'd already started working. Not to be outdone, I told him about how much scenery I'd taken in. How much background I could fill in from just my short walk here. I also put down my oyster fork and opened my notebook, like I was ready to start taking furious notes and show just how serious I was. Just as serious as him. I ate two more oysters, as delicious and delightful as the first.

After listening to me rattle on, he swallowed the last of his wine. "Well, I can leave you to it. I am more tired than I thought, and we should get an early start tomorrow. Apolline doesn't strike me as the sort who sleeps away the morning."

"Oh, okay." This, strangely, was when my heart sank. Just a little. I was enjoying his company more than I thought. More than I wanted to. "Are you sure you're not trying to lose me again?"

"No. I'm tired." He stood and pushed in his barstool.

"I'm teasing. Au revoir."

He nodded and turned to go. But then I stopped him. "What time tomorrow?"

"We could meet for breakfast at nine?"

"That sounds good. Au revoir."

He smiled again. "Au revoir."

He strode out of the wide doors and disappeared in the promenade crowd.

I ate another oyster and took up my pencil, scrawling out as many details about the place as I could think to note. I would need settings and backdrops for everything I'd write here. I watched the crowd and tried to note faces. A few were perhaps familiar from Paris, and I wanted to notice as many as possible in case some of these faces became familiar in the coming days. And while paying my check, I talked to the bartender for a few minutes about what he thought of the new casino coming, how long he'd worked here, and if his views represented that of the community at large, in his estimation. By the time I left, I had a solid start, and I reveled in the pleasure of accomplishment. I was the most productive reporter in the world.

Outside, the sky was fully dark now. The half moon clung to the top of the sky. And cast just enough light to illuminate the white caps rolling in at their regular intervals. Traffic on the promenade had eased; the shows had started and the gaming tables were full. Underneath all the chatter of tourists and music from the hotels, ran the slow rhythm of the waves breaking. I let it drown out all the lingering noise in my mind. I walked back to the hotel, upstairs, and into my room without more than a glance down the hall toward Benoit's.

Chapter Eight

The pain awoke me a few short hours later from a dead sleep. It was a shooting, searing intestinal pain that shocked me with its urgency. I pulled on my robe and slippers and darted into the hallway. The facility was shared but mercifully empty at that hour. Not that I had any time to check or care. With great exigence and as much speed as possible, I made it to the toilet. I will not tell you what happened after that with any specifics. I will only say that my experience in those wee hours was so painful, so dark that I feared I would not make it out. Death I would have welcomed.

Just before dawn, empty and exhausted but still cramping, I peeled myself up off the cold bathroom tiles. I cleaned up as best as I could and went back to my room. Had I contracted dysentery? A killer virus on the verge of sweeping the continent? Some exotic beach-dwelling parasite? I was so violently ill that it had to be medically significant. I collapsed in my bed, a husk of my former vigorous self, and fell asleep despite the continuous rumble of my inner organs.

When I awoke later, it was to sunshine pouring through the window and hard knocking on my door.

"Don't come in!" I groaned miserably. "Do not disturb!"

"Not a chance, darling." A muffled, yet dastardly familiar voice came from the hallway. "You missed breakfast. It's past ten."

"I'm quite unwell." I couldn't let him see me like that. "I'm very sick. I need more time. I can meet you later."

"We're worried, dear. If you don't open the door, I'll go get the concierge," called another voice. Apolline.

"Okay, okay. Just give me a second." I struggled to stand on my weak legs. To preserve my last shred of dignity, I wrapped myself in the quilt from the bed before unlocking and opening the door.

"Bonjour, mademoiselle," Benoit said cheerily. He stopped short then and recoiled upon seeing me, undoubtedly crusted in vomit and god knew what else. My feet were bare, my hair uncombed, and certainly not presentable in any sort of professional sense.

"Oh, my. What happened to you?" Apolline barged in and surveyed the scene.

I sat on the edge of the bed and pulled the quilt around me tighter. "I've come down with something terrible. Keep your distance. I don't want you to get it."

"What's wrong?"

"I've been up all night vomiting and... sick in worse ways. I feel like my insides are bound up in knots. It's probably contagious." The taste in my mouth was so foul, and it was as if all my blood and energy had been sucked out by a vampire.

"The oysters."

"Oh," Apolline shook her head. "You ate oysters?"

"No. I don't think that's it. This is much more sinister than a bad oyster."

"I bet that was it," Benoit said, ignoring my protest.

"That's why I don't eat them anymore." Apolline shook her head with grave seriousness. "I ate a bad shellfish once and thought for sure I was turning inside out."

"I ate a bad piece of fish in Marseilles during my service, and I still haven't forgotten it."

"Oysters can do this?" It didn't seem possible. I shuddered.

"Absolutely. All it takes is one bad one."

"You could have mentioned that last night when I was eating them!" I said to Benoit, who was examining the surfaces of my room.

"That's the sort of thing you eat at your own risk, honey. Everyone knows that," Apolline tutted.

Benoit nodded.

They were right. He shouldn't have had to tell me. I wouldn't have listened anyway. I'd been such a spiteful cow, and this was my punishment: explosive sickness and complete humiliation. I never imagined a fresh oyster could be this dangerous, even a bad one. They'd all been so delicious. I let my head fall back. My mouth was so dry. And my stomach was still roiling. A sob emerged from me then, though it was tearless and parched. I was such an idiot, and it had all been too much. "How could I have been so foolish? When we have so much work to do!"

"It's okay, darling." Benoit sat down next to me and looked questioningly at Apolline.

"I was up all night, and I feel terrible!" Another ugly sob wracked me.

"It's okay."

"I'll go get her some hot coffee and toast," Apolline said, heading for the door.

"And maybe some cold water." Benoit, with an unprofessional level of tenderness, put his arm around me. Then he leaned in and cooed. "It's okay."

"It's not okay!" A single, fat tear squeezed from my eye. "I feel like an idiot."

"Oh, stop." He laughed. He was laughing at me, squeezing me against him.

I had bruises the size of fists from my fall at the train station. Everything on my body hurt, and I was so pathetic. But there was his heartbeat again. The warmth of him. I stopped crying. I didn't laugh, but listening to him laugh made me feel better.

"The worst is surely over. But you're probably exhausted and dehydrated. You won't feel well for a while." The weight of his arm on my shoulders was heavenly. "And you may never eat oysters again. At least not for a long time."

"I thought you were so unadventurous and unrefined when you wouldn't try one last night. I'm such a self-righteous bitch."

"Ha. I might not use those words." He squeezed me closer. "It will be all right. And you can take the day off."

"I'm sorry." Taking a day off was the last thing I wanted to do. I'd already cost us a day of work with my trip to the newsstand. "This is shaping up to be the worst work trip ever."

"Oh, don't worry. We're here for three weeks. It's only just begun. When was the last time you were sick?"

"It's been a few hours. It was still dark when I came back to my room."

Apolline returned then with a server carrying a tray of coffee and baguette and a glistening carafe of iced water. He set it down on the nightstand and left to bring a fresh pitcher of warm water and towels.

After pouring me a cup of coffee, Benoit said to Apolline, "Why don't you go ahead down to the casino while the light is still in your favor. I'll see that she gets settled and meet you there in time to get the tour?"

"I should do that," Apolline said with a business-like nod. "As long as you're okay here?"

"I'll be right behind you."

I noticed that Apolline's camera box and tripod were sitting on the floor right inside my door. They were all ready to go to work, and I was perhaps the furthest away from that that I'd ever been.

Benoit stood while she picked up her things. "Feel better, dear."

Then it was just me and Benoit. I tucked deeper into the quilt. "I can settle myself, you know."

He cut me a piece of bread and placed it on a plate. "I'm not so sure by the looks of you."

I turned toward the mirror for the first time that morning and was shocked by how gray I looked, rather like the offending shellfish. My hair was like a pile of yellow straw. I exhaled a pitiful sigh. "I'm sorry again. You must think I'm a disaster."

He set the bread on my bedside table. Then he sat in the armchair and rifled through the papers he must have brought up with him. "Drink some more coffee. I don't want to leave you until I'm sure you're on the mend."

I nodded, mortified speechless, and sipped my coffee. My stomach growled then at the decibel of the lions roaring in the city zoo. Sometimes you could hear them from blocks away. I instinctively put a hand over my stomach. There was no way he didn't hear that. But I didn't think I was going to get sick, so I took a bite of bread.

Benoit watched me. "That grumbling might continue for a while. Just don't venture too far from the facilities, and you should be fine."

"You don't have to sit with me."

"If you're still not able to hold anything down, then you might need a doctor."

Oh, I hoped not. This could not get any worse. "I think I'll be okay. I just want to lie here."

"I'll sit with you for a while and read the paper, if you don't mind."

"How long?"

"An hour or so; long enough to make sure you can hold down that coffee and bread."

"You've been sick like this?"

"Yes. Probably worse. In some places, drinking the water can do this to you." He sat back in the chair and stretched out his legs. They were so long. His socks were navy blue, half a shade lighter than his pants. His ankles were thick and manly. And his boots were broken in but polished black. "We were awaiting transport in Marseille, and I spent the first night in a restaurant eating the most delicious seafood bisque and the rest of the weekend regretting it. It nearly killed me. Not literally, of course, but I had never been so sick in my life. I've learned to be more careful."

"I never imagined I'd have to worry about it."

"One never does, perhaps. The folly of youth."

"How old are you again?"

"I'm thirty-two. Much wiser than you're... what? Twenty-three years?"

"I'm twenty-four."

"Well, darling, you're still young. And, not to sound like an old man, but there is a lot of learning that happens after twenty-four."

I sat up and looked at him. "I'm not too young. For anything."

"No, not at all," he said with a defensive edge. "I didn't mean to imply."

"No." I lay back down. "You didn't. I'm just making sure."

"Stating the obvious, darling." He held up the paper. "I can read you the headlines, if you like."

I nodded and nestled in while he read from the first page. Maybe I was too sick to care, but I actually didn't mind his presence. I had slept in front of him, after all. Propriety was no longer with us. So I listened to the smooth drone of his voice. And I watched him until he noticed me staring. My stomach kept growling, but I didn't get sick.

It was nearly lunch time when he uncrossed his ankles and pulled his legs in to stand. "I should get to work."

"Okay." A pang of disappointment hit me. I had been enjoying his company.

"Do you need anything else right now?"

"No. I'm going to try to sleep."

"When we're done at the casino, Apolline and I will come check on you." He was moving toward the door now, putting on his straw boater hat.

"Of course. Merci."

After he left, I groaned into my pillow. I felt dizzy and light, mostly because of the sickness, but also kind of because Benoit was being so nice. With him gone, the room suddenly felt empty. In an odd way, he was growing on me. He'd been very kind to me, over and over again, since we left Paris. Working with him was probably not going to be the living hell I'd feared.

I felt guilty for not going with them to the casino, for taking the day off work, but even the idea of getting dressed exhausted me. I sat up for a sip of water. Then I settled back into bed. The hotel sheets were crisp and soft, worn from frequent washings. Guilt be damned. I was so grateful that he'd agreed to cover for me today while I rested. And then I promptly went to sleep.

I awoke a few hours later to a gentle knock at the door. After orienting myself for a moment, I got up and answered it. It was room service, which Benoit and Apolline had probably arranged for me. The young man was wearing a stiff uniform and had a stack of newspapers and a fresh pot of coffee.

"Merci beaucoup," I said. The disease had subsided considerably. "The other pot of coffee has surely gone cold, and that smells wonderful."

He smiled. He was a tall, thin young man, maybe seventeen or eighteen. As he cleared my half-finished cup of coffee and the pot and arranged the fresh, I asked him if he lived in town.

"I do, madame. My father is a carpenter, and my mother works downstairs in the kitchen."

"Oh? How nice. I am a reporter from a paper in Paris."

"Monsieur Levin mentioned that; that you and the other woman are here with him for work."

"Yes. We're writing about the new casino and about the town."

"Yes, madame."

"What do you think about the new casino? And what do your parents say?"

"Oh, it's a good thing, madame." His northern accent pinched the vowels in his words. "For everyone in town. It's good that you're writing about it too. The more people who come, the more customers."

"Yes."

He finished tidying up. "Will that be all?"

"Oui, merci." As he turned to leave, I stopped him. "What was your name again?"

"Pierre, madame."

"Very good, Pierre. And do you know if Monsieur Levin and Madame Trouvé have returned yet?"

"Not that I'm aware of, madame."

I thanked him again as he left the room. The coffee was hot and aromatic. The first sip further revived me and settled much easier than my last attempt.

I hadn't had household staff since I was a child. We had a housekeeper, but she didn't wait on us. Now there was Madame Tremblay and Cook and Claire at home, but they didn't clear my dishes or bring coffee to my room. Not the way this young man had, asking me if I needed anything and addressing me so formally when I was such a mess. It was nearly dinnertime, and

I was still dressed in my robe. Perhaps I would rather like hotel life.

I read the papers and washed and dressed in a fresh nightgown. I was wondering what I should do about dinner when another knock came at the door. This time it was Benoit.

"I've brought you some chicken soup."

"Merci. I was just starting to think about food. That smells perfect." Even though he said he'd check on me, I had expected Apolline to be doing the actual checking. He was a man, and stopping in on the sick often fell on the woman's shoulders by default. I was surprised he'd come alone. Pleasantly so.

"It should go down easy enough. Are you feeling better?"

"I am." I wished I'd put on a proper dress. How many times could a man see a woman who was supposed to be his equal in her night robe? There had to be some professional standard that this blatantly violated.

"Wonderful. You look better."

He turned to leave, but then I asked him to wait. I didn't want to bring it up, but I also had to. "I feel like some professional boundaries have been crossed. I'd rather you hadn't found me in that state. You're my colleague."

He smiled. "I'm sure. But don't worry. This sort of thing happens all the time when there's travel involved. You really get to see firsthand what a person is made of."

"Fantastic!" I laughed. "My humiliation continues."

"I'll still see you as competent in the morning." His smile warmed me; it was like a magic spell.

"I suppose I'll see you a little differently. You've been very kind." I didn't love admitting how wrong I'd been about him. Not at all.

"Really? You must not be fully recovered yet. Or perhaps there's been some damage to your brain."

"I'm being serious. Don't make it harder."

"I'm only teasing you. But I'm glad to hear your opinion of me has improved incrementally." He shrugged. "It's not easy being the most horrible man in the room."

"You're not."

"No. But you must admit, now that we're having a moment of honesty, there have been times in our brief acquaintance that you've thought so."

"You are right. I'm sorry." I looked down at the cup in my hands. I had been truly awful. "Now please let me process the emotions that have come with admitting that. Let's talk about something else. How did today go?"

"It went well." He produced a notebook from his pocket. "I brought my notes if you'd like to go over them."

"Yes! Tell me everything while I eat my soup."

He settled into one of the two chairs at the small, round table, and spread his notebook open. He used unruled paper, which intrigued me almost as much as what he'd written. His handwriting was uniform and pleasing to the eye, so disciplined that he didn't need lines to keep it straight. A detail that perhaps only a person obsessed with stationery and its applications would notice or find fascinating. I half-heartedly tried not to like him even more because of his delightful note-taking methods.

He'd taken several pages of notes on the interior and layout of the two gaming floors. And he'd asked most of the necessary background questions. It seemed all we really needed to do was attend the opening and get a few more interviews from patrons and maybe workers. We decided that he should cover the business side, while I wrote about the first night from the perspective of a patron. We talked all this out in about half an hour, during which it occurred to me that he was a competent and solid teammate—since I had to have one.

And then the strangest thing happened as he was leaving. I was up and moving around by then, almost fully recovered, and I walked him to the door. We were standing there, saying goodnight, when he paused for a beat. His hat was off and in his hand. His hair was not so straightly combed into place, and his collar and cravat had been loosened in a casual, end-of-the-day sort of way. His neck and throat held my eye for a moment before my gaze drifted upward toward his mouth. His lips were full and soft, perfectly lined by his trim mustache. Then that compelling mouth quirked into a confident sideways smile. He was watching me looking at him.

Then his eyes fell to my mouth. Did he want to kiss me? He looked a little like he did.

And then I was thinking about him doing it—leaning in and meeting my mouth with his. Him wrapping his arms around me. Me pressing into his body. I wanted to kiss him… which would surely be a complete disaster. I cleared my throat and pulled my eyes away, pulling out of the reverie as quickly as I'd fallen in.

"I should…" He pointed toward his room but didn't finish his sentence.

"Oui, merci again."

We laughed briefly, awkwardly. Then he nodded and walked toward his room. I closed my door and leaned against the back of it, dizzy.

Had we almost kissed? It felt like we had almost kissed. Why did I have to react to him? Every single time? We couldn't have a normal, professional, neutral conversation. It always had to be charged with something confusing and powerful and un-ignorable. It was exhausting.

Chapter Nine

By breakfast the following morning, I was feeling much better. I apologized to both Apolline and Benoit again, and then managed to avoid them for most of the rest of the day.

I walked around the little town, seeing parts that looked familiar from when we arrived and wandering off to different places. Paquin was always telling me that the key to finding good stories was to never stop looking with fresh eyes. Being in a new place made this incredibly fun.

Cabourg was nothing like Paris. Newer, except for the very old parts. Shorter in stature. And not nearly as diverse. But for a bourgeois family, it seemingly had everything required for a fun vacation. Boat rides, plenty of sand and water, live entertainment, attractions. I bought a choux bun at a patisserie and spoke to the owner about the new casino opening. I poked around in the bookstore and found a volume of local history. Then I went back to the hotel and sat at one of the tables on the promenade and read about how the small seaside village with medieval churches and inns had transformed into a vacation destination. And then I went upstairs to flesh out a few story ideas in my notebook. After a day of difficult travel and a day of the worst sickness imaginable, spending time exploring and thinking made me feel alive.

I wrote to Madame Tremblay about my illness and thankfully swift recovery. I hadn't had time to miss home yet, but that night when I was getting dressed for the casino opening, I missed having Nadine's help. I'd worn my most professional evening wear option the first night in town. Instead of repeating it already, I decided to wear one of the dresses Nadine had given me. It made more of a statement, like everything associated with Nadine. The garment was plainly and elegantly cut with a low scoop at the neck and narrow skirt. But the color was the same fiery pink as a radish. Quite the opposite of my gray standards.

Without Nadine to tell me how lovely I looked and bolster my self-esteem, I questioned my choice a thousand times. Then I was still fixing my hair when Apolline knocked on my door. I told her to go ahead without me. I'd meet them there. I was, once again, off kilter.

Benoit and Apolline were at the bar when I walked in the casino twenty minutes later. The gentleman they were with was sharply dressed in the same blue and gold as the decor; he had to be the owner. He was talking and gesturing around the room with the grandness of a proprietor.

As soon as I started toward them, Benoit's gaze came to rest on me. Something in his face changed then. His eyes darkened and smoldered as they swept me from head to toe. The dress! I didn't falter; the appreciation on his face emboldened me. If he was doing this to throw me off balance, then I would play right back. But it was getting harder and harder to tell if this was a game or something else. Because the pleasure I felt at drawing his eye had ignited my whole body.

"Ah, you made it," Apolline said. She introduced me to the casino owner, Monsieur Lefeuvre, who smiled and kissed my hand. His wandering eyes suggested he also appreciated my dress.

Benoit, in turn, greeted me with la bise. This was a casual greeting that people often exchanged, even in professional settings; Paquin had greeted me similarly. But this time, when Benoit greeted me with kisses, it was charged with something else. A frisson of energy sparked when his lips brushed my cheek. When he pulled away, Apolline was watching us with a curious expression on her face. Not unhappy, and not surprised either. Curious.

Before the pause of my entrance stretched any further, I asked if Monsieur Lefeuvre was pleased with the turnout so far.

"I am quite pleased!" He raised his hands to indicate the crowd around us. With a full house, the opening was a success.

As planned, we split up to get everything we needed. While Benoit was interviewing Monsieur Lefeuvre and getting the view behind the scenes, I would be talking to patrons on the floor. Apolline, who'd brought her sketchbook, would be here and there throughout the night. Thank goodness, we all got to work.

Le Diamont Casino had been conceived and built with every detail designed to encourage patrons to continue playing and, ultimately, lose money to the house. The seats were comfortable. The games lively. The drinks were free as long as you were placing bets. The room was full. Perhaps more people were milling about and taking it all in than there were at the gaming tables. But that would likely change as the night wore on.

One thing was for sure, I didn't have any trouble getting the gentlemen on the floor to talk to me. The dress again! I'd never worn it in a professional situation before. I would have to remember to thank Nadine.

I spoke to a group of students from Paris who'd come up for the weekend. And I spoke to an actress I knew from the city and her new aristocrat gentleman friend—patron, she'd said when introducing me to him. Some local government officials were there and pleased to share their views with the readers of *L'Entreprise*. I filled a notebook in about two hours.

The casino had paid the paper for advertising and our coverage, which was common practice for all the newspapers. Amongst all the news that people often didn't want us to print, there were stories like these where interested parties paid for the exposure. Some papers even went so far as blackmailing interested parties—politicians, businesses, private citizens from prominent families (and by prominent I mean rich)—when scandal struck. Pay us or we print the story. *L'Entreprise* didn't do so much of this, at least not in my experience. It remained to be seen how much *L'Etoile* did. And there never seemed to be a shortage of advertisers willing to pay to reach our readers.

When I was sure I had everything I needed, I found Benoit at the bar with the casino owner.

"We were just wrapping up," Monsieur Lefeuvre said. "I hope your evening was enjoyable?"

"It was, merci. I have plenty of material for a compelling story."

"Good. Let me buy you two dinner." Monsieur Lefeuvre puffed up magnanimously. "I regret I can't join you because I'm meeting with my manager in a few minutes."

"Is Apolline still here?"

"No. She went back to the hotel as soon as she finished with her sketches." Benoit watched me expectantly. "Will you have dinner with me?"

"I'm starving," I said.

"Good." Monsieur Lefeuvre led us past the gaming floor to a dining room that sat off to the side of the bar. He thanked us and told us to enjoy ourselves. Then a host sat us at a small table against the wall. Away from the games, it was far more subdued than the rest of the place. A pianist played on a small stage. There was an electric chandelier on the ceiling and a lush orange rose in a vase on the table. The atmosphere was anything but professional, crossing into romantic territory for sure.

After we were seated, the host promised that a server would be along shortly and departed.

"You look stunning in that dress, Vanessa." Benoit leaned over the table as he spoke, his eyes catching and holding mine. "I've been wanting to tell you that all night. That color. It's absolutely ravishing on you."

I blushed at his effusiveness, the intensity of his gaze. "Stop. We're working."

"I'm just making an observation," he said innocently. "I am an observant fellow."

"Aren't you."

The server arrived with a bottle of champagne, eager to tell us all about the dishes. We both ordered chicken and roast vegetables. Then when we were alone, Benoit told me about his evening with the casino owner, who had inherited the money he used to start the business. And I told him about the students who'd come from Paris and lost all their money. The conversation was strictly professional, but I felt anything but. I tried to suppress it, but the way he sat and his gestures and the smooth sound of his voice aroused more than my mind. The more we talked, and the more wine we drank, the more I thought about the way he'd looked at my mouth the other night. The way he looked like he wanted to kiss me. And the way I kind of wanted him to.

The server brought dinner, and we ate for a while. The food was delicious, casual fare served simply. I didn't usually write about restaurants, but I could easily put something together about this place to go with our larger dispatches.

When Benoit filled his champagne flute, he topped mine off as well. "Have you been to the beach before?"

"Oui. I was nine. My father took me to Nice. And we didn't stay in so nice a place. But we were right by the water."

"Do you swim, then?"

"I do. They taught us at the orphanage as well. But I don't have a bathing suit." I'd seen some in a shop window earlier that day. "What about you? Do you swim?"

"Of course, I swim. I was in the military."

"Oh, that's right. I suppose they require that in their training. So you have a bathing suit then?"

"I never go anywhere without it." He said it like this should be obvious. Perhaps at the beach it should have been.

"You know, maybe I should buy one." The store's display had been tempting. Or maybe the champagne was getting to me.

"Since we're supposed to be working?" He sipped his wine.

"Yes. Working."

"You keep saying that. But the lines blur on assignment."

"Oh, really."

"Yes. Everything becomes research." He leaned in as he spoke.

I cleared my throat. It seemed to be closing up or catching or something. "Everything?"

"Everything." He looked me right in the eyes and lowered his voice as he said it. He was a walking double entendre. My stomach fluttered.

"Tell me about it. Your military days in the Far East."

"What do you want to know?" He smiled, thrilled that I'd asked.

"I don't know. What did you do there?" I leaned back in my seat and twirled a loose strand of my hair.

"I was in public relations, you know. In Vietnam and then later in Laos. And much of the fighting took place before I arrived. So work-wise, it wasn't so terrible."

"Except you were writing about military actions instead of casino openings." I tried to imagine him in some remote jungle surrounded by snakes and exotic birds and people speaking a strange language.

"I was. And when my two years were up, I went to work as a correspondent."

"And kept traveling."

"Yes."

"So where did you go then?"

"Italy. Greece. Egypt and all points in between, really."

"You've been to so many places." I'd read his stories. I knew he'd been everywhere. But I wanted to know what he'd say about it. He, like every man once you got him going, liked to talk about himself. He inflated as he entertained, and I didn't mind watching.

We finished the bottle of wine and our dinner while he told me about travel and work. When the server came around, he asked me if I'd like more wine. I did, but I felt mildly guilty about ordering a second bottle during a professional dinner. But Benoit didn't hesitate. Probably no man would, when I really thought about it. Monsieur Lefeuvre wanted us to have a good time. Another bottle of wine was nothing to him, especially not when *L'Entreprise* would be singing his praises to all of Paris for the next month.

The server cleared our dishes and promptly returned with the wine. When he'd gone, I asked the question that I'd often wondered about Benoit. "Why, after such an exciting career, going here and there, did you settle into culture pages? It seems so boring in comparison."

He sipped his wine and eyed me for a moment over the glass before answering. "As a younger man, I did aspire to write the hard stories. I wanted to be just like Zola. Now I think I would rather write about Zola's books than be him. It was fun while it lasted. But I'm at a place in my life where I want a slower pace and deeper work. Something that might give me time to write a book. And I grew tired of touring. Plus, culture news is important; locally it's more important than distant lands, as far as I'm concerned."

"I suppose I understand that. You've seen it all then?"

"Well, not everything." He arched an eyebrow and twirled the stem of his champagne flute between two fingers. "But let me ask you the same question. If you're so taken with the idea of traveling more, why do you want the editor position?"

"Me?" I hadn't really thought about it, aside from the clout. "I'm not sure who would hire a woman who's hardly been out of Paris to write about travel. The only reason I'm here is because the paper arranged everything for me. And no one would take me seriously. Whereas, I've been at *L'Entreprise* for years. People take me seriously there."

He shook his head.

"You don't believe me?"

"Well, it's not that I don't believe you." His face was flushed from the wine and food. His eyes joyful. "I wish you were wrong, but in all likelihood, you are right. It's harder for women, even though it shouldn't be. If I were an editor, I'd hire you as a correspondent."

"Not so fast. You're not going to be an editor, remember? I am."

He shrugged and drank the rest of his wine instead of responding. "Shall we walk back to the hotel?"

"Okay." My glass was empty too, but the bottle wasn't. "What about all this wine?"

"The staff will drink it."

After thanking the staff and Monsieur Lefeuvre, we walked out of the casino and onto the promenade. Groups of people still walked and milled about. This was not Paris nightlife, but it was nightlife. Because Benoit and I were both staying at the same place, and therefore headed in the same direction, there was no reason to discuss whether or not we would walk together.

"Do you mind if we take the beach?"

"It's dark."

"I'll protect you." He said it so innocently. "And there's no better time for a walk on the beach. Trust me."

"Flinging me into the sea would be a convenient way to ensure you get to stay at the paper and I don't."

"You're right. But I like your company. And if we can't be there together, then I'd rather beat you fair and square. Plus, I heard you can swim."

Of course, I trusted him to walk me half a kilometer to the hotel. While I wanted to kill him, or at least I used to, he didn't seem to want to kill me. He'd brought me soup, after all.

We took the stairs down to the sand, where my shoes sank, and the air was heavier with the salty smell of the water. He offered me his arm; I hesitated for a second and then took it. Why not?

The breeze pushed the wisps of my hair, and the sand shifted under my feet. For whatever reason my whole body tingled with the awareness of him. His footfalls next to mine. The feel of his jacket. His arm; his shoulder. He was a magnet for my attention. I couldn't seem to exist in his presence with any sort of neutrality. For all that doctors made of the restorative properties of the ocean, proximity to the beach had done nothing for my sanity.

I couldn't stop thinking about him, wondering what he was thinking. Feeling tingly about my hand in the crook of his elbow. I was the one being strange. He had been nothing but a perfect gentleman, while my thoughts had been racing all over inappropriate territory. This was not a romantic rendezvous. It had been a professional meeting. But colleagues didn't usually offer an arm or walk quite so close. It was like my brain had been completely scrambled by him. In a constant state of fluster. It was most unwelcome. And yet I was helpless against it.

The sky was dark, but there was enough moonlight to see the shadows of his face. It was a perfect face. He must have felt me staring because he looked down at me and both smiled and furrowed his brow.

"What?"

"What what?" I snapped my gaze away like a naughty child caught red-handed.

"What are you smiling about?"

"I wasn't smiling."

"You were," he insisted. "You're enjoying yourself. Admit it."

"What do you mean enjoying myself? What are you suggesting?"

"That you don't hate me."

"You've misread my smile, if that's what you think."

"Stop being so grumpy."

I scoffed, pretending to be dumbfounded by the accusation. "I'm not being grumpy."

"You absolutely are. And I caught you enjoying yourself. Dare I say: enjoying my company."

"No. You definitely shouldn't dare." I started to pull my hand away from his arm, but he caught it and held it.

"Stop. I won't tell anyone. Besides, we're here." He nodded toward the stairs closest to our hotel and steered me that way without letting go of my hand.

"Fine. You're right. I was enjoying your company. But I don't expect it to last."

"You wound me with your cruelty."

I immediately knew it was true. I was being cruel. I didn't exactly want to be, but it was maybe my natural state. "I'll make it up to you. Join me for one more drink before we head upstairs?"

"What? Is this an invitation?"

"Yes, it is." I laughed. "One drink. That's it."

"You're quite skittish, you know."

"Well, you, monsieur, are a flirt! I need you to take me seriously. Professionally."

He stopped me then and tugged me so I was facing him. "I take you seriously. Have I given you reason to think I don't?"

My mouth opened to list examples, but I couldn't think of any; there weren't any. "No, not exactly. But it's something I have to be aware of constantly, as a woman in a professional setting. It's my greatest hindrance."

"So that's why you're so uptight. You're afraid people won't take you seriously." It was like all the pieces of his mystery were falling into place.

"People don't take me seriously often. Believe me. This is something you know nothing about."

"Maybe not." We continued up the stairs, his hand on my hand where it was holding his arm. "But you don't have to worry about me not taking you seriously."

"I'm not sure I believe you after all we've been through. After all you've… seen."

"I have seen some things, that's for sure."

I tried to tug my hand away, but he caught it again.

"I'm teasing you, Vanessa. I like you." We'd stopped again, at the top of the stairs now, and we were facing each other. "I like you very much. And your professionalism continues to impress me. But you must lighten up. You're a human being. Sometimes we are felled by shellfish. Sometimes by gravity. That's life. You won't lose my respect for being human. And I do know exactly how serious you are."

"Good. Fine. Okay then." Did he say that he liked me? And why was that the one sentence that stuck out? This man reduced me to a mess every time. Still, he didn't seem deterred by my general bitchiness. He didn't even seem to hold it against me.

"Okay then."

The hotel dining room was nearly empty at that hour. The piano was quiet. The servers were doing more cleaning up than serving. Except for two gentlemen at the other end who appeared to be deep in quiet debate, we were alone at the bar. He pulled out a stool for me and then sat in the one next to it. The chandelier sparkled and cast a twinkling glow on every glass in the room.

"Whiskey, neat," I told the barman, who was short and thick and built like he might spend his off days in a boxing ring.

"I'll have the same," Benoit said. He drew a cigarette from a slim silver case in his breast pocket. Snapping it open with his ink-stained hand, he offered me one.

The bartender put a short glass of brown liquor in front of each of us. The burn from the first sip was heavenly. I took a second drink, the burn a little duller after the sharp shock of the first, but fortifying nonetheless. Benoit had both forearms resting on the bar, and he rotated his glass in his wide, manly hands. His wrists were so broad.

"You said that you like me. When we were outside."

"I did." He smiled his devilish smile, likely pleased that it was bothering me enough to bring it up again.

"You made a pass at me when we first met. Do you even remember?"

"I remember. We were backstage at the Comédie Française."

"I'm surprised."

"That I remember? Why wouldn't I?"

"Because you strike me as the kind of man who makes passes at many women all the time."

"What?" He winced. "What gives you that idea? I resent the accusation."

"Oh, I've offended you?"

"You have."

"Stop it. I'm not blind. You ooze flirtation in every interaction with every woman. You even flirt with Apolline."

"Well, I am a man. And why shouldn't I flirt with Apolline?"

"She's married!"

He looked at me hard and licked his lips. "What if I told you that I'd been very taken with you when I saw you at the theater, and I'd been trying to think of a way to approach you all night?"

"Oh, like I'm special." I ramped up my show of disbelief.

The color on his cheeks rose. "Mademoiselle, you are absolutely special. I've never met anyone quite like you. And if I haven't made you feel that way, then it's my fault."

He was being serious, and now I felt foolish. Boorish, even. I didn't know what to say.

When I didn't speak, he continued. "But don't worry. I know you don't like me. And I respect you, remember? I can stop trying to get you to like me back."

Was that what he'd been trying to do? Get me to like him? I shouldn't have liked him. Liking him was a bad idea. He was really the only thing standing between me and what I wanted. But my immediate reaction was no. No, I didn't want him to stop trying to get me to like him. Because I did like him. I knew I shouldn't, but I did. The thought of him not liking me felt sad and lonely. Liquid courage burning in my gut, I said, "I don't want you to stop trying to get me to like you. I do like you. A little."

He smiled broadly and victoriously. "Only a little?"

"Oui. And I prefer not to talk about it."

"I see." He grinned like a cat that finally caught the mouse. And then he didn't say anything. Finally, I'd shut him up. We sat there, side by side, and drank our whiskeys in companionable silence.

After we left the bar and were heading upstairs, a strange urgency came over me. We were about halfway up the three flights to our floor, and he was walking a few steps behind me. I stopped and turned around to face him. He stopped one step below me, right at eye level now. Close. Again.

His eyes were blue and bright around dark pupils that expanded as I stared into them. I didn't break eye contact, and he didn't either. He had one of the hotel room carnations pinned to his lapel and its subtle spicy scent reached me. We'd been this close now countless times. It was no longer an unfamiliar place. Dare I say it wasn't even uncomfortable any more. But—and I'll never know where my sudden boldness came from—I wanted more. I wanted to be closer. And so I tipped forward and kissed him.

He flinched when my mouth collided with his, like he might pull away; but I already had my hands on the sides of his head. In an instant, he understood what was happening and put his arms around me, holding me close. I wanted to sing, he felt so good. I leaned against him with all my weight and let him press my lips open with his. His tongue swiped mine, and my knees almost collapsed. It wasn't enough. I wanted more.

My hands fell to his shoulders, pulling him closer. Holding me in place with one hand on my waist, his other began to wander toward my front. When he grasped my breast with the sweetest squeeze, I almost fell apart. His mouth pressed and kissed me into an oblivion of arousal. His breath was hot and liquefying. Without loosening my grip on him, I pulled my mouth away from his, no longer able to breathe. And his lips fell to my neck. I tilted my head back so he could keep kissing, like I'd gone completely mad. And the only words in my head were finally and yes.

Complete madness was the only way to describe it.

Footfalls coming from above stopped him, and we both froze and held our breath to listen. Someone was coming down the stairs. He righted me and released me, while I smoothed my dress and hair. We continued upward, reaching our floor as the gentleman heading down passed us with a polite nod.

"What happened back there?" Benoit said casually when we'd reached my door.

"I'm not entirely sure."

His hair was messy where my fingers had slid through it. His mouth was red and bitten. He eyed me, looking for something in my face. I didn't know what. Did he want me to invite him in?

Before I could speak, he took my hand and kissed it and said goodnight. He walked away. Two doors down, he stopped at his door and smiled sheepishly. Then he blew me a kiss, opened the door, and was gone.

Alone in the hallway and seemingly frozen where I stood, I shook my head to clear it. My heart raced in my chest, like I'd been running for my life, or headlong into something. A worn floral carpet ran the length of the hall, and the walls were paneled in oak wainscoting. The sound of someone moving around upstairs carried down through the walls. I was astounded by how moving, how right that kiss had been. Completely astounded. It must have been all the champagne.

In my room, I undressed and saw to my toilette. Then I lay down in bed in the darkness and relived the weight of his hands squeezing me. That kiss. It unleashed something—a raw passion that had been latent inside me. There was no way he couldn't be thinking about that kiss. He'd been just as starry-eyed as me at that moment we broke apart. That tragedy of an interruption. What if no one had come? I might have let him pull up my skirt right there, I was so gone in that kiss. I was not supposed to like Benoit Levin. He was my rival, not my love interest. But the truth was that I liked Benoit Levin very much.

Chapter Ten

I was still a mess from that kiss the next morning. What had come over me? I certainly wanted to do it in the moment. But the idea had perhaps struck me so fast that I'd not fully considered the consequences. Now there was work to do, and I had already missed a day of it. So I dressed sensibly in gray, braided and pinned up my hair, and then went to face Benoit on the most professional terms. Because that was the thing. I hadn't just kissed someone; I kissed a colleague. Unlike any other kiss I'd ever shared, I couldn't run away and hide from the awkwardness.

The hall was empty, and I went down, walking back through the scene of our crime in the stairwell. I held my breath as I passed it. My heart fluttered, though that had to be because I'd been moving so quickly. I was merely winded. I wasn't palpitating over the thought of kissing that man. Or anguishing at the thought of never getting to do it again.

Irregular heartbeats, excessive sweat, shortness of breath. Benoit Levin was becoming a physical ailment in my life.

There was only one logical conclusion: I needed to end whatever this little flirtation was before it went any further. If I didn't, it could derail my whole life. I needed to tell him as soon as we had a moment alone. Before he could flirt or look at me with those blue eyes.

Benoit and Apolline were sitting in the hotel dining room by a window with a view of the promenade. They had coffee, but hadn't ordered yet. He was dressed smartly in a lightweight navy blue suit. This time, he had it paired with a blue shirt and a blue cravat that I liked. That I'd started cataloguing his garments only strengthened my case for keeping our hands to ourselves. I was relieved as always to have Apolline there as a buffer.

"Bonjour," I said cheerfully, drawing their attention from the menus.

"Bonjour," Benoit said. His eyes met mine with a curiosity that I promptly looked away from.

"Bonjour," Apolline said.

I sat and situated myself, carefully keeping my head turned away from Benoit. He went back to his menu, I assumed from what I saw in my periphery.

"Apolline, have you been in touch with anyone from the paper?" I pretended to be deeply curious in the goings on back at the office.

But Apolline shook her head. It had been a silly question, asked because I had been silly and needed to say or think of anything besides kissing. I looked at my menu.

Apolline said, "What time are your machines coming?"

"They should be here anytime now." Benoit put his menu down. "I told the concierge to send them up."

"What machines?"

"I've borrowed a typewriter for each of us."

"Oh." I hadn't even thought as far ahead as finding a typewriter. I never imagined he'd take care of it for me. I had been so worried about kissing him and so self-absorbed that I hadn't even thought to ask. My brain was being sabotaged by desirous chemicals of my body's own making.

"We can't exactly work without them."

"No. We can't."

"Do you have typing to do?" He asked with an amused quirk of his brow.

"I do."

He nodded and smiled, as if everything were right in the world. "I figured you would."

The thoughtful bastard. Kissing me senseless and then helping me with work. I needed to end this. That kiss needed to be forgotten and never spoken of again. Making it clear that kissing had been a mistake would alleviate all of my messy, unprofessional thoughts.

Mercifully, the server came and took our orders, which were simple. Coffee, baguette, and fruit all around. Benoit ordered a side of bacon. And Apolline asked for a glass of orange juice. The server departed; Apolline and Benoit opened and began reading the day's papers.

"I am done with *Le Matin*, if you haven't seen it yet," she said.

"Oh, yes. Merci." I took the paper and read the front page with the deepest focus, not wanting to look at Benoit or send any other signals to him besides disinterest. I squinted a little as I read, exuding the need for no interruptions. I didn't even look away from my reading when the server returned with breakfast.

The melon and berries were sweet and the coffee dark and rich. I ate and perused the paper. The news reports from China, a double suicide in Saint-Quentin-sur-Isère, and the morning editorial. Nothing about Louise Montmorency or Antoine de Larminet in the gossip columns. Or Charlotte Deveraux. It would be nice to know what was happening with her. She'd been so upset that morning she left Paris. Then Antoine, when he came looking for her, had seemed just as anguished. What a mess.

Antoine de Larminet—now there was a man with a typewriter. Charlotte was dizzy with excitement and affection over it. It had truly been a thoughtful and perfect gift. Now that someone had been so thoughtful with me, I felt even worse for Charlotte. No one had it easy. Nadine told me that she'd been running out of money, which surprised me. I hadn't known or even considered that. Another case in which I failed to see past myself.

Outside the window, the beach was sparsely populated at that early hour, except for a few intrepid shell collectors and families with young children to entertain. And the morning sun danced between the marching clouds and across the water, making the waves flash like coins.

"Well, I believe I'm off. I have a few pictures I want to try to get." Apolline had finished her breakfast and was gathering her things. She was always thinking about the light, which worked best with her camera equipment only during certain times of day.

"Of course," Benoit said, standing for Apolline. "We'll see you at lunch?"

"Oui. À bientôt."

She'd hardly gone when I panicked and stood as well. I wasn't ready to be alone with him yet. "I should go too, to clear a place for the typewriter on my table."

"Okay." But he put a hand on my arm to stop me from leaving. "How are you this morning, darling?"

"I'm fine."

"You seem tense."

Why was I always so transparent to him? I needed to get this over with. I sat back down, and he did the same.

"Listen," I said, steeling myself. "I'll make this brief. What happened last night: it can't happen again."

He sank into his chair. "What if I disagree?"

"What? You can't." I huffed. "We made a mistake."

"So you don't care about my feelings?"

"Don't make it sound so harsh. I can only care so much when you could be sabotaging me for a job. I can't compete with you properly if we're…"

"If we're what?"

"You know." If I said it, I might try and do it again.

"Never?"

"Well…" Never? That's what I'd meant, but was that what I really wanted? I was losing my nerve. "I want us to get through this trip and work well together."

His brow furrowed as he considered this—no doubt seeing the room for possibility that I'd left in there for him. I liked him. I just couldn't let myself get carried away. And I certainly couldn't let him get carried away. Who knew where that would lead? He was far too dangerous.

"I think you must admit that this is going well."

"What is going well?"

"Us."

"Working together."

His smile faltered slightly, like he really was disappointed. "Of course, working together—"

"Well, working together is going better than I had expected." I could admit that much. He'd been a star coworker the whole time. "But there can't be anything else besides professionalism between us."

He narrowed his eyes and pursed his clever, perfect mouth. "I have a counteroffer."

"A what?"

"A counteroffer."

"This isn't a negotiation." Was he really going to argue?

"No. It isn't. It's feelings. Messy ones. And an attraction that is very real. Palpable." The words rolled off his tongue.

"So?"

"So, my proposition is that we do the exact opposite. That we indulge in some more kissing. Much more if it goes well and we are so inclined."

I gasped at his brazenness. "Well, I am not inclined."

"Your behavior yesterday suggested very strongly otherwise."

"It did not."

"It did."

"Well, that doesn't mean it has to become…" I waved both hands at once like I was conducting a symphony. "Something grand."

"It doesn't have to be something grand." His eyes roved over me like he was considering where to bite first.

"Then what would it be, exactly?"

"It would be two people, away from their everyday lives, in a new place together, seeing what happens."

I am not proud to admit that his offer was quite tempting. I'd grown rather comfortable with his presence over the past few days, and he was not in any way an unappealing person. Very well shaped and appealing, in fact. Symmetrical. Strong. Slightly rugged and yet refined. Difficult to resist in a particularly manly way.

But indulging myself in what sounded a lot like a casual vacation affair was not the way to get him out of my mind. It would be quite the opposite. It would kill my brain, hinder my output, and therefore surely endanger my career and chances of beating him for the promotion. And I was in a precarious position at work.

There was also the issue of my never having gone to bed with a man before. If I forgot to mention that, it's because I never really gave much thought to going to bed with any man ever. Obviously it wasn't that important to me. But I was thinking about it now. Very much.

This too had to be a warning sign. This man had scrambled my brain. I could not let him scramble it any longer.

Before I could continue my protest, a bellhop arrived at the table. "Monsieur, mademoiselle, excusez-moi. Your delivery has arrived. We are taking the machines upstairs right now."

"Merci," Benoit said.

I stood, grateful to have a reason to pause this conversation.

Benoit stood as well, then he gestured for me to go first. As I passed him, he said softly, "You can think about it."

"Oui," I whispered. Think about it. Ha. I couldn't stop thinking about it. That was the problem.

Once the typewriter was installed in my room, I spent the rest of the morning typing up all the notes I had on the opening night. I had a few follow-up questions, which I'd have to sort out, maybe later that night. But I had a good start. I needed to be careful and solid on this one. I had to prove myself and my capabilities to my editor. It was not in my favor that Paquin was leaving. Vartre was Benoit's editor. If she left the paper to follow Paquin, she'd not necessarily get a say in her successor. But she could put Benoit in a better position to step up, and whoever made the decision would surely choose their own man over the woman whose biggest supporter was now working somewhere else. It was getting so hard to tell anymore how things would work out, and all the striving that had sustained me for so long had started to feel a little pointless. Like the thing I'd been striving for no longer existed, at least not in the way I'd thought it would.

Instead of meeting Benoit and Apolline downstairs for lunch, I went out for a walk. I needed to get out of my own head. The sun was high and bright, and the street wasn't empty, but it was far from a bustling Paris street. I walked toward the Grand Hôtel, which was the axis of several streets that jutted away from the coast and fanned out, like spokes on a wheel. It was an odd choice of focal point for a town; more common choices were a church or a government building or a castle. But for a vacation town, perhaps a hotel made perfect sense.

When I came again to the women's boutique with the swimwear display in the front window, I stopped. I had almost forgotten about the bathing suits. I could swim, but I'd never had specialized clothing like this. The bathing suit in the middle was navy blue silk with a wide white collar. The skirt and shorts were trimmed in white ruffles. It was the one, of the three bathing suits, that I could picture Nadine choosing. I needed to try it on.

Inside the shop smelled like lemon furniture polish, and a smiling attendant greeted me right away.

"Is the bathing suit in the window ready to wear?"

"The one in the middle?"

"Oui."

"It is. Would you like to try it on?"

"Oui. Merci."

"I saw you looking at it." The clerk, a fashionably dressed woman in her thirties, eyed me from head to toe, gauging my size, surely. She exuded professional competence. She probably sold bathing suits to women from Paris just like me all day long.

She showed me to a fitting room, which was equipped with a full-length mirror. I tried to avoid impulse purchases, especially things that wouldn't be useful longterm. I had never needed a bathing suit in Paris before, and I wasn't sure I ever would. But it seemed like a shame to come to the beach without one. The women on the beach in their bathing suits looked so free and at ease. They weren't here for work, obviously. They were on vacation. But I wanted a little slice of that for myself. I wanted to wear something skimpy and sit by the ocean in the sand. I wanted to swim in the water and feel the sun on my bare skin.

God help me, but as I removed my skirt and blouse, my treacherous brain imagined what Benoit might think of me in a bathing suit. That kiss had been a revelation. And he seemed to feel the same way about it. He was right: the chemistry between us was undeniable. But was it a positive chemistry or a corrosive, destructive one? It surely had to be the second. Sleeping with that man, my nemesis, would be a terrible idea. It would wreck my career. And if he was as thrilling as my imaginings, then my brain would surely be damaged. I'd probably want to marry him and have his children.

The skirt fell to my hips and the shorts underneath landed at the bottom of my plump thigh, leaving so much bare skin. I did prefer to be covered, but as I considered myself in the mirror, it seemed I didn't mind showing some leg either. While I was there in the shop, I bought two skirts that were split into what were essentially billowy trousers. Gray, of course, to match everything else. When I got home to my bicycle, these garments would, I was sure, change my life, even if I never wore the bathing suit again.

Unlike Benoit. He would not change my life. I would not allow it. And so I spent the next two days avoiding all situations that could result in us being alone. I set off with Apolline every morning after breakfast. I begged off with her every night after dinner. A handful of times I caught his questioning glances, but I hoped my actions spoke the words I didn't say. I didn't want to have a sexual relationship with him, but strangely I couldn't completely eliminate the opportunity either.

We did work well together, though. The three of us established a bit of a routine. Breakfast meetings in the morning. Phone calls to the office from the front desk. Then working in our respective rooms—or in Apolline's case, out and about with her sketching implements and camera. We helped each other with ideas and collaborated on stories. There was no animosity or romance. Pure professionalism. It was incredible. But oddly not enough.

We usually had dinner together in the hotel—me, Benoit, and Apolline—at the end of the day. At least when we weren't otherwise engaged in reporting. But covering culture outside of Paris was quite different. There were no salons to attend and fewer main events. The artists were local rather than national. And for the first time in a long time, it felt like I was making discoveries. No one in Paris had seen the local painter's seascapes or read the local writer's novels. A few of my pieces had been more touristy dispatches geared towards interested travelers. Or aspirational travelers, as the case often was. And I liked exploring. I liked the discovery of talking to the curator of the local gallery and the producer at the theater, capturing their passion and what they had to offer. It was fun.

One night at dinner, we were sitting at what was shaping up to be our usual table, finishing our coffee, when Apolline asked Benoit about his time in Vietnam.

"The country is different in every possible way from France, from anywhere in Europe." He spoke with enthusiasm and reverence. "With deep jungles that go on for kilometers and underwater crop fields that they waded through to farm. It was amazing. The food, the flavors—it was unlike anything I'd ever eaten."

"Oh, that does sound fascinating. I've only been as far as London." Apolline had grown quite fond of Benoit over those few days. She gazed at him like a proud mother and patted his hand when he showed his deep goodness, which he did often. He was a good man. Interesting, curious. He liked to get Apolline talking, and she flourished under the attention. And I enjoyed both of their stories. I liked hearing about their lives. Even his. He won everyone over. It was like magic. The most wonderful man in the world.

Even though he'd won me over as well, I still hadn't crossed that last line into his bed. And, I suppose, because I hadn't given him explicit permission to, he stopped flirting with me.

I'd noticed immediately. Not only noticed, but I'd obsessed over its absence. No sultry glances. No double entendres. No nudges or raised eyebrows. No fooling around at all. He treated me respectfully and with cool detachment.

I tried to think about other things—about what I should write to Charlotte, about how things were going at home, about work. I kept busy with my own research and writing. It had gone quite well. But he was never far from my mind. Even knowing it was a terrible idea, a small part of me reconsidered whether or not professionalism could be put off temporarily.

I was powerless against him it seemed. Whatever energy existed between us had morphed into a complete infatuation. At least for me. With him on his best behavior, it was hard to know what he was hiding from me in his ridiculously handsome head.

Chapter Eleven

We were talking about shopping in town—not doing it ourselves, but whether or not Cabourg had anything to offer that Paris didn't—when I mentioned that I'd purchased a bathing suit. "I've never seen anything like it in Paris shops, though maybe I've been in the wrong shops."

"Wait." Benoit put a hand on my arm. We were at breakfast in the hotel. "You bought a bathing suit? Then we should all take the afternoon off for a swim."

"I can't swim," Apolline said with a shrug, having the sense to decline immediately. "I like the beach. And I love that the water is different every time I look at it, but I am not going in."

When Benoit looked at me, I said lamely, "I should finish some work."

"You are ahead of deadline. You can take a few hours off for a quick swim. You'll want to try out your bathing suit, won't you?"

He was right. Our trip was nearly half over already. "I will."

"And you can't go alone. It's safer to swim with someone."

He wasn't wrong, though somehow I suspected swimming with him would be dangerous for me as well.

When I didn't protest, he said, "Wonderful. Let's go after lunch."

"I'll look for you when I'm out on my walk," Apolline said.

Our conversation moved on; then we wrapped up breakfast and got to work. I spent the rest of the morning thinking about getting out of swimming in the ocean with Benoit. I let my mind wander through every possible excuse—physical ailment, late-running interview, revision emergency, feigned exhaustion, food poisoning again, complete disappearance. But no matter how much I thought about not going, I could not convince myself not to show up. I was the one who'd brought up the bathing suit, after all. A woman who didn't want to swim didn't bring up her new bathing suit. It was as if I'd gone completely off the rails of good sense.

I cannot deny the pleasure of walking down to the beach with my terry cloth robe wrapped modestly around me and nothing underneath but my bathing suit. The anticipation of being so scantily clad in Benoit's vicinity gripped me. He was waiting for me by the promenade stairs, as we'd planned. And he was wearing his own quite revealing swimming costume. He smiled as soon as he saw me, and even before I'd reached him, his eyes were visibly darkened with what had to be desire. He probably looked at all women like this, maybe a hundred women a day, but he was so good at it that I felt beautiful. And I loved my new bathing suit even more than I had when I bought it.

"I was sure you wouldn't come out, darling."

"I almost didn't!"

"I know." He had shapely arms that suggested athleticism and calves that quite honestly took my breath away. Were all men's legs like that? They couldn't be. And I couldn't take my eyes off them. They were an absolute marvel. When I finally did, making my slow way up to his face, his delight was apparent.

"You like my bathing suit."

I laughed. "I do like it."

All around us, people in similar dress were lying on towels and splashing in the water. Not everyone was dressed for swimming, but most were. And there were little tents where people could change their clothes.

He looked down the front of me, all covered in white cloth. "I look forward to seeing yours. There are chairs where you can leave your things. Shall we?"

I followed him to the line of chairs our hotel set up every day for guests. They were nearly full, but we found two empty seats at the far end of the row. I slipped out of my shoes, which were filled with sand. Then the only thing between me and water was removing my robe. Which I did quickly and without attention to sex appeal. I untied the belt and slid it off my shoulders, and then I hung it on the back of the chair.

He watched me; I could feel his gaze on my skin. He wasn't shy about appreciating what he saw, which was flattering now instead of frustrating. It's not every day a girl wears so little in public; it was nice to know I looked good. I waggled my eyebrows playfully and then made my way to the shoreline and let the water run over my bare feet. It was cold and almost fizzy. The chill cooled my whole body and made my skin prickle with goosebumps.

"Let's go out further," Benoit said, smiling and shivering.

The water was cloudy and gray, blurring my feet more the deeper I went. When we were up to our knees, he took two fast, leaping steps and dove into an oncoming wave. He was nothing but a blur of bubbles and stirred up water, then he emerged with a burst of breath, still smiling. His hair was plastered to his head, and water ran down his face in rivulets that sparkled in the sun. Meanwhile, I was standing there lamely, too chicken to follow him.

"It's not so cold once you get used to it."

"Isn't that what they all say?"

He laughed. "Come on. Do you want me to pull you in?"

"Just give me a second." The water was up to my mid-thigh now, higher—and more intimately chilling—when the waves passed. A couple ran by, splashing and chasing each other in that sickening, playful way that couples do. They laughed and swam away together. For the briefest second, I was jealous of their easy togetherness. How they were so carefree. What was it like to feel that with someone? Anyone. Benoit was a few meters away, still watching me.

I took a deep breath and closed my eyes, then dove in with my hands straight out over my head. The water surged around me, freezing and enlivening. I opened my eyes, paddling and kicking hard the way the nuns had taught me in school. Not far up ahead were Benoit's bare legs, glowing white in the water. The salt stung, and so I stood, pushing my head above the surface. My thick blonde braid floated around my shoulder. I wiped my eyes and blinked away the salt.

"It's refreshing, isn't it?"

"It is. But I don't remember it being so salty."

With the waves, the water was at my shoulders in the valleys and so deep at the peaks that I had to float up off the sandy bottom to keep my head out. We stood there for a while, saying nothing and enjoying the feeling of being in the water. Of cooling off so thoroughly.

"Do you want to swim a ways? We could stay parallel to the shore."

"Yes." I was always a decent swimmer, and by decent I mean not at risk of drowning. "But you don't have to wait for me. I'm probably slower than you."

"I won't leave you to swim alone. It's not safe."

"Well then, I suppose I'll race you." I dove in without waiting for his response; with a body like his, I assumed the only advantage I'd get was that of surprise. My form, especially in the current, wasn't elegant or strong. And he quickly overtook me. But when he was only a few meters ahead, he rolled onto his back and smiled. Gloating.

"That you've physically bested me doesn't mean you'll ever best me again." I panted out the words between strokes, which weren't as furious now that he'd unofficially won.

"I would never assume so. I know better."

"Good." I swam to him and faced him. I planted my feet in the sand, which shifted and swirled away in the waves. The current seemed to be pushing me toward him. Or him toward me. And then we were standing quite close. The fabric of his bathing suit stretched across his chest; the creamy skin of his shoulders and arms exposed. He was pale with blue undertones from the cold water. When I looked up at him, the sun gleamed, and I had to shade my eyes.

He opened his mouth to say something, and then took a step back. He changed his mind.

"What?"

"Nothing."

"Tell me." I wanted, more than anything in that moment, to be standing so close to him again, the water swirling between us.

"I don't know." He pushed his wet hair back from his face with both hands. "You never really gave me an answer, for one. I thought you were thinking about my counteroffer, but you've been avoiding me for days. Now here we are, you agreed to meet me for a swim. I assumed, and perhaps wrongly, that you came because you have something you need to say."

He wasn't wrong. Not indulging myself in this man would be the wiser choice. But my physical longing for him was making it difficult to think. Forgetting it, ignoring it wasn't working. I also had a growing feeling that this trip and what happened on it didn't really matter. We'd go back to Paris and who knew what would be happening at work. Sure, our editors thought they had it all figured out. But how much did they really know about what the owners were working on or thinking up. One of us could get the job, but someone else just as easily could. Either way, we would have to break up once we were back in Paris. Here at Cabourg, though, we could simply see what happened. See what came of it. See how we felt. Right there, in the water, I wanted to very much. "So…"

"So?"

"So, I understand what you're asking of me. And I can't say that I'm not interested."

He smiled at this. Came a little closer.

"But in these matters, I am…"

He tipped his head, waiting for me to finish saying what I didn't want to say. I'd never had this conversation with a man before, and I wasn't sure how he'd react. He could lose interest, or make some misogynistic comment that would make me change my mind. That would end the flirtation before it went any further.

"I am not experienced." I looked down at the water and wanted to sink into it.

"Oh," he said thoughtfully. He hadn't considered this, I'm sure. Then he said in a tiger-like purr, "I'll be gentle."

I gasped and shivered, only in part because the water was cold. At the same time, parts of me ached for him to touch me. But there was no reason to think too far ahead. "Then I agree only to seeing what happens."

He nodded. "Okay. That's good. I like that. So, in that case, perhaps we can have a drink together after dinner tonight. After Apolline has gone off to bed."

"I would like to have a drink this evening."

"Good." His smile widened. "And then we can see what happens."

"And then we'll see what happens."

"I know what I want to happen now." He had not stopped grinning, but now his gaze dipped down to my mouth.

"What is that?" There was no one around us, and we were out so far in the water that probably no one was paying attention. Not that anyone cared about either of us.

"I want to kiss you here in the ocean."

A bigger wave came and the water pulled us toward each other, so close now that I had to put a hand on his chest to keep from rubbing up against him. The pull was so strong and intoxicating that all I could mutter out was a breathy oui before I was in his arms. His eyelashes were stuck together in spikes from the water, and it dripped down the side of his forehead and off his ear lobes.

"I want you to kiss me," I said, the words coming out huskily and wanting. Then, like two stags fighting in a meadow, our mouths crashed together. His lips were cool from the water, but his mouth was warm inside. His breath was hot and tinged with cigarette smoke and salt. The water sloshed around us. And my leg found his and nearly wrapped around it. There was no skirt between us and a whole sea around us. I was wet and freezing. It was an incredible kiss. But before it escalated to something far more inappropriate in a public setting, he set me down and broke away.

The water was colder without the warm contact of his body. But as I slowly regained my senses, I was relieved that he'd stopped. I couldn't let myself get carried away. I needed to keep my wits about me. And he'd made his point about what I should consider. That kiss and everything it evoked in me, between us, was what I could choose to continue. Or choose to deny myself.

We swam for a while longer and then walked back onto shore. Children played in the waves and piled sand into buckets. Other people were lounging on chairs with books in hand.

Just then, a waving arm a few meters up the beach caught my attention. It was Apolline. She tucked her camera box into the cavernous bag on her shoulder. When it was secured, she headed straight for us, holding her skirt aloft only high enough to keep it from brushing against the sand.

"Did she just take our picture?" I took a step back, putting distance between Benoit and me. What had we looked like, standing that close?

"Probably not. But maybe." We started walking toward her.

"How was the water?" Apolline said when she reached us. She was wearing a straw hat with a wide brim and the same green dress she'd had on earlier.

"Brisk," Benoit said at the same time I said, "Freezing."

"Well, it's so blessed hot that I may reconsider wading out there myself."

"I think I'll go get my robe," I said, feeling suddenly underdressed now that I was out of the water. They walked with me up the beach.

"You know, on the other side of this channel," Apolline said, "they use horse-drawn bathing machines that drop you into the water where it's neck deep and you don't have to walk in your bathing suit where everyone can see you."

"Really?"

"I've heard that before," Benoit said. "They're very uptight about seeing bodies."

"Everyone has a body, but heaven forbid we should see it. But you know how those Protestants are." Apolline huffed. Then she gave me a cautious look. "No offense if you're Protestant, dear."

I shook my head.

"I'm Jewish; culturally more than religiously," Benoit said when she looked at him. "But some countries don't let you swim at all."

"That's true," Apolline said. "Anyway, I brought the camera down to look for pictures. The light is so clear and less sharp now that it's a little cloudy."

"I may sit in a chair and read for a while."

"I may join you," he said noncommittally.

"Well." Apolline shrugged. "If I don't see you two when I come back through, I'll see you at dinner."

We agreed, and she ambled off, unconcerned. If she had seen us out in the water in less-than-professional circumstances, she certainly didn't care. And then Benoit and I were alone again.

"Would you like to sit for a while in the chairs?"

"I would. Very much." We'd reached the chairs now. The warm, loose sand coated my feet like sugar on a candy. I slipped on my robe, feeling immediately less vulnerable and swirly. Perhaps the sun on my skin was more powerful than I imagined. The beach chairs were comfortable and shaded by pretty striped umbrellas. I let my head fall back as I took in the vast landscape of sea.

The silence that settled between us was part expectation. And also some relinquishing. Benoit always seemed confident, but now there was a vulnerable tension in his gaze. He was nervous, and it was fascinating.

His long, lean feet were also coated in sugary sand. And sprinkles of it clung to his shapely, delightfully hairy calves. I pulled my gaze away. I couldn't just sit there and ogle him.

There was a family not far off in front of us; a mother and father, a young girl, and an even younger boy, holding hands and splashing in the breaking waves. The ever-present threads of loss tightened around my heart the way they always did. I hadn't had a family anything like that in a long time, and yet the ghost of it is always there. I sighed and looked back at Benoit.

He'd been watching me. "Did your family ever look like that?"

"If it did, I was too young to remember."

"What do you remember about your mother?"

"It's just glimpses now, really. I remember her sitting in her chair and sewing. I remember her and my father, walking in front of me on the sidewalk. I remember her room and the things she kept on her dresser. A little oval box with a lock of my hair in it from my first haircut. A ring she wore on her finger. The feeling of her."

He frowned slightly and looked out at the sea. The family had moved on.

When he didn't say anything, I asked, "How is your mother doing?"

"I had a letter from my sister this morning. She's no worse."

"It must be frustrating to be away, especially when you took your position to stay in the city." This trip was an inconvenience for him.

He shrugged. "I told Vartre that I would take this trip and no others. She understands the situation."

"And what kind of care does your mother require?"

"She can't be left alone anymore. She's liable to wander off and get lost or start a fire or any number of unspeakable things. It's like she's become a child again. And her ability to remember the rest of us comes and goes."

"That's terrible." I brushed sand off the arm of my chair. It was wooden and low to the ground with a seat and back made from blue canvas. The blue and white striped umbrella snapped taught in the breeze and then relaxed.

"It is. I am losing my mother as we speak, and it's something I can't seem to stop worrying about. I don't know what I'll go home to. Everything could be the same, but there's a chance that she won't know who I am. There's always that chance."

"I'm so sorry for bringing it up."

"No. It's okay. I enjoy talking to you, as you know, and talking about it helps. It keeps me from dwelling on it. You're a good distraction."

"Oh, am I?"

"Yes. Very."

"You know, your mother might not approve of me. I'm not Jewish."

"No, she probably wouldn't. Nor yours of me, most likely." He frowned and patted my arm. "Sadly none of them are in any position to weigh in."

"Well, I'm sorry your mother's unwell. And it's good of you to take such good care of her. Many in your situation would have the parent institutionalized." The homes for mentally infirm people had a reputation for being far worse than the worst orphanages.

"I couldn't do that, as hard as it is. We need help at all hours, though. Especially with me gone."

And it was why he needed the editor position. That part neither of us acknowledged.

"But that's enough about me. How are things at home with the infamous Charlotte Deveraux?"

"I'm not sure. She left Paris shortly after my story was published. The vicomte's son then threw over Louise Montmorency and went after Charlotte."

"Really? I wasn't sure he had it in him." Benoit leaned back in his chair and squinted out at the water.

"Do you know him?"

"I know as much as anyone else. I was surprised that they are involved. And perhaps even more surprised that he's serious about her. Serious enough to brush off the marquis's daughter."

"Charlotte is quite talented. And pretty," I said defensively. "I can see why he fell for her."

"Good for her, I say."

"I agree. It's a far better outcome than I had predicted. I wonder if my overstep pushed it along."

"Maybe. Does she see it that way?"

"I don't know. Either way, it doesn't change the fact that I should have talked to her about the story before publishing it."

"How did you two leave things?"

"With her screaming at me." I cringed, and he furrowed his brow. "She left Paris and went home. I need to write to her to explain everything. I got her address in Vernon before I left. But I just haven't done it."

"Are you unsure what to say?"

"I don't know." I buried my toes in the loose sand. "I guess I plan on starting from the beginning. I didn't mean to hurt her. But I was such a mess—largely because of you, I must clarify—that I didn't let myself think about it."

"Do you do that a lot? Make yourself not think about things?"

"I suppose I do. That and make it worse." Sometimes, and for no real reason, I made enemies of people who could have been friends. I judged harshly when I should have asked more questions and been more empathetic. I was as hard on other people as I was on myself. Looking back on what I did to Charlotte, I would not make the same decisions I'd made a few weeks ago. Not that I wouldn't have written the story, or a version of it. But I would have spoken to Charlotte first. It had been a journalistic oversight, especially considering I had access to her. I was wrong.

"I think you should go write to her now."

"Right now?"

"Yes. You've allowed it to fester for too long now. And it's clear you're avoiding it because you're afraid that you've irreparably damaged your relationship with your new friend." He leaned forward in his chair and turned to face me. "And the timing is good because she's probably getting what she wants. She has one of the richest men in Paris knocking on her parents' house in Vernon. He's thrown over the most eligible bachelorette in the city. It will be the most talked-about union in Paris this fall. Charlotte has everything to look forward to. Your crime is a minor offense in her mind right now. But you've lost sleep over it for how many nights? You have to let yourself off the hook. Stop being so hard on yourself. Write a genuine, heartfelt apology letter, and then let me undress you tonight in my hotel room."

My jaw dropped. But it didn't sound like a terrible idea. My stomach fluttered. "Whatever happened to seeing what happens?"

"I've recently learned the benefits of thinking ahead." His eyes gleamed. "But first you have a letter to write."

"You're right. I should get it over with."

"Let's go now." He leaned forward and readied himself to stand.

"Now?"

"Yes. Now." He pushed up out of the low seat and offered me a hand. It was sandy and warm. I longed to feel his hands drag across my skin.

There were outdoor showers for rinsing off the sand, and we headed in that direction. "We could talk through your letter, if you like, while we walk. The way we do any other story."

"So obviously 'Dear Charlotte' is the starting point."

"Obviously. And then you need a compelling opening."

"Yes, get to the point in a quick and interesting way. And take full accountability rather than shift blame."

"Since it's an apology," he said.

He was half-teasing me, but it did help. I didn't know exactly what to write, but I had to stop putting it off. Further delay would make things worse. And I had gained some insight into my misguided motivation, which would make my groveling more effective. At least I hoped.

"Merci."

He raised a thick eyebrow.

"For what you said about my situation with Charlotte. I have been such a mess over it that I needed to hear an outside perspective."

"It's nothing."

"Maybe not to you. But I have a cold heart. So I couldn't get there on my own. Anyway, it's important; not nothing."

"You don't have a cold heart, Vanessa." He stepped closer.

I almost argued, almost insisted that I had no heart at all. But something happened to me when he was that close. It had happened so many times now that I could recognize it, even if I didn't know exactly what it was. A slight easing of something. A lightening of the fight within me. A letting up. I didn't hate it.

"You're just not easy." He looked deep into my eyes as he spoke. "There's nothing wrong with that."

Inexplicably—again!—his words made me want to soften and melt into a puddle. "Well, thank you for that too."

Chapter Twelve

As we climbed the stairs to our rooms, Benoit's hand found mine. A lightness enveloped me, like I was floating up the stairs instead of walking. Although he could have, he didn't press me up against the wall in the stairwell for a kiss. And when we reached my door, he didn't ask to come inside. I was mildly disappointed, but also relieved. There existed between us at this point a tacit agreement. He kissed me quickly, once on each cheek, and then he walked away. I was in my room and closing my door before he reached his own.

I wrote to Charlotte, completing a bad draft and then revising it to something that felt authentic and caring and humble. Then I wrote to Nadine, explaining my latest personal revelations about being hard on myself and others. There was a reason I was distant. My whole life had prevented me from getting close. I wanted to be better, and I needed these women in my life.

Then I bathed and scrubbed and moisturized every centimeter of myself. And I dressed like a woman who was going to be undressed by a man later. With attention to detail and enhancing the experience. I pinned up my hair, and it was time for dinner.

When I stepped out into the hall, Benoit was also coming out of his room. This happened often with him two doors down. He smiled and took me in. I was wearing one of my regular gray ensembles, dressed up for the dinner hour with earrings and the bodice instead of a blouse. It was nice to be taken in by him.

All of my arguments against this man had fallen away. Our job situation was so unpredictable, that whether I slept with him or not, it was going to be professionally uncomfortable for the foreseeable future. We were so far away from home that nothing really mattered. He also was very kind and smart; his personality was appealing when I stopped actively hating him. His physical presence stoked a reaction in me that was not at all unpleasant. And I was quite certain I would enjoy him. That we could enjoy each other.

I was ready. Because that's what this ultimately was about. Whatever this attraction was between us, I could no longer ignore it or pretend to hate it. I needed to confront it head on. One night of seeing where it went, and he'd be out of my system for good. It was my only chance to get my life back. And then it would be done.

My last remaining hesitation was that he'd hijack my brain. But he'd already done that, hadn't he? A while ago. I hadn't been able to think straight since he walked into the office that first day the paper was sold. I was already a goner. The only way forward was to, as he said, see what happened.

He was dressed in his dinner jacket with a flower from one of the hotel bouquets pinned to his lapel, and his eyes sparkled as he took me in. My breath rushed out of me and my whole body flickered on in his gaze.

Before reaching me, he smiled slyly and then stopped and knocked on Apolline's door. Walking down for dinner together had also become part of our routine. We eyed each other while we waited outside her door. He looked handsome as always, and he seemed to appreciate my toilette as well, though we didn't speak. Then Apolline opened the door and joined us, chattering away about how hungry she was and how many pictures she'd gotten that day. Making her pictures required a process of light and fixative that could only be performed with the right conditions and equipment. She had no idea yet what any of her photographs would look like because the only place in France that could process the film was back in Paris. All her work was a mystery until some time in the future. Apolline loved to talk about it. She'd been hoping for a processing lab at the paper, but the editor she'd been talking to about it left two days after the takeover.

Downstairs, we parted ways so I could post my letters at the front desk, and then I met them again in the dining room. When I arrived at the table, Benoit was saying, "It's a capitalist endeavor as well as a democratic institution."

"Oh, not this again," I said, and they both looked up at me. They had been rolling over the same discussion of ethics in journalism for the past several days. Apolline, I'd gathered, liked the American approach to the newspaper business. Undercover investigations, exposés, and sensationalism drove American papers. We had much the same in France, and Benoit loved to point out that our readers also liked reading about grisly murder scenes and heinous crimes. They liked stories. But France, more than America and Britain, had a deeper legacy of speaking truth to power. He'd mention Zola soon if he hadn't already. Benoit's take, always, was that the work held some responsibility to prop up democracy, inform the masses, and hold government accountable.

"We can't help ourselves," Apolline said. "Shop talk."

They carried on while I half-listened. I ate my ratatouille and chicken, which was herby and similar to what we'd had every night so far. The whole time, Benoit's carnivorous gaze was on me. He didn't touch me or neglect Apolline in conversation, but his subtle attention and awareness consumed me. I drank three glasses of wine.

When the server came to clear our plates and offer coffee, Apolline declined. "None for me, thank you. I believe I'm ready to go up."

"No coffee, Apolline?" Benoit said when the server departed. "This is early even for you."

"I know. But I had a lot of sun today." Apolline moved her napkin from her lap to the table. "You two enjoy yourselves."

We said goodnight in turn, and off she went.

"And so it's just us," Benoit said as the server returned with our coffees.

"And so it is." The server placed a delicate cup and saucer in front of me. He served another to Benoit and left a tiny silver pitcher of milk on the table between us. Then he was gone again. My mouth had become so dry. I stirred a spoonful of milk into my cup, but then the spoon slipped from my fingers and clattered when it hit the saucer and landed on the table.

"Are you nervous?"

Although it didn't feel terribly different from any other time I was alone with him—internal fluttering and sweaty palms and scrambled thoughts—I was nervous. Not that I could ever admit it. "About what?"

"Anything."

"I'm not nervous, exactly. But I'm not exactly not nervous either. You are quite the seducer."

"This isn't something I do often, you know."

"Oh, really? That makes me special?"

"We already knew you were that." Benoit reached across the table and took my hand. "But I mean it. This isn't something I do. I meant it when I told you that I've been interested since I first saw you. I've come to like you very much, Vanessa. Working with you has been a pleasant surprise, even if you can't say the same about me."

Hearing him say these things was a little like drowning. I didn't want to think about feelings. Or what it meant if he had feelings for me. I didn't want to examine how I felt about him for one second longer. I just wanted to get on with it. If this whole trip had been the clunkiest, most fitful foreplay ever, then I was ready to get to the main event.

"You know, I believe I'm finished with my coffee. And if you want to see this through, then I suggest you come with me now."

His jaw ticked. I'd baffled him. But that was entirely enough smooth words and seduction. It was time for action. To emphasize my point, I stood and stepped away from the table to leave. For the briefest moment, I feared that he'd changed his mind and wouldn't get up. But then he did.

We crossed the dining room and lobby with purposeful strides, heading straight for the stairs. There was a gentleman coming down as we started our ascent. Benoit followed me a stair or two behind. When we were alone, passing the landing on the second floor, I looked over my shoulder at him. His face was serious, maybe even nervous. When he noticed me, his serious mask cracked into a wickedly handsome smile. "I feel like I'm chasing you."

I laughed and paused a few stairs from our floor. I leaned on the rail as he stepped up to my level. "Now you've caught me."

"I have." He leaned into me and kissed me. This time there was no question, only certainty.

I put my hands on his lapels and gripped the fabric. Our mouths, searching each other more frantically with every passing second, said everything that needed to be said.

We were both breathing heavy when he broke away and leaned his forehead on mine. "I want you to come back to my room. Or take me to yours. Whichever you prefer. If you prefer it."

I did very much prefer that we continue, but I hadn't considered location at all. Because of work, we'd been in and out of each other's rooms a handful of times already. Admittedly, I had imagined lying with him on various surfaces. But I wasn't sure I wanted him spending that much time in my room, exposing myself in this intimate way even if we were about to be intimate in other ways. "Your room."

He nodded and stepped ahead of me. "Right this way."

Our hall was thankfully empty and the thin rug down the center muffled our steps for the most part. He had his door open in no time. Inside, he closed the door and lit the lamp on his desk. Papers were scattered here and there, newspapers and typed manuscript pages in various states of editing and finalizing. His room was nearly identical to mine.

"Would you like a glass of wine?"

"I would. You keep wine in your room?"

"I bought it today in a shop down the street. I sometimes like to have a glass."

"I would like one, merci."

He poured the wine and passed me a glass. I took a mouthful; it was red and bold.

"Is there anything you'd like to talk about?" He said, eyeing me over the rim of his drink.

"I'm not asking you for anything. I guess I should clarify."

"Well, I suppose I am not asking you for anything tonight either, Vanessa. But if we're clarifying, then I should say that, depending on how things go, I might ask you for something in the future."

"What do you mean?"

"I mean this for you is, at least in part, about getting something over with. But I can't promise that I will see it that way. I am even hopeful you'll change your mind. Depending on how things go."

"On how things go." I took another big gulp of wine.

"And how we feel afterwards."

How we feel afterwards. "I don't think we should talk about any of those things right now."

"Since we haven't started yet."

"Oui." I put my wine glass down on a pile of papers on his desk.

This was enough of a starting flag apparently because he set his glass down too and then pulled me into his arms. We kissed again; a firm, confident opening to whatever happened next.

It's true that I didn't know what I was doing. But when I envisioned doing this with a man, I always imagined his nakedness coming first, and then my own second. I was comfortable with the idea of doing it that way, and when I wordlessly took over the situation and steered it in that direction, he complied. He removed his hands from my body so I could slip off his jacket. When it was free, I hung it over the back of his chair. Then I untied the knot at his neck and slipped off his cravat. The buttons down the front of his shirt allowed me to take my time. And when I pushed it open and slid it off his arms, I touched the bare skin on his back. He was warm and firm. Seeing him like this, chest naked and covered in dark, soft hair, surpassed anything I could have imagined.

His sharp intake of breath when I grazed my hand down the front of his pants eased my performance anxieties. He liked what I was doing. Even experience, which I presumed he had plenty of, didn't lessen these small pleasures of touch and sensation. I started working his pants open and could feel him hard underneath. And you don't really have to know much to find such a state compelling. When I grasped him, he groaned and his head dropped forward. And suddenly I had never been so excited to do something in my entire life. I wanted him and whatever might happen. When his pants fell and he stepped out of them, not a scrap of clothing left, he was glorious.

"Is it easy for you? To be naked in front of me?"

"As long as you're next, I'll be fine."

"I am next."

"Trés bien." He stepped forward and pulled me in against him, kissing me fully and assertively, like a warm-up exercise. And then he was working on the buttons at the back of my bodice. It had quite a few. I had to put it on backwards and then spin it around when I had them all fastened. He stopped kissing me to pull the garment away, and he placed it neatly over the back of his chair on top of his jacket. Then he unfastened my skirt at the waist and helped me step out of it. I'd kissed boys and gone beyond kissing even, involving various degrees of bodily exposure, but no man had ever seen me like this. He admired the view only long enough to hang up my skirt. And then he made fast work of removing my corset and petticoats. The underwear and stockings, my frilliest, he took a little more time on, doing each leg one at a time with both hands and then taking down my underwear with both hands as well.

"I remember picking these up off the floor of the train station," he said with a sultry smile.

"Very funny."

"I've been thinking about them ever since. He kissed the top of my thigh as he stood back up.

We faced each other, right next to his bed, and not only were our clothes removed, but everything else between us was gone too. How had I ever hated this man? I didn't hate him. Not at all.

Our eyes met, and we stared at each other for a moment. He pushed me toward the bed, and so I climbed onto it and lay in the middle with my head on the pillow. Then he climbed over me. When we were face to face, he said, "You're so beautiful, Vanessa. But now how do you feel being naked in front of me?"

"It's easier because you're naked too."

"Ah? See." He kissed me on the mouth; a quick peck. "How nice it is, not arguing or competing. Being nice."

"Are you going to be nice?"

"I am always as nice as you let me."

"In that case, I want you to show me how nice you can be."

He waggled his brows and moved down, stopping to kiss briefly each sensitive part. His mustache raked against my skin. Then he was there at the absolute most sensitive part, which he found and gently took into his mouth for a kiss as well. It happened fast, in a few deft tongue movements. A rushing, pleasant agony that escalated to an eruption. My vision blurred and the world went white for a blissful second. A brief, fast explosion of sensation that made me pant and lace my fingers through his hair.

When the waves within me subsided, he crawled over me until we were face to face again. "I know how to be very nice."

"I can see that."

We stopped talking then. And after a few deep kisses nudged my my legs with his knees and nestled his hips there. Then he pushed in slowly and kissed me on my neck. It was a lovely, invigorating feeling that only became more pleasurable as he moved. What was at first like scratching an itch became so intense I began to lose myself completely in it.

He stopped kissing me and we were face to face as we moved together, closer than we had ever been. Though it occurred to me then that I'd been in his face many times by that point. When you are that close to a person, every emotion bares itself in the flicks of the eye and the ticks of the jaw. I had glimpsed his vulnerability so many times, and now here it was, on full display. Mine was too, I imagine. Something primal and animal took over then until I was lost in another explosion that sucked me from my body completely. I moaned involuntarily, and he silenced it with a kiss. I was breathing heavy but quiet and pliable as he kept going. And so I watched him close his eyes and grimace before he pulled away and his body clenched as he finished on my stomach. I was too physically spent to wince or say anything about this unexpected completion, but I was pleased that he didn't leave all of that inside me. He rolled away and lay there panting for a few moments before getting up to find a towel. He cleaned me off and got back into bed, curling into where I was still flayed and limp.

He brought his face close to mine and whispered, "Are you still here?"

"I am." I turned to face him, though I wasn't sure how to look him in the eyes. I just did it.

I smiled, and he smiled too. "I like being naked with you."

"I like being naked with you too, it turns out."

"Good. Because I hope that we can stay like this a while longer."

And we did. For quite some time. Long into the night. Until we had seen what could happen in many different ways.

He was asleep on his stomach, arms curled under his pillow, breathing slow and steady when I got out of bed. The sheet had slipped down, exposing the broad plane of his back and shoulders. After marveling at his sleeping form for a moment, I dressed and crept from his room to mine in the dawning light. Once inside, I opened my curtains to let in the pale new day. I undressed again, having only put clothes on in case I encountered an early riser in the hall. I hadn't, thankfully. I would not flout propriety completely just because I'd lost my virginity. Not that anyone cared much about that. I didn't, but I'd lived with all sorts of girls who'd had all sorts of experiences. And I'd heard many stories about how it might go. I was pleased that it had been so satisfying and fun.

But in all the stories about sex that I'd heard, no one ever told me that it involved looking deep into the other person's soul. I had seen Benoit in a way I'd seen no one else. And he'd seen me. That had felt more exposing than having his face between my legs, exposing in ways that I had not been prepared for. I had never been so vulnerable in my life. I had never given of myself or taken from someone else in that way. It had all been quite stirring, and I still wasn't sure what to make of it. This was why it was best for me not to wake him before I left. I wasn't quite ready to face it.

I had a friend at the Saint Genevieve's who was my age, older than most of the other girls. She had arrived a year after me. But she had been with a boy before, a neighbor she grew up with in the hayloft of his barn, before she was orphaned. She told me they agreed to marry when they both came of age. She said she couldn't imagine marrying another man after what they'd done, and I had thought at the time that she was being a sentimental fool. I believed sex was a purely physical act. So why, now that I'd done it, did it feel more than physical? Why did it feel like one of the most important things I'd ever done? I had never been precious about my virginity. The nuns, because the girls had come from such a range of backgrounds, had to be practical about it. But now that I'd done it, the world did look brighter somehow.

Chapter Thirteen

Over the next few days, Benoit and I slept together many more times. Every night in either his room or mine, and once during the day after an argument about who should call the office. It had been both exhilarating and unseemly. A blissful stretch of days focused on only his body and mine. Sex. Who would have guessed.

One night, after we'd finished and were catching our breath, he propped himself up on an elbow to face me. "I don't want one of us to quit if the other one gets the job."

"What?"

"Remember? We agreed that if one of us got promoted over the other, then the one who didn't get it had to leave."

Of course I remembered. "Why? Do you know something?"

"No. No. I'm just enjoying working together so much that I don't want a silly agreement to be taken seriously."

I didn't want to talk about work. As close as we had gotten so many times during that handful of days, we hadn't talked much about what we were doing or what it meant, professionally and certainly not personally. It was as if the future didn't exist. As if nothing mattered outside the two of us when we were in the throes of it. And we were so often in the throes that conversations about problems were easy to put off and ignore. I wanted to continue ignoring it now.

I rolled onto my side so we were lying face to face. Under the blankets, I found his chest and placed my hand over it.

"Fine. You don't have to leave *L'Entreprise* when I get the promotion." Honestly, if I got the promotion, I wouldn't have any trouble being his boss. I learned in his bed just how easy he was to tell what to do. No trouble at all.

"But what if I get it? You won't leave?"

I would never have any credibility if I were having a relationship with my boss. That was if I managed to hold onto the rage that would surely result from him being picked over me. I would never be able to work with him again, let alone be in the same building.

I moved my hand down his stomach and scooted closer. He hardened as I stroked him, ending that conversation before I had to answer. When I stretched to kiss him, the topic was forgotten. Or at least we stopped talking about it.

And, fine, I must admit that part of the reason we hadn't talked about work and what would happen when we got back to Paris was that I intentionally kept him from bringing it up. Instead of arguing, I distracted him with sexual acts. Instead of talking, I dove headlong into the other thing.

That part was fabulous. He worshipped me unabashedly and with enthusiasm, always kissing and petting and marveling at me in bed. And then he suppressed all of that bubbling heat into little more than glances when we were with Apolline or out working.

The closeness happened every time. It was different each time and not always so intense, but it was there. The becoming vulnerable. The full show. Allowing him to see. I was still not used to this. While I enjoyed it, it also scared me. It was a dangerous feeling. Something that could destroy me if I let it, and so I was determined not to. We would stop as soon as the trip was over. Everything would be different back in Paris. Vacation would be over.

Cabourg was a temporary detour from the usual way of things. Back at home, back at work, there was no way I could continue sleeping with him. The fact that our jobs were still at risk only made this more so.

To be honest, the only regret I had in those frolicking days at the hotel was not sleeping with him sooner. I had wasted so much time and mental energy trying not to give in to this man, when I could have been enjoying myself with him the whole time.

Sex also kept me from thinking about the fact that I hadn't heard from Charlotte or Nadine. Nadine and I had parted on decent, though tenuous terms, much of which depended on Charlotte. There had been plenty of time for my letters to reach them and for them to respond, unless they were not responding. Or unless they weren't sure what to say, what to decide about me. I desperately wanted reconciliation, but every time there were no messages from Charlotte, I had to confront the possibility that she might not forgive me. And if I wasn't able to reconcile with my friends, then what kind of person did that make me? I was sure not a good one. Cold was my first thought.

Sleeping with Benoit did not make me feel cold. Quite the opposite. Again, the perfect distraction.

Two nights before our scheduled departure, Apolline, Benoit, and I were having dinner at our usual table. Work had gone well over the trip. Surprisingly well. Benoit and I had each filed the same amount of stories. And the way we'd collaborated on them all had made everything we sent back to Paris much stronger and better to read. We worked together like a team. And we had nearly finished the job. When we were done talking over what we had left to do, Apolline excused herself and went up to bed.

This had become my favorite part of the day, when all the work was done, and we were finally alone. I wanted to climb across the table and into his lap. Imagining this, the satisfying way I would fit straddling him, the feel of his dinner jacket under my hands and the awareness I'd surely experience of the hard body underneath all those clothes. It was such a strong, compelling vision that I gulped down the rest of my wine.

I waggled my eyebrows at Benoit. "Are you ready for bed as well?"

He bit his lip. "Can we have one more drink before heading up?"

"Of course," I said.

"I've enjoyed these past few days, Vanessa." He smiled harmlessly. Something was bothering him.

"I have enjoyed them as well."

"I am glad to hear that. Because I want us to continue enjoying ourselves, each other, when we go back to Paris."

"That would be nice, but it's not possible. You live with your family, and I'm not allowed overnight guests. Where would we even go?"

He held up a hand to stop me. "I'm not talking about that."

"Then what are you talking about?"

"Vanessa, darling. I want to come to your home and present myself to the woman in charge there, who in this situation acts as a guardian on those kinds of matters, right? And I want to present myself as a suitor."

"What?"

"I will bring flowers and send letters and romance you, Vanessa. That is what I want."

"Flowers? That's ridiculous, and you know it."

He slumped like I'd hit him. "Why?"

"Because we are enjoying each other on this trip because this is not real life. It's the beach. It's a strange blip in time in which our interests aligned. Going back to Paris, back to everyday life, our interests don't align there. This won't work in Paris."

"No, perhaps creeping from hotel room to hotel room won't work in Paris. But we are good together, Vanessa, and no amount of time with you feels like enough. And that's not going to change no matter where we are. For me, this is not a blip in time, but a beginning of something that could be life-changing for both of us."

I sat there listening to him say all these decidedly wonderful things that I had not considered. The idea of him arriving at 77 Rue de Fortuny with a bouquet of flowers and kissing the hand of Madame Tremblay was both intriguing and unthinkable. "I'm not so sure I'm looking for life-changing, Benoit."

He sighed but didn't say anything. He sipped his drink, and then he reached across the table and took my hand. He held it there for a long time, looking at me so intensely and sorrowfully that I had to avert my gaze. His hand was big and warm. I'd grown accustomed to the feel of it, but still every time he touched me it was a thrill. Then he pulled his hand away and swallowed the last of his drink.

"If you'll excuse me, Vanessa, I believe I'll turn in early tonight. I'll see you tomorrow at breakfast as usual."

"Wait. What?"

"I'm off to bed."

"Well, do you want company?"

"No. I don't. And I think it's best that we end that part of our relationship."

"You're breaking up with me?"

He looked so hurt. "Vanessa, you can hardly call it that."

"We have two more days before we have to go back to Paris." He wasn't making any sense.

"For someone who is so observant, Vanessa, you are being frustratingly obtuse." Anger tinged his voice. He leaned in close and said, "I am not comfortable with the arrangement you're proposing. You're using me for sex, and it doesn't feel good."

My breath hitched. "I thought we were using each other."

"I told you that first night that there may come a time when I asked you for more. This was it, Vanessa. And you have declined."

"You're right. I have." I don't know why I said this. Even as the words left my mouth, I recognized how indignant and selfish I sounded. My behavior was poor; but I'd said it anyway. There was venom in me that escaped sometimes even when I didn't want to be so harsh.

"And I misjudged you, for which I am very sorry." There was a pained crease in his brow when he stood, nodded, and walked away that I very much regretted.

I sat there dazed for a minute. Then I got up to follow him. But when I reached the lobby, he was speaking with the concierge at the front desk. I hesitated because the affair had to end. We couldn't carry on; this was what had to happen. Wavering would only weaken my stance. Some distance was perhaps called for, an evening apart, time to sort out my feelings. We could talk about it more in the morning.

In my room, I lit the lamp and undressed and curled into bed. It would do me good to spend a night alone. Everything was fine. We still had two days. This wasn't really over.

But then it was over, because the next morning he was gone.

When I joined Apolline at breakfast, before I was even seated, she told me that Benoit was on his way back to Paris. "He got a message late last night and had to go home."

"What? He didn't tell me."

"I bumped into him when he was on his way out this morning and told him I'd pass the word along." Apolline spooned jam onto her slice of baguette. She was wearing her linen suit, this time with a crisp white shirt. "He was in a hurry to catch the first train. He should be getting on it now."

"Did he tell you what happened?"

"His mother fell, it sounds like. He wasn't sure how bad it was yet."

"It wasn't for work?" Sadly suspicion was always my first reaction. But that was how I kept myself from heartbreak: by pretending I didn't have one. "Or because he's mad at me?"

"No."

"Do you believe him?"

"Believe him?"

"Yes. Do you think his mother really fell?"

Apolline recoiled. "You think he lied to me about something like that?"

"No. I guess not. But he'd been trying to talk to me about work. And supposedly our editor is leaving soon." Even as I explained this to Apolline, the problem sounded thinly contrived. "I'm just saying that, if he was called back for work, it could be that something's happened. A big decision has been made."

"I don't think so. He said his mother fell, and I believe him."

"I suppose I do too." I unfolded my napkin and placed it in my lap. Then I swirled milk into my coffee. When I looked up, Apolline was gaping at me. "What?"

"I thought you liked him?"

"You did?" We'd not acknowledged our affair in front of Apolline. "What gave you that idea?"

"Are you mad, dear? It's obvious. You two are always bickering in that flirtatious way." Apolline straightened her shoulders. "Plus he told me you'd been spending time together."

"Oh, did he?"

"He did. Not details or anything. He was asking for advice."

"Advice about what?" My words came out sharp. I was surprised that Benoit had spoken to Apolline—anyone—about me or us. That anyone could know.

"What to do when you like someone and she doesn't like you back."

My mouth fell open. "And what did you say?"

"That it was obvious you liked him back."

"It is not."

"Oh, it is too." She pursed her mouth. "And now I have an even clearer view of the problem."

"And what problem is that?"

"That you're unable or unwilling to admit how you really feel."

It was impossible that Apolline had cracked the code on me. And yet she had summed it up quite neatly. "So you think I've pushed him away?"

"No. I don't know what happened. Did you push him away?"

Had I? I had. But what I didn't understand, at least not yet, was why. "I have to work with him. That makes things difficult."

"You're right. It does. But for some people, work isn't everything." Apolline bit into her baguette.

"It feels so risky. Letting myself hope for anything but work. I guess because I can control it a little better."

"My dear, have you learned nothing in the past few weeks?" She wiped her mouth with her napkin. "Our stable workplace was disrupted because some man with too much money decided he wanted to buy it. Nothing is under our control. Nothing. Not really. No one knows for sure what's going to happen."

"I never would have predicted that I'd be engaged in any sort of non-work dealings with him. Of all people."

"I don't see why not. Sure, a man from work is never ideal. But no job is permanent. That may be difficult for you to understand because you're young. I've worked for four different publications in twenty years."

"What about long marriages? You have one of those."

"I do. Because we choose each other over and over. No newspaper will do that for long. They get rid of you as soon as you're too expensive. What's important to me is having someone along, no matter what the world dishes out. It's better that way."

"It doesn't exactly sound romantic."

"No," she said thoughtfully. "But it still is."

We finished our breakfast, but before leaving the table, Apolline said, "You know, if he does get this editor's position over you, I wouldn't take it personally."

"Why?"

"Well, you're an ambitious woman. And I don't want you to take what I'm saying the wrong way. But you may have had a chance before we were bought. Now, though, if it's between you and Benoit, and his lot are making the decisions?" Apolline shrugged. "Then you might be wasting your time wanting something you don't have a shot at getting. Not only is he a man, he's their man."

"I appreciate your candor, Apolline."

"Something to consider."

So it was just me and Apolline for the next two days.

The last story I was working on was about the Grand Hôtel, which had been written about a thousand ways already by every publication in Paris. And it was grand, to say the least, stretching along the shore like a seaside Versailles. The lobby was draped in burgundy curtains and a dazzling crystal chandelier hung in the center. Every night, the dining room was like the Paris social scene relocated. But a diplomat who kept a place outside of town held weekly gatherings that thinned the hotel crowd on those nights. I visited the hotel twice before I found a unique story to tell about the place: I followed their main attraction stage performer through the course of her regular day and wrote a profile about her. She was a singer from a hamlet outside of Lyon who was passing through on a tour that would take her to London and eventually Oslo.

Apolline and I followed the same routine as we had been, except without Benoit. He didn't show up at breakfast or knock on my door before dinner. He was never there in the hallway. I didn't bump into him in the hotel lobby or pass him on the street when we were out working. An older couple moved into what had been his room. My swims in the ocean were less invigorating. My work felt less interesting, less sharp. Apolline and I didn't talk through our stories or bounce ideas off each other. He was gone, and everything about the trip dimmed.

Though I did get to know Apolline quite well.

"I believe my daughter is a lesbian," she announced with very little preface over dinner on the last night at the hotel. Now that it was just the two of us, we were seated at a smaller table by the bar. We couldn't see the pianist anymore because of a large potted palm tree, but he was playing something tinkling and soft.

"What makes you say that?"

"My husband caught her with the neighbor's maid. He's been absolutely beside himself about it. That and she says she'll never marry; been saying that for years."

"And how do you feel about that?"

"Worried, mostly. I fear she'll suffer greatly for it."

"So, and this is a selfish question perhaps. But why did you suggest introducing her to Benoit? Why did you talk about how marriageable she is?"

"Just because she's a lesbian doesn't mean she isn't marriageable."

"Well, no, I suppose not."

"And she's like all women. If she isn't in a good marriage to a decent man, then who will keep her safe?"

"Can't she keep herself safe?"

"I suppose she could. But she would have to be in the right position. I don't think she's cut out for journalism, and I've done everything I can to teach her to draw without it catching on in any professional way. But she'd be a wonderful mother."

The server came and cleared our dinner plates. He offered coffee, and we accepted.

"At first, I admit, I thought you might be a lesbian," Apolline said when he'd gone.

I laughed. "What do you mean?"

"I mean you disliked Benoit so much that I thought for sure you had to be one of those girls who isn't interested in men at all."

"I'm not a lesbian, Apolline. There's nothing wrong with that, but I'm not."

"Well, I know that now. After a few days it was pretty obvious that you felt the opposite of how you let on about Monsieur Levin."

"What exactly was obvious?"

"My dear, I've never seen a pair of idiots more in love than you two."

Love?! I was surely not in love. I definitely couldn't fall in love with him. Because falling in love meant getting married and having children and family responsibilities in the best case, and constant heartbreak in the worst. Even if people agreed not to have children, children still had a way of coming. After the way we'd carried on for those handful of days, I could have been pregnant already. I would have to stop working—the only thing I've ever really, truly loved and excelled at—to take care of his children. Our children, but still. Maybe it was different when you fell in love. Maybe, when you fell in love, it didn't feel like you were giving anything up. Which was why I never wanted to do it.

What Apolline probably didn't understand was that people are unreliable. They are selfish and cruel. They move on from things. They put people in bad positions, often unintentionally. And even the best people, the ones who love us, have to go. They die. Or they get sick. Or they get pulled away from us for this or that reason. Or they stop talking to you as soon as you aren't perfect. I could not attach myself to anyone. No one ever really belonged to me, could ever be fully relied upon. My parents, who'd loved me completely, left me. If I fell in love with him, I would lose myself and everything I worked for. I couldn't let myself do that. It would ruin me.

But I did miss him. Unfortunately, even in his absence, I had plenty of time to think about Benoit. I thought about everything, replaying our intimacies, our conversations. Longing might be a more appropriate description than missing. A mundane pallor fell over the hotel and the town and even the beach. The sunsets were less colorful. The tufts of clouds less striking. Even Apolline wasn't as enthusiastic about much without Benoit's invigorating presence. Though I will admit that the train ride home went much smoother without him. I missed him so much that I was beginning to wonder if Apolline was right. That no matter how much I didn't want to fall in love, it was too late. Maybe I already had.

Chapter Fourteen

The backyard was empty when I returned to 77 Rue de Fortuny. The tomato vines in Cook's garden stood taller and bore more fruit than when I'd left. What remained of the lettuce had flowered. I clicked my tongue to draw out the cat, but she didn't come.

Cook was in the kitchen, getting ready to run her errands, when I came in. After hugging me and asking me about my trip, she said, "I've got some bad news, I'm afraid. I haven't seen the cat in five days now."

"Oh, no. Do you think something happened to her?" I hadn't thought much about the cat while I was away, but I'd never fathomed she wouldn't be here.

"I don't know. I keep leaving out a dish for her, and it goes untouched."

Cook and I talked for a few more minutes about what might have become of our kitty and what we might do to lure her back. Perhaps she hadn't thought as much of us as we thought of her. Or, god forbid, something terrible happened.

"Don't worry too much about her," Cook said. "She's a smart kitty. And she survived just fine before finding her way to us."

Cook left to run her errands then, but the news of the missing cat dampened my return.

I found my mail stacked on the table in the foyer. None of the letters were from Benoit. Or Charlotte. I trudged upstairs and didn't encounter a soul on my way to my room. The place was in a rare, though not unheard of, state of quiet. After the clamor of train travel all day, I didn't mind.

My room was exactly as I'd left it. My stacks of papers were all still there, including one of Benoit's work on the nightstand. Everything I'd been reading and thinking about before the trip felt like another life. A different person had read all his stories in that stack. It was foolish, but my first thought was that of course I was a different person. I mean for goodness sake, I had lost my virginity! I had been thoroughly ravaged. Ravaged by the wrong man—there was no such thing as the right one—but ravaged nonetheless. Of course, I was a changed woman.

This had to be why I couldn't stop thinking about Benoit. About how lonely I had felt since we parted ways. The feeling like I wanted to tell him something but he wasn't there. Looking for him in every room I entered. Wondering what he'd think or say about this or that. Wanting to hear him laugh. The sensation of his hands on my body. The sensation of standing next to him. The sensation of him being in the room. This was because of the physical intimacy we'd shared, nothing more serious or detrimental to my way of life than that.

The agonizing part was that we hadn't talked after our argument. Had I known it would be so long before I saw him again, I wouldn't have said some things. I would have worked harder to contain my impulsive negativity. And so I was looking forward to seeing him at work and having a chance to break the silence.

That night at dinner, Nadine and Madame welcomed me back warmly. Diane and Catherine still had family in the city—even more family than there'd been when I left, apparently. So they were having dinner out.

"I've heard from Charlotte," Nadine said with a bright smile. "She's engaged to the vicomte's son! She's coming back to the house to stay for a few months until the wedding. And he's paying for everything."

"That's amazing!" I was genuinely happy for Charlotte. Relieved as well.

"It is." Madame, who sat at the head of the table in her usual spot, nodded approvingly.

Nadine passed the chicken to me. "She doesn't hate you, you know. But she's mad. And if she hasn't written, then it's probably because she's still trying to figure out what to say."

"I understand." And I did. I wanted the absolution that would come with Charlotte responding to my letter. But that was a selfish want. Being forgivable had to be tied up somehow in accepting Charlotte's timeline for forgiving me. I would have to be patient. I chose a slice of breast meat and passed the chicken to Madame.

"I believe Catherine will be leaving with her family when they go," Madame said as she accepted the dish from me. "Back to America."

"Will she? Did she say that?"

"She did. It's why her family came in the first place."

"Diane's not going, though?" Nadine asked.

"Last time I saw her, she insisted she wasn't," Madame said. She was wearing one of her plain work dresses, but she'd taken off her apron and fixed her graying hair in a fresh bun for dinner. "But one can never say with Diane."

Diane seemed never to be satisfied or tired. She'd had several different jobs since moving in and it hadn't been a year. She'd always struck me as a frivolous sort of person. But since *L'Etoile* took over *L'Entreprise*, I appreciated her ability to keep going after a setback. And, as Apolline had said, not everyone cared so much about work as I did. Work wasn't everything.

"It will be strange without Catherine," I said. She was always up for anything, and she'd often accompanied me to shows I was writing about. It was hard to imagine the sisters living separately. "I've grown quite fond."

"Well, she didn't come here intending to stay," Madame said. She poured wine into each of our glasses as she spoke. "I'm more surprised that Diane isn't going too."

"I suppose that's true."

"Catherine doesn't have it easy." Nadine wrinkled her nose. "She fancies her step-brother. He's here too."

"Oh," I said. "I think she told me about him. Or at least I knew there was someone back in America. But a step-brother? How tragic."

"I don't think he's really a step-brother. I think he's her father's fiancée's stepson."

"Interesting." It took a second to work through all those steps.

"He came all this way," Nadine said. "To get her back."

Madame tutted. Like me, she held herself above romantic notions. Though one of her letters to me in Cabourg had mentioned dinner with Monsieur Gauthier, which made a total of two confirmed dates with the same gentleman.

It was certainly a romantic gesture: transatlantic travel. Not that I needed anything like that. Quite the opposite, in fact. Benoit and I didn't need such gestures because romance had nothing to do with it. Staunch as my view on that was, however, I was still thinking about him. I had admittedly imagined a bouquet of flowers on my desk when I returned to work.

Dispelling my pervasive thoughts about Benoit Levin had been my motivation for sleeping with him in the first place. I had anticipated that the act would make him less interesting, would release the mental hold he had on me. But that hadn't worked. And even though I was back in Paris, far away from the hotel in Cabourg, he was on my mind.

The next morning, my first day back to work, I dressed smartly in my new split skirt and my favorite white blouse. After sleeping in my own bed and sifting through my emotions, what I really wanted was for Benoit to still want me. I refused to believe I was in love with him. Even if I was, I could talk myself out of it. A small and barely acknowledged part of me was coming around to the idea of us continuing our affair in some way here in Paris. Not flowers and drawing rooms, for sure, but a little something. An occasional friend, maybe? And I felt mildly guilty about what he'd said about using him for sex. I hadn't meant to make him feel bad, and I hadn't exactly chosen my words correctly when I was trying to explain it to him. The only thing I knew for sure was that I was confused—about my feelings for him, my feelings about everything, how to proceed, what I really wanted, and what he meant when he said all the things he'd said. I couldn't bring any of this up at work, of course. But maybe we could meet afterward for dinner.

Cook had already gone to the market by the time I came down, and there was still no sign of the cat in the yard. But the heat of late summer seemed to have broken in Paris, and there was a hint of cooler weather to come. My bicycle ride to work, in my new riding garments, was just as wonderful as I'd hoped. I'd missed my usual rides through the streets of Paris, waving at the familiar people, the rumble of my tires on the pavement, the ding of my bell. As much as I had enjoyed traveling, being home was pretty great too. Maybe it was the existence of both that made the whole traveling endeavor so grand.

When I reached *L'Entreprise*, I steered my bicycle into the service yard and parked along the edge of the loading bay. Work was the same and different all at once. The familiar smell of ink and paper that permeated even the lobby. The click of my shoes on the stairs and the cool marble handrail as I ascended. But there were faces I didn't recognize, desks in places I didn't remember them being. More of the business of combining two publications.

Benoit wasn't in the pen. My desk was empty, and he wasn't seated at any of the others. I had beaten him in. Either that or whatever happened to his mother was serious enough that he was still engaged.

I went to the editors' office to check in with Vartre, who would be the only one in there now that Paquin was gone. When I reached the open door, though, Benoit was inside. He was sitting at the desk. There was only one of those now. And he had the same clean, freshly dressed morning appearance that I'd become so achingly familiar with over the past few weeks. His brown hair was smoothed into place. His jawline was freshly shaved, his mustache neat. But his eyes, when he looked up at me, seemed tired.

"You're back," he said and stood abruptly, like I'd caught him in some devious act.

I was still trying to determine what exactly I was looking at. "I am. Where is Vartre? And why are you sitting in her desk like it belongs to you?"

He put his hands up, as if he were surrendering. "Vartre is gone. She left while we were still in Cabourg."

I swallowed hard as this revelation sank in. Had he double-crossed me? The sickening realization roiled inside me. I'd been even worse than a fool. "So this was why you had to rush home. To assume the position."

"No. My mother fell. That was why I had to leave. They gave me the editor position yesterday."

"Why did they do that? Why didn't they wait for me to come back?"

He opened his mouth, but nothing came out. Like he didn't want to admit to something.

"Was this the plan all along?" While I'd been concerning myself with feelings and affection, he'd been getting promoted. "I was never in the running for the job. And you made me promise to quit when you knew I wasn't going to get the job anyway."

"Vanessa. Now that's not fair. I didn't know I was going to get it when we made that deal. And I regret making it; I've already said as much."

"So when exactly did you know the job was yours, then?"

He hung his head. "I wasn't sure until I got back, but Vartre told me it was probably mine a week ago."

Hot rage rushed through me. "And you let me carry on thinking I still had a shot? You despicable bastard."

"Vanessa. Please. Let me explain." His words were tinged with desperation, but also an aloof coolness. I wasn't getting a warm welcome from him; so much for flowers on my desk. "Vartre was leaving; she didn't know anything for sure."

"And you slept with me—seduced me!—knowing full well that you had what I wanted. The whole time!"

"Vanessa, darling," he scoffed. I'd offended him. "You're making this all sound much more sinister than it really is. And you had to know that I was the more likely candidate. The paper you worked for is gone. The people I have worked for for years are the ones running it now. They chose me over you. They know what I'm capable of, and they picked me. I'm sorry that you didn't get what you wanted, but I'm not sorry to have this job. I need this. My mother needs care."

"I can't believe you. You were working against me this whole time."

"Vanessa, we were working against each other. What would you have done differently if the situation were reversed?"

I didn't answer his question. I was too busy being self-righteous to consider it. Instead, I stepped closer so I didn't yell. "I had sex with you. Something I've never done with anyone else. And you knew it would come to this."

"Forget about our deal, darling." He changed tack, trying to appease me. "It was stupid to make that deal. I was playing around. I don't want you to quit. I want you to stay here and do whatever kind of work you want. Whatever moves you. I want to give you creative freedom."

"But with you as my boss. The man I slept with. No one in this place will ever respect me."

"But no one has to know." He threw his hands in the air, frustrated. He also checked his volume. "And we're no longer sleeping together, remember? What happened in Cabourg stayed in Cabourg. You said yourself that it couldn't come to Paris."

"That is such bullshit, Benoit. I can't work for you. You know I can't. I came in here this morning thinking we could reconcile in some way. My head full of romantic notions that we could keep seeing what happens. I was changing my mind. And you were setting me up to fail."

Benoit's brow creased and his mouth pulled in a stricken line. His blue eyes pled with me not to take this personally, to reconsider. Even troubled, his face was one I wanted to hold in my hands and kiss. But I should have known better. People were unreliable. They let you down. They hurt you, even when they don't mean to. I knew better. Still, I'd let him get to me. He'd tricked me. Or he held something back from me. And we'd had a deal. Leaving this job that I loved so much, that I'd hung so much hope on, was the last thing I wanted to do, and now I had to do it. I couldn't not do it. Regardless of the timeline of our relationship or this professional outmaneuvering, I had to quit.

When I turned away from him, he came around the desk and reached out a hand to stop me. "Vanessa, I understand why you're upset, but you've got the situation wrong."

I recoiled from his touch.

"Vanessa, wait. Don't leave like this."

"I quit, Benoit." I was unreachable in my anger and offense. "You knew when you kept this from me that this is what would happen. And now it is happening. You win. I quit."

My heart galloped as I charged out of his office, down the hall, and across the pen. I didn't keep anything at the paper. The desk where I wrote didn't even technically belong to me. It was just where I sat when I was here. And so my departure from the building was swift and clean. There was no box of personal effects to pack or emptied flower vases to awkwardly carry out. I just picked up my bag, slung it around my shoulder, and walked back downstairs. My job had been everything to me for so long that I never imagined how efficiently it could be gone. No physical cleaving required. No tricky detachment. I just walked out, retracing the steps I'd only taken minutes before on my way in. It was an unceremonious departure that was so easy it hurt all the more.

And the whole time, running my hand along that cool marble banister, shoes clicking on each step as I descended the stairs, I wanted nothing more than for him to come running up behind me. I didn't care about the job or who got to be the section editor or any of that. I wanted him to try to catch me. The hardest thing about crossing the lobby and pushing out that back door one last time was that he wasn't coming. That I'd messed it up so bad he was letting me go.

I rode my bike all the way back home, parked it, and made it up to my room before my crying started. Crying that lasted for the rest of the day.

By that evening, a strange numbness had settled over me. I thought about doing something to remedy my situation—like looking for jobs or making flyers for the missing cat—then became so overwhelmed that I started crying again.

Nadine must have heard me because she knocked and then opened my bedroom door. "What's wrong? Can we talk?"

"Oui." I sat up, wiped my eyes, and smoothed my hair. It didn't stop my tears from welling.

She stepped inside my room and closed the door behind her. Almost as soon as she sat beside me, I crumpled again. "Is this about Charlotte?"

"No. Not really. I mean, what I did to her is part of it. I quit my job this morning. The same job I was so obsessed with keeping that I did something so horrible to someone. To Charlotte." I sniffed and choked on tears as I rambled. The more I talked, the more I cried. "And I know it all turned out okay between Charlotte and the vicomte's son, but that doesn't undo the fact that I did it in the first place. I did a terrible thing. I'm a terrible person. Maybe not all the time, but sometimes I am. I hurt people because I was so obsessed with my work. And it was all of no use because I quit."

My shoulders quivered, and Nadine put her arm around me.

"Oh, dear. It will be all right. You're not a terrible person. You did something you regret, and you'll learn from it. That doesn't make you horrible. You're a work in progress. We all are." She let me cry, drawing firm, reassuring circles with the palm of her hand between my shoulder blades. "And don't worry about work. You'll find something else fast enough. And maybe Charlotte can help? She knows the people at that ladies magazine."

"If she doesn't hate me." My words came out in a bursting sob that didn't stop or ebb for several minutes. Nadine let me cry and kept rubbing my back.

Several minutes later, she said gently, "Vanessa, it will be okay. You aren't unforgivable."

Another sob clenched me. I wasn't unforgivable. It was such a simple thing to say, but it meant so much to hear. I had been bumbling through everything since the newspaper was taken over. It was like that crumbled and took out everything else in my life with it. Everything was gone. Everything I'd worked so hard to achieve. Everything that had been at risk since the paper was bought. All my worst fears had come to fruition. All the worst cases that had been lingering on my horizon for weeks were here now and fully realized.

"So why did you quit your job?"

"Remember what I told you about the paper being bought and combined with *L'Etoile*?"

"Oh, yes, and that handsome man who wanted the same job as you."

I nodded and wiped my tears on my well-used handkerchief.

"What happened?"

I explained everything to her then, about how that miserable trip somehow became so incredible. And how that made everything else so much worse.

"So I quit, because I am mad at him and because that was our agreement." An agreement that he did try several times to annul, in all fairness. When it came right down to it, I'd lost my position and a significant source of income and personal pride in a hot, passionate flash. I had always thought of myself as level-headed, practical person. I had never concerned myself with frivolous entanglements or romance. And yet I had just quit my job—the thing I loved most—over a man. Something very terrible was happening to me, inside me. Apolline's words on the train kept circling around in my mind: *I've never seen a pair of idiots more in love than you two.* I certainly felt like an idiot.

"And you told him that you don't want to continue the affair now that you're back in Paris?"

"Yes."

"But you were having a good time, it sounds like. And now that you aren't coworkers, it might be okay."

"No. That's definitely not a good idea."

"Why not? The sex is no good?"

"No. I mean yes. The sex was good. It's not that."

"Then what is it?"

"I'm still mad about work. And I can't fall for him. I need to forget about him. That's what this whole mess is about. That's why I slept with him in the first place, so I'd stop thinking about how much I wanted to. Now, I guess because he was my first, my feelings are confused. But I most definitely should forget about him."

"Well, Vanessa, that's not going to happen if you don't get out of bed."

And so my mission, from that moment on, was to forget about him. What happened in Cabourg was staying in Cabourg. It was over. A blip in my existence that was over and completely unrelated to anything else in my life.

"How do you forget about a man, Nadine?"

"I'm sure we can figure it out! But start by cleaning up your face and coming down for dinner."

Chapter Fifteen

Nadine had a number of ideas for forgetting about a man. And she had theater tickets, so she insisted we start right away. After dinner, she got dressed and then came to my room to help me. Nadine said I should wear the magenta dress because if I was attracting attention, then I would be too busy to dwell on a past lover. I wanted desperately to believe her, and so every time I looked down at myself, I pushed the memory of Benoit's face and his words—*you look stunning*—from my mind. Every time I put him out of my mind, I got one step closer having him gone completely. Didn't I? Surely, sometime soon, this would work.

We caught a cab on Avenue de Villiers. As it conveyed us to the Cartier Theater in the Latin Quarter, I told Nadine about my bathing suit and swimming in Cabourg. I left out the part about being in the water with Benoit.

The theater was a small, smoky, bohemian place with aging burgundy damask wallpaper and black beaded lanterns. And while the operetta did distract me temporarily, it was a romantic comedy, and the happy ending brought thoughts of Benoit spiraling back. Of kissing him in the ocean. Of the deeply satisfied, very pleased-with-himself look on his face after that first time together. The sound of his pleasured groans. The feel of him in my arms.

Nadine knew several of the actors in the company, and so after the show we agreed to meet them at the café across the street. We arrived first and had our drinks when the lively troupe of actors and musicians came pouring in about twenty minutes later. They were scrubbed clean of stage makeup and in plainer clothes than their costumes had been. Nadine introduced me to everyone, and any friend of Nadine's was a friend of theirs. It was easy to be part of their boisterous group because they all wanted the spotlight, and I could simply watch and enjoy.

Nadine and I were at the bar getting our second glasses of champagne when she put an arm around my shoulder and pulled me close to whisper in my ear. "My friend Henri likes you."

"What? How do you know?" Henri and I had gotten into a conversation about cats and my missing one. He was handsome and had kind, suggestive eyes. And he liked cats.

"He told me that he thinks you're pretty." Nadine cocked her head to the side and raised the perfect red arches of her eyebrows. She was wearing a silver gown. Her hair comb had a black silk flower on a long wire that arched up over her pile of red hair and quivered as she nodded encouragingly.

I laughed. "I told you it's the dress."

"Maybe. But he's fun. Why not talk to him?"

I ventured a look back at our table. Sure enough, he was watching me. Our eyes met; he smiled and held his tumbler of liquor aloft. I turned back to Nadine. "If he thought you were pretty, would you be talking to him?"

"Oooh, good question." She squinted while she thought about it. "I know him better than you, which admittedly includes a reputation for taking women to bed. But I don't currently need the services of a man to wipe my slate clean."

I laughed again. "I don't need my forgetting to come with chlamydia."

"So don't sleep with him! Just go talk to him. Let him flirt with you."

"Maybe you're right."

"I'm definitely right."

"Fine."

When we went back to the table, I sat next to Henri, who gave me all of his attention. He'd played the male lead in the operetta with enthusiasm and convincing vigor. He had a deep, room-filling singing voice. And it was nice, especially after cataloguing all these positive attributes, to have his attention and obvious affection. He listened to the shortened version of my career drama. I left out the part about Benoit. And Henri asked with genuine interest what my plans were now that I had left. When the conversation lulled, he leaned in close and said, "You look stunning in that dress."

Something inside me squeezed. And definitely not because I was thrilled to hear these words from this actor. Did he have to say it like that, word for word? Again, I decided not to think about Benoit.

I took a fortifying gulp of my champagne and smiled and desperately tried to adopt a flirtatious air. "Tell me about being an actor, Henri. A leading man."

He carried on about getting the role and preparing for it. He was dressed in a burgundy dinner jacket with an elaborately tied mauve cravat. His black silk top hat sat in front of him on the wobbly table. Every time he moved to emphasize this or that drama in his story of being an actor, the table tipped where one leg was uneven. I sat and listened to him. I asked questions to keep him going. A few times I thought he'd make a good interview for a story. If I still had a job. He would be perfect to write about. The whole production deserved some press, in my opinion. But none of my professional ideas really stirred me the way work used to. It felt shallow and uninteresting, and it wasn't enough to keep my thoughts from wandering. A part of me wasn't there—not at that café or even at the paper. A dastardly part of me was still back in a hotel room in Cabourg with Benoit Levin. All the while, Henri carried on.

"They say, Vanessa, that the key to playing a romantic lead is convincing the audience to fall in love with you alongside the love interest character."

"Is it?"

"So tell me. Did you fall in love with me a little tonight?" He looked so earnest; truly a talented actor.

"Oh, Henri, I'm not sure that I did." It would have been much easier if I had.

He frowned so dramatically that I wondered how much of his story of himself was also an act. "Perhaps you like me enough to join me at my place after this?"

Here it was, the very thing that might actually erase the feel of Benoit's hands on my skin. But the answer was a resounding, respectful no. He took it in stride. And Nadine and I went home.

The house was dark and quiet. We came in through the front and went straight upstairs.

"Did it work? Forgetting him?" Nadine asked before we went to our rooms.

"Maybe a little."

I slept well that night and awoke with a renewed sense of purpose. Instead of languishing in bed, I got dressed and went downstairs to breakfast. I was still thinking about Benoit, admittedly, but I was also dressed and ready for the day, which was proof that I was at least making some forward motion. My mission was showing progress. My job and Benoit may have been gone, but I was moving on. However, I wasn't exactly sure what moving on should entail.

When she found me lingering after breakfast, Madame Tremblay asked if I wanted to help her with errands, and I jumped at the chance.

The flower market, though I rarely had reason to go, was a wonderland of blooms. Stall after stall of roses in every color, bundles of lavender and daisies, bouquets of carnations and sunflowers and hydrangeas. Perfume from each flower hung and mingled in the air.

When we came to a seller with mums the colors of spices, Madame threw up her hands.

"Oh," she exclaimed. "The first signs of autumn. They're so pretty. If I buy two, Vanessa dear, will you carry one?"

"Of course."

Madame crouched down for a better look at the flowers, muttering to me and herself about which plant to choose. When she stood up, she asked what color I liked.

"The purple is my favorite."

"I agree. We'll take these two." Madame furrowed her brow. "Do you mind if we come back for them?"

"I can give you an hour," the vendor said. He was a short man with a straw hat and clean canvas apron. He smiled and chatted with Madame while she paid him. Then we were off again.

Madame was a consummate housekeeper. She liked to keep a few bouquets around the house and came to the market every week. The fragrance was heavenly especially on a warm summer day. And it was a pleasure being with her while she did this work she loved. She'd been giving me a short course in flower arranging all morning. I wished I'd brought a notebook and pencil so I could take notes for a story.

I had been playing around with the idea of pitching some pieces. That's what Charlotte did. She wrote fiction—short stories and serials—that she submitted, and I had begun to think I could do the same with lifestyle stories. Benoit had talked about his experience with this, selling ideas to the news agency and specific publications. Along with my income from my trust, I could maybe do that instead of get a job at another publication. The freedom might be nice. It was different, but maybe doable. My idea of success was starting to change. Instead of being the best in the office, I could design my work around my life.

"Madame, did you always know you were meant to do what you do?"

"What do you mean?" We were perusing a stand of dahlias so perfect they seemed unreal.

"You know, keep the house, make it nice. Buy the flowers. Did you always know you wanted to do this?"

"I don't think I did. At least not at first. My husband and I had plans to travel more, maybe live abroad. His father died, then, and we put it off to help his maman with the house. Now that she and my husband are gone too, I can't imagine myself doing anything different. At least not anymore."

"Why?"

"Oh, love, I suppose. I still love him too much to get rid of the place." We moved on to a rose stand, where bushels of petals and bouquets of every color were on display.

Love. I wondered what it would be like to make a life with Benoit. How that would be so different from anything I'd ever imagined. "How did you know you were in love?"

"In the beginning?" Madame raised a bouquet of blush roses to her nose. Her eyes rolled back in her head. "Oh, that's heavenly."

"Oui. How did you first know?"

"I don't think it was instant. And maybe I didn't know until I was too deep in. I just kept wanting him around. And he kept wanting me around too. I never had to doubt that. He just became the person I always wanted to talk to."

Madame grabbed two more bouquets of the same roses and was ready to go. She went to pay and then started haggling over some greenery, while I watched a couple on the other side of the booth. The woman had her arm linked casually in the man's, comfortably possessing him. And he was obviously delighted to be possessed. They were discussing something, and she smiled up at him with such an achingly sweet, dreamy look that an agonizing sense of loss seized me. I was back in that chilly water, so close to Benoit's wet, underdressed body, and he was smiling at me with that same open affection. He put me right in his pocket in that moment there in the ocean. I slept with him the first time that night. And then after all that fun we had, he told me he wanted me, and I told him I didn't want him. He was the one who got called away, but I was the one who fled. And still, I was constantly looking for him in every crowd, around every corner. Had I been wrong? Was I in love with him? Oh, god, anything but that.

When we made it back to the house, armfuls of flowers in tow, there was a letter for me on the table. I recognized the *L'Entreprise* stationery and Benoit's handwriting and stopped short. I put down the flowers and picked up the letter. He'd written to me. Finally. I didn't realize how much I wanted to hear from him until right then. I tore open the letter, desperate to see what he'd written, what feelings he'd profess after all these days. But as I read, my heart sank.

Vanessa,
I hope this letter finds you well. I regret that our last meeting ended so poorly and with your departure from L'Entreprise. I have a vision of what the culture section can be, and I would like another chance to make you a part of the team. Can you come to the office for a meeting to discuss this opportunity?
Sincerely,
Benoit Levin, culture section editor

My hands shook, and the air felt thick in my lungs. I had been squirming around in my feelings for days, and he wrote to offer me a job? I read the short, business-like missive again and again, searching for some subtext or sign of romance. There was nothing. Every sentence included words like "team" and "opportunity." I had been hoping for, waiting for him to appear, ready to put everything that had happened behind us. But he wasn't going to do that. The letter was maddening to read. And it paralyzed me with a different question: how to respond?

I didn't. Not for days. I went out every night with Nadine or Diane, flirted with men and danced until my feet ached. I went to cafés and saw shows. Nadine introduced me to new people, who were interested in me and curious about my work. I tried as hard as I could to be energized by the commotion of my life. And I was, a little. But largely, I found that no matter where I was or what I was doing or who I was talking to, every thought in my mind was about Benoit Levin and what I wanted to say to him about his stupid job offer.

Did I want to go back to work at *L'Entreprise*? No. Oddly enough, that wasn't the problem. I wasn't going to work for Benoit. *L'Entreprise* wasn't the same paper any more. The publication, the place I loved, was gone for good. There was nothing left for me there. I wouldn't crawl back to an institution that would never truly support me. I was moving on.

Finally, I got up one morning, mildly hung over and yet crystal clear, and I wrote to him. No, thank you, was the gist of the letter. If he wanted to be cold and professional, then I could be cold and professional. I was a master of cold and professional. Not a problem at all. And it did feel good to get that out of the way. That left only the disappointment that he'd written me about work and nothing else. No feelings. No longings. No yearning. I was the one doing all of that. After thinking for so long that work was most important, suddenly it wasn't anymore. All I cared about was Benoit. I was mad and maybe in love and confused most of all. And I had no clue if he still cared about me.

There was still no sign of the cat, so after posting my letter, I went out on my bicycle and rode toward the river. I followed it across the city all the way to the twelfth arrondissement. Saint Genevieve Maison des Filles Immaculeés sat on a quiet, tree-lined avenue not far from the Place de Bastille.

The orphanage was housed in a long, stone building that stretched out like an open arm from the side of a pointy church. I parked my bicycle in the portico at the entrance closest to the offices and went inside. The cool, hushed halls were empty, but the sound of children playing carried in from the courtyard. When I asked if Sister Clothilde was available, the tidy receptionist, who was new since I'd last been there at Easter, asked if I had an appointment.

"I don't, but I used to live here, and she often sees me without one, if she can. I won't keep her for long."

"Ah, of course. She's in her office."

Sister Clothilde was reading when I knocked on her open door, and like always, she wasn't surprised to see me. "Vanessa, my dear, come in."

She stood and greeted me with a cordial pat on the arm, and then she ushered me into the seat across from hers.

"Merci, Sister."

"You look well." She watched me as she retook her seat. The worn wooden desk between us was bare except for a stack of files. A simple wooden cross loomed on the blank white wall behind her. "I saw in your articles that you were at the beach. How grand that must have been."

"It was. But I've recently left the paper."

"Oh?" She listened and nodded thoughtfully as I explained most of what had happened at *L'Entreprise*. And most of what happened between me and Charlotte. I was not the sort of person to confess my sins to a priest, but Sister Clothilde had served as a repository for my guilt and problems on many occasions. When I got to the part about being jobless and not knowing what to do next, she told me not to worry so much about that.

"Having a goal and a focus, as you've always had, is important for a person. It is fulfilling to work toward something. It gives us meaning and purpose. But breaks are okay too. Not knowing what to do next is okay. We sometimes need these fallow periods to gather strength and prepare."

"Yes. I know. It will work out soon." I looked down at my hands folded in my lap.

"Is there something else bothering you?"

"Well, maybe. Yes. There was a gentleman, at the paper. He went with me and the illustrator to Cabourg. And we grew quite close… romantically."

Sister Clothilde nodded and squinted her eyes, like she was trying to gain a clearer picture of the situation I was describing. Romance wasn't exactly her area of expertise.

"We were in competition with one another, essentially. And he won. He kind of cheated, but not really because the game was rigged in his favor the whole time. His paper was the one that ate ours, you could say. And he's a man. Anyway, when I found out about this, it upset me. A great deal. I blamed him for everything. I don't think I was wrong for doing so. But I can't seem to let go of it either."

"I see." She smoothed her hands across the desk. "And what is it exactly that you can't let go of?"

"Well, him, really. I can't stop thinking about him."

"You know, dear, that blaming people who are important to us can be quite troubling. And if you blame this gentleman for how things transpired, then I encourage you to consider what you would have done if the situation had been reversed. What if the game had been rigged in your favor? What would you have done? And sometimes we find, especially in the people worth keeping, that right from wrong isn't always clear."

"How do you know if a person is worth keeping?"

She scoffed. "Vanessa, dear child, I have known you for many years. You have always been hard on yourself and just as hard on others. And I have seen you struggle to form alliances. It is always you against the world. So even though I have never met this gentleman and don't know a thing about him, the simple fact that you're here bringing him up to me must mean he's the sort of gentleman worth another chance."

I nodded and swallowed a lump in my throat. She was right, of course.

"And it can be frightening, especially for someone like you who has lost so much, to be vulnerable and trust in other people. But relying on others makes us stronger, not weaker. And forgiving is as much about freeing ourselves as it is about freeing those we forgive."

I nodded again. "You're right."

"Oh, goodness, now that's something I'm not sure I've ever heard from you, Vanessa Marnet. Admitting I'm right?" Sister Clothilde laughed. And then she yelled through the door to the receptionist. "She says I'm right, Sister Amie! Can you imagine?"

"Ha!" Sister Amie called back. "They don't usually say that, do they?"

"That's how we know you're all grown up." Sister Clothilde smiled at me.

We chatted for a few more minutes, but she had an appointment with the priest. She hugged me, and then just before we parted ways, I remembered the other reason I'd come. "Can I borrow the printing press?"

"Of course, dear. It's right where you left it."

The tabletop press and all my supplies were, as she'd said, tucked in the storage room cabinet. I cleared the end of a long table and set everything up. Then I arranged the type on the plate and got to work.

An hour later, I rode back across the city with a stack of flyers in my bag that read:

Tuxedo Cat Missing from 77 Rue de Fortuny
She's obstinate and only loves us for our table scraps, but we miss
her terribly. Please send immediate word of any sightings.

I handed one to every person I passed in the neighborhood, and left one in every shop. No one had seen the cat, but everyone promised to keep an eye out for her. Chances were she'd be close. Probably mooching off some other house full of soft hearts.

I think Cook was half convinced that the cat had left us for a more luxurious situation. Someone had taken her inside, maybe. Or she'd set up in a yard with more rats. This was a possibility, and I told myself that I would accept the cat's rejection if it were the case. Passing out flyers was important even if it only brought the knowledge that the cat was happy and well somewhere. But something told me that she needed me. So I looked for her under every bush and in every garden I passed. I even looked up into the trees, just in case she'd gotten stuck.

There was a letter from Charlotte addressed to me waiting on the table in the foyer when I returned home. Finally. After taking the last few flyers down to the kitchen for Cook, I went up to my room and opened it.

Dear Vanessa,

It's fine! I mean, it wasn't fine at first. And it wasn't fine for a while, which is why you haven't heard from me. But it's fine now. Please, let's just put this behind us. I feel like your sincere and wonderful apology letter has healed my heart. And the potential of our friendship is more valuable to me than revenge or spite. I hope that we can be friends.

Nadine tells me you've moved on from the paper. And to prove that I come in peace, I have already written to my editor at La Fronde to tell her about you. Her name is Anais Blanchet. I think you should send her something. Something fun. And use my name. I won't be back for another week, but she's expecting to hear from you.
Charlotte

I sighed with relief and then sat down to write her back. Her letter lightened my spirits dramatically. I didn't want any hard feelings. And her words were genuine and quite generous. It reminded me of Nadine telling me that I wasn't an unforgivable person. I would be a fool not to keep Charlotte as a friend, even if I didn't always know exactly how to do it. I could be better. Once I finished a letter to Charlotte, I spent the rest of the day and most of the evening writing an essay about swimwear fashion. I wrote it with pen and paper, then I rewrote it and had it ready to send to *La Fronde* with the morning post.

Chapter Sixteen

I was straightening a cabinet for Cook later that day when Madame called down to the kitchen that I had a guest. As I came up, there was a small woman in a navy blue skirt and striped blouse chatting with Madame in the foyer. It was Apolline.

"Bonjour, Vanessa." She greeted me with la bise and passed me an envelope. "I brought you something."

Tipping my head toward the drawing room, I asked if she wanted to sit.

"I can probably find you some coffee," Madame offered.

"Oh, no, merci. I've been out running errands all day, and now I'm eager to get home."

Madame stepped away, leaving us there in the foyer. The envelope was as large as a full sheet of paper, looped closed with a piece of string.

"Those are pictures from our trip," Apolline said. "I took some to Benoit as well."

I nodded and turned the package in my hands. I needed to open it, but something made me hesitate. Here was Cabourg, finding me in Paris again. "You're still at the paper?"

"I am. Though it's quite different these days. You're not the only one who has moved on."

"Do you see Benoit there often?"

"I do." She nodded at the envelope, still unopened in my hands, and perhaps read my mind. "You don't have to open it now; I have to run anyway. Just thought you'd like to have it."

She turned to go then, and I walked her down to the door. "It's nice to see you. So much has changed that Cabourg feels like a dream."

"Oh, yes. Back to the real life. Have you found work then?"

"Maybe. I sent a pitch to *La Fronde* this morning. My housemate has written for them before and promised to put in a word on my behalf with her editor. I have other ideas that I didn't get to at *L'Entreprise* that I might try to place elsewhere. And I've even been thinking about traveling more, maybe writing about that."

"That's good to hear, Vanessa. You seem to be doing well."

"Well enough, at least now. I did spend a few days crying in bed. Now I think it will be okay."

Apolline patted my arm. I opened the front door and walked out with her. The sun was high and warm. Madame's purple mums were holding court on the stoop.

"Well, dear, if I hear of any opportunities, I'll let you know."

"Thank you." We were on the sidewalk now. "Does he ever mention me? Benoit?"

She smiled knowingly. "Not usually. But when I gave him the pictures, we did talk about you for a moment."

"What did he say?"

"Oh, that he was sorry about you leaving. He also mentioned that you two are no longer speaking. He seemed to regret that too."

None of this was revelatory. But what did I want him to say to Apolline? They worked together. Still nothing I'd done had effectively put him out of my mind, and I wanted to know if he was suffering too. Or if I had ruined it.

Even after everything Nadine and I had done to help me forget, Benoit Levin was all I could think about. I was as sad and bereft without him as I was the day he left Cabourg so suddenly. The ache was familiar now. I had not awoken one single morning and not wondered about him. I had not gone an hour without coming across something I wanted to tell him. Nothing had worked. In that moment, there on our stoop, I wanted Apolline to tell me what to do. She didn't, of course. She just patted me on the arm again and then stepped into her waiting carriage.

I held off opening that envelope until I was upstairs in my room. But as soon as I closed my door, I unwound the string and unfolded the flap. Inside were three photographs. One of Benoit and me walking side by side, coming out of the water. Waves lapped at our knees. Again, I didn't regret that bathing suit one bit. I looked fabulous. And he was looking at me, smiling conspiratorially. My eyes were downcast, but I was obviously smiling. There was a shadow of delight on my brow.

The next picture was of us sitting on opposite sides of a bench. I didn't even know she'd taken this one. We had been arguing about something, which was why he was sitting so far away from me. The image captured so much. My face was turned upward and away, completely unaware that he was staring at me, smiling with the same abject affection and regard. It was emanating from him. Oddly, I remembered having the argument, but not what it was about. The tenderness in the way he was looking at me surprised me. But here it was, printed on Apolline's chemically reactive paper.

I had been a fool not to acknowledge his feelings for me, or to keep it at a distance—whatever I'd been doing. He really meant what he'd said about wanting to be with me here in Paris. This wasn't a fling for him. But when he tried to tell me that, I brushed off his feelings. When he had been vulnerable, I had closed him off.

I had pieced together a picture of our last few interactions. It was clear that we had miscommunicated. I didn't handle emotional moments well, it seemed. Whatever he knew about what was happening at the paper, it had been bothering him. He'd tried to talk to me about it. Then he'd asked me for something I wasn't ready to consider, that I hadn't even fathomed. And I messed it up.

I had been so disappointed by the lack of emotion in his letter. I'd been wondering why he hadn't come for me. Why he wasn't standing outside my window or tying bouquets of flowers to my bicycle or writing me heartfelt letters. But I'd been stupid about that too. He hadn't come begging me to reconsider because I hadn't given him any reason at all to believe he'd succeed.

And it had all gone to hell over a job. I let it happen. I even made it happen. I was the one who walked out of there and refused to listen. I didn't regret my choice to leave, but I had been wrong about not hearing him out. I was wrong for shutting down. Because I was undeniably in love with him. Love! And love was not something I could think myself out of or persist against.

The third picture was another I hadn't noticed Apolline taking. In fact, the background wasn't familiar to me at all. She must have taken it when I wasn't around. It was of Benoit, dressed up and smiling in what was a fine portrait. He was staring right at the camera, so when I looked at the picture, he was looking right back at me.

I can't exaggerate the agony I felt seeing his face. Not only was I in love with him, but I'd been so cruel to him, that there was a chance he wouldn't love me anymore. He may have ruined me, but then I ruined everything. I lay on my bed and curled into a ball, staring at that picture of him until it was time for dinner.

That night was Catherine's last in the house. She was going home to America, and so, except for Charlotte, who was still in Vernon, we were all dining together one last time. Catherine and Diane had been spending most of their time at the hotel where their family was staying. It seemed so strange to be losing one of them because they were always a pair. Diane was staying on, and she was no longer engaged, even though she was never really engaged. A long story, as it always was with Diane.

"Are you excited to be going home?" Nadine asked her when we were all seated around the dining room table. Even Claire and Cook were there—they were always welcome to join us for dinner, but they usually ate beforehand so they could clean up and finish their work.

"I am. It's been so long. And I never intended to stay away." Catherine had dark eyes and long, light brown hair. She was slightly taller, slightly thinner, and ever so slightly prettier than her sister, a burden that Diane bore in good spirit.

"So will you marry your step-brother?"

"I don't know about that." Catherine blushed. "But I'll resume my life there. And then maybe we can get married one day. Maybe."

"Have you told your parents?"

"No. No." She shook her head firmly. "We don't want to say anything until we're sure. Can you imagine? Telling our parents that we're in love and then not getting married. I couldn't do that. So, Diane, don't mention it, please."

"I'm not going to mention it." Diane scoffed. Her dark brown hair was swept up in a mass of curls and she was wearing a new red dress. Their father had taken them shopping. "I've been keeping it a secret for this long. And you don't need to worry about me. I'll be on the other side of the Atlantic, remember?"

Catherine, who was also in a new dress, smiled at her sister condescendingly and then turned to me. "How's it going since you left your job?"

"And why did you leave your job again?" Diane asked. She'd been absent for most of my professional and personal mess. "I thought you loved that place."

I sighed. Work wise, I was fine. I was actually a little relieved not to be there suffering through that terrible takeover. It was over now. I didn't have to worry, and I had a better grasp of my opportunities. It was almost silly how little any of that mattered to me anymore.

"I did love it. But I've recently been the victim of a shocking revelation: I am in love with the man who would have been my boss, if I'd stayed."

Everyone at the table looked at me like I'd lost my mind. Even Madame and Cook were giving our conversation their full attention now.

"You're in love with him?" Nadine purred. She'd been unsatisfied with the results of her efforts to make me forget Benoit. Her eyes were wide, as if she'd not considered things were this serious.

"I know exactly how you feel," Diane said. "Did you tell him?"

"No. In fact, I told him quite the opposite because I was being so foolish about everything. And now I don't know how to undo the whole mess." Ending things had been all my idea. But it had been a terrible idea. In all matters dealing with that man, I had been a fool from the word go.

"Have you written to him?" Diane asked. "I've been writing to Guillaume every day in hopes that he'll forgive me. He's still at the beach with his family. Cabourg—the same place you went, Vanessa. His family goes every year."

"Oh," I said to acknowledge the coincidence. Diane was exactly the kind of person I could imagine spending a summer at Cabourg. "But I'm still coming around to the idea of being in love. I didn't think it was possible, to be honest."

"Oh, Vanessa," Nadine said. "You're not that cynical."

"I really might have been." My face crumpled, and I swallowed hard to fight back the tears. So many tears. Where did they all come from?

"Oh, honey," Madame said soothingly.

"Do you think that losing your virginity to someone can make you feel unreasonably attached to the person?" I pushed out the words between sobs like I was begging for them to be true.

Madame's gaze swung heavenward, and she put a hand over her heart. I wouldn't normally bring this sort of subject up at dinner. But my feelings had become an unruly force within me.

"But you haven't mentioned him in days. I thought you were doing so well," Nadine said.

"Just keeping it to myself."

"I had no idea."

"I was trying so hard. I really was. But today Apolline came by, that's the illustrator who went to Cabourg with us. She brought me a few pictures she took with her camera while we were there."

"Can we see the pictures?" Diane asked.

"Yes, we need to see the pictures."

"After dinner, maybe?" I said.

"No, I think we need to see them now," Nadine insisted.

"I would like to see them too," Madame said.

It took a beat for me to realize they really meant now. I ran upstairs and came back a minute later with the envelope. I passed it to Nadine first. And while she opened it and flipped through the pictures, I refilled my wine glass.

"Oh, dear. You two are adorable, Vanessa." Nadine looked at the top picture—the one of us on the bench—and then passed it to Catherine, who was sitting next to her. The second was the picture of Benoit and me coming out of the ocean. Nadine gasped. "God, look at this. This is your bathing suit? You have to let me try it on."

After a close look, she passed that one on and came to the third, the portrait. "Ooh la la. He's handsome, isn't he?"

"Don't I know it," I said.

"Oh, let me see that one," Diane said with her hand out. Nadine passed it to her, and the pictures made their way around the table to everyone.

"So what now?" Nadine said. "You're having second thoughts about wanting to forget?"

"You could say that." I took a drink of wine. "I just don't know what to do?"

"Be more specific," Catherine said. "You don't know what to do about what, exactly?"

"I'm in love with him, even though I don't want to be. And I'm so confused that I'm not even sure why I don't want to be in love with him anymore. Then if I am in love with him, what should I do? He probably hates me."

Nadine held up the picture of him looking at me from across the bench. "This man doesn't hate you. Anyone who looks at you like this will at least be willing to hear you out."

"So I should talk to him."

"Yes. There is no one else you should be talking to about all of this but him. Tell him how you feel. Tell him how complicated it all is. See what he says."

"But how should I approach him to say all of this?"

"Writing is not enough, especially if he's here in Paris," Diane said.

"You know where he works," Nadine offered.

"No. I can't go back to the newspaper office. I left there in a huff that I don't want to undo."

"It's not exactly a professional conversation."

"Should I go to his house? It's not far."

"You know where he lives?" Nadine asked. Her brown eyes were bright with ideas.

"I do." It was strange having everyone's attention at the table, having them all talking about me and my problems. I preferred to be the quiet observer, and the dinner was supposed to be about Catherine. But this time I didn't brush it off or even want them to talk about anything else. And it reinforced what Sister Clothilde had said about having people around us who make us stronger. I did feel stronger being there with all those women trying to help me.

"What if you show up and he's not there?"

"His family will be there. I met them."

"Maybe it should be more romantic?" Catherine said. "More meaningful than knocking on the door."

"There's nothing more romantic than a straightforward, well-intended call during appropriate hours," Madame chimed in.

"You're right. But I left it quite poorly with him." For Madame's sake, I didn't say that he said I'd used him. "When it comes to him, I've been wrong about so much already."

Hating him had been my decision from the start. I made him my enemy when all he had really wanted was to get closer. All of my reasons for doing so had fallen away. And before, when he told me he wanted to still see me, I didn't think that's what I would want. I thought I would come back to Paris and be my same self. But I was not the same at all. I was completely different. And this new version of myself was very unhappy with the previous version's decisions. Again.

"Something bigger, then, to make more of a statement," Diane said dreamily. "Oh! Like an ad in the paper pronouncing your affection."

"Maybe start small."

"I still think a visit is the best approach," Madame said. She stood and picked up a handful of dishes to take them downstairs. "I've got an early start, mademoiselles."

Cook and Claire followed her out to start cleaning up.

"We'll all bring down our plates," Nadine said as they filed out.

Diane turned to me. "So what will you do?"

"I think Madame is right. I should go to his house." I needed to jump on my bike and go to him. I needed to tell him how I felt.

"Will you go now?" Diane asked.

"I don't think you should go now," Catherine said, eyeing her sister. "It's been over a week, hasn't it?"

I nodded.

"Then it would be a little dramatic to go rushing over so late."

"She's right," Diane relented. "First thing in the morning, you should go to his house."

"I agree," Nadine said. She rose and started stacking her plates to carry down. "And ask him on a date. Then that can be over-the-top romantic."

"So what should the date be?" I stood too.

"Oh, that part will be easy," Nadine said, dismissively.

"Oui!" Diane clapped. "This is Paris!"

Chapter Seventeen

It was raining the next morning. A gray blanket of low clouds covered the city in an indecisive drizzle. Despite the poor weather, I got up and dressed and went down to breakfast. My plan to find Benoit had hardened into determination overnight. And a calm steadiness and assuredness burned inside me. I would find him, hopefully at his house, and tell him how I felt. I had sorted out all my conflicting and assorted feelings into a clear arrangement of hopes. I hoped he'd be there. I hoped he'd see me. I hoped he'd be willing to hear me out. And I hoped that I still had a chance.

After my coffee and baguette, I set out on my bicycle for Benoit's house. I rode up Rue de Fortuny and down Boulevard Malesherbes. Then I took Boulevard des Batignolles all the way to Benoit's neighborhood. It was Sunday, so the streets were clearer than usual. The rain, though misty and light, showed no signs of stopping. Not the best bicycling weather. But I'd waited so long. It had taken me all this time to understand myself and what I needed to say. I didn't want to wait any longer. Even waiting for a cab seemed like an unnecessary delay. And I needed the bicycle ride to burn off my nervous energy.

It only took a few minutes to reach Benoit's apartment on Rue Blanche. I hurried inside the street-level door just as the rain started to pick up, and I left my bicycle at the bottom of the stairwell. I was damp, but not soaked. I paused for a breath when I reached the top of the stairs. The door on the landing seemed different, though I couldn't say exactly how. I hadn't committed it to memory. Or now I was looking at it from a completely different perspective. A completely different Vanessa. A hopeful woman instead of an annoyed coworker. Loving not hating. How different that made everything.

I raised my fist and knocked on the door. A moment later, there was someone on the other side of it, unlatching and opening. And then there he was. Benoit. Not exactly like I'd left him, standing in his new editor's office; a more disheveled version of him. His hair was shaggy and uncombed. His shave wasn't clean. He was dressed in his shirtsleeves, and there was no sign of a cravat.

"Oh," he said with a combination of surprise and disappointment, which pricked at my heart and confidence. Had I been wrong to come? Maybe he didn't want to see me. Maybe I had really lost him. But I had to try; I had things I needed to say.

"Bonjour."

"Bonjour, Vanessa." He smiled, overcoming the shock of seeing me at his door. "What are you doing here?"

"I need to talk."

He looked hesitantly over his shoulder. "That's wonderful, darling. But I'm not sure this is the best time."

A bang, perhaps a door slamming, came from somewhere inside the house. Followed by a moaning scream that didn't sound childlike.

"Is everything all right?"

"No. I'm afraid it isn't. We've had a rough morning. A rough night. A rough couple of days."

"What happened?"

He looked nervously over his shoulder again and then opened the door wider. "Please, come in."

I hesitated. "I have so much I need to tell you. If now's not a good time—"

"No, no. It's fine. You're here now, and I want to hear what you have to say. It's just that my mother isn't doing well. The woman we had looking after her left a few days ago, and we haven't found anyone to replace her yet. The children have been a terror. And so I'm afraid the house is in shambles."

"How is your mother?" We were inside the foyer with the blue pagoda wallpaper and the pretty green fern, which looked less lush than I remembered it, like maybe everyone had been too busy to water it.

"She's recovered physically from her fall, but mentally she's more distant than she was before. Her confusion has worsened, and she needs constant supervision. She's not even sleeping through the night." He ushered me into a small parlor with a window that looked down on the street. I sat in one of two matching velour armchairs, and he took the other one. "With the caregiver gone, the burden has fallen on my sister, who has the children to look after as well. I've been helping, but it's not easy with work."

"How long is she gone?"

"For good, I'm afraid. She and my sister didn't get along all that well. And she wasn't very patient for someone whose job it was to take care of people."

"Oh."

"But I don't want to bore you with the details. What can I do for you?"

The way he said it was more professional than friendly. Though he was receiving my early, unannounced call with perfect manners, it was not the reception of reunited lovers. I looked down at my hands. I shouldn't have expected anything warmer. I had walked into the midst of what seemed like a family crisis. He had his hands full. I couldn't ask him for more than this. I needed to say what I'd come to say. "Benoit, I'm sorry. About how things between us turned out."

"What do you mean?"

"I mean that things are different now. I am different from how I was when we were in Cabourg."

"You made that quite clear, darling." There was a hint of pain in his words.

"I know I did. And I know I said I didn't want to be with you, as well as some awful things about getting you out of my system and all of that. But I've gained some perspective since leaving the paper—"

A child screaming interrupted me. It was muffled by the apartment's interior walls and spaces, but still loud enough to unstring my thoughts.

He picked up the thread that I left dangling. "After your clipped response to my letter, Vanessa, I'm surprised that you're here."

"I know. I was short. But I was mad." I shifted in the chair. "But I'm not here in a professional capacity. And I don't want to talk about work. The reason for my visit is personal."

Another shriek rang out, this time closer and more desperate than the previous one. And it was followed by another howl, perhaps from a different child.

"Forgive me." Benoit stood, concern creasing his brow. "I better make sure everything's okay."

I stood as well, and instead of waiting there, I followed him through the door. We were in the hallway, almost to the staircase, when another scream came from somewhere upstairs.

He was surprised when he realized I was following him, but he didn't stop me.

"I meant what I said. I don't care about work. I'm here to talk about the way I left things in our personal affairs."

"The personal affairs you ended, you mean."

"Yes, those affairs." We had reached upper floor of the apartment, where we encountered his sister, Rachelle, headed for the nursery where the children were in tears.

"I'm sorry," she said. "I thought they were both down, and I went to bathe mother. I didn't realize you had company."

"It's fine," Benoit said, scooping up a teary, red-faced toddler. And then to me, he said, "We're a bit short-handed, as I mentioned."

His sister smiled at me with faint recognition. She was also more disheveled than she had been when I met her. Her braid had come completely loose on one side, and strands of her dark hair spilled around her face. There may have been some baby spit-up in it as well, but she was moving so much it was hard to tell. "I'm sorry to disrupt your visit."

"I came unannounced. It's completely fine. I don't mind at all." And I didn't. I liked very much getting this glimpse of Benoit's household, this glimpse of his life.

"Well, perhaps Benoit told you, our mother's caregiver departed quite unexpectedly, leaving us in a lurch."

"Our housekeeper helps when she's here. But she's out running errands."

His sister went to put the quieted baby down. "I can't leave Mother alone in the bath any longer."

She tutted at the child, whose face was peaceful though streaked with tears. But as soon as she put the baby down, the frantic crying recommenced.

"Darling," Rachelle said in a tortured voice. "I'm sorry, but I have to check Granny."

Benoit, who was still holding the other crying baby, looked on helplessly.

"Here," I said, surprising myself. "I can take her."

I reached for the child, who turned her pouty little face to me. She regarded me with suspicion. She also, mercifully, quieted. She was light but also solid in my arms. Her brown curls were damp with sweat from her fit, and her cheeks were red and mottled. Her little dressing gown had ridden up to reveal very chubby thighs. I hadn't held a baby since I left the girls' orphanage. It was a familiar weight that human women like myself had perhaps evolved to appreciate. I had read Darwin. I pulled her in close and rested her bottom on my hip.

"What's her name again? I seem to have forgotten."

"Brigitte." Benoit watched me get acquainted with his niece, who was watching me intently and thankfully no longer crying.

"Bonjour, Brigitte. Enchanté. I remember now." I looked at the baby in Benoit's arms. "And this is Claude."

"Oui." He was quiet now too, watching his uncle through teary brown eyes. He had two fine wisps of hair flaring out from behind his ears, and he was dressed in a nautical ensemble that reminded me of my bathing suit. The collar was crooked; a rumpled little sailor. They were adorable children.

Benoit's sister thanked me and begged off, hurrying back to their mother.

And then there we were, Benoit and me, standing in a messy nursery, each of us holding a baby. The rain had stopped now, and the clouds must have shifted, because the room brightened.

It was an odd moment. If there had been any remaining barriers between us, they were all gone now. Completely crumbled. I was seeing him exactly as he was. And he was seeing me too.

"You're a natural." He waggled his eyebrows.

"Stop it. I've had practice. There were plenty of little ones who needed carrying around the orphanage."

"Ah! I could have guessed. Though you never talk about your days at—what was it again?—the Saint Something Maison des Filles Innocentes."

"Yes, something like that." I smiled, so happy to be in his presence. I'd ached for this.

"I wondered if it was an off-limits topic."

"Not for any reason. We just hadn't gotten to it yet."

"Thank you for helping. And I'm sorry our talk has been so thoroughly hijacked."

"You really have your hands full today."

"I do. And for the foreseeable future." He shrugged. The little boy was playing with the collar of Benoit's shirt, quiet and content. Whatever happened to make them both cry had been forgotten. "I will have to start all over with my search for help with my mother."

Just then, a small, wet hand landed on my cheek. Not a slap, but a deliberate touch, as if Brigitte was making sure I was real.

"Oh!" I looked at her brightly. The best idea dawned on me. "I know someone who might be able to help."

We sat on the floor with the children, enticing them with toys while I explained what Apolline had told me about her daughter needing a position. And later, when Rachelle had settled their mother and come back to the nursery, I left to pay a call on Apolline. Needless to say, she was thrilled to see me.

I returned to Benoit's apartment with Apolline's daughter, Collette, a few hours later. She was a sturdy, tall girl with a wide, appeasing smile. By this time, the housekeeper was back from her errands and a thin sense of control had been returned to the home. They put Collette to work right away. And I volunteered to straighten up the nursery—not because I hoped one day I'd have a nursery filled with my own children to clean up after, but because it felt nostalgic. I'd had a nursery like this in my house once, a long time ago. And it was nice to be around the business of a family again, even a family in the midst of a crisis. I put blocks in a basket, folded diapers and tiny shirts, and arranged stuffed animals on shelves, returning the room to some semblance of order.

Later, I found Benoit in the same parlor where we'd started my visit. This time he was smoking a cigarette. He stood when I came in.

"May I join you? Only for a minute."

"Of course." He held out his cigarette case. I slid one out, and he struck a match to light it for me.

I sat across from him. This time we were in opposite chairs from where we'd been sitting this morning when I arrived. "I won't keep you."

"Please. You've been a great help today. Thank you, again, for Collette. I never would have known a solution was so close at hand." He smiled, and his eyes were as sincere as they were sparkling blue. He still wasn't wearing a tie. And his hair still wasn't combed into place. "I owe you one."

"No, please. You don't owe me anything." I smoothed my hands down the front of my gray split skirt, pushing down my instinct to leave without saying it. But I couldn't. "And remember, I told you I didn't come in a professional capacity."

"Our personal affairs, right?" I had his full attention now. "Tell me what you want to say about the way we left our personal affairs, Vanessa."

I took a breath to steel myself. All the words I'd arranged and planned in my head had dissipated over the course of the day. Suddenly, I couldn't remember where I'd planned on starting. So I just started. "I want to take back what I said about not wanting us to… see what happens… between us now that we're back in Paris."

He watched me intently as he smoked, but didn't react or respond.

"I thought that was what I wanted, for us to be done. But I was wrong. Quite wrong." As the words came out, I gained steam. I sat up taller in the seat, looked him right in the eyes. "And the fact is that I can't stop thinking about you. I can't stop wanting to see you and talk to you. I've been in agony for weeks now because I screwed up so badly. I want to take all that back."

"And then what?"

"And then, I want you to come to the door of the house where I live. I want to introduce you to Madame Tremblay. I want it to be just like you said it could be before I messed everything up."

"But what about the job? I should have told you as soon as I knew it was likely I'd get it. I'm sorry about that."

"I don't even care about work anymore. I mean, I do, but not really. Not about *L'Entreprise* or the editor job or any of that. I was using it as a crutch to keep people away, to keep myself alone and safe in my aloneness. It's easier that way, at least it is when you know how painful it is to lose people." I swallowed hard. I didn't want to cry, but it seemed that was all I did lately. "I just don't want to be without you in my life anymore."

He put his cigarette out in a brass ashtray and leaned out across the space between us with his arms outstretched. "Come here."

I rose from my chair, put my cigarette out, and reached for his hands. He pulled me over and into his firm lap. I put my arms around him, and it was such a relief to be so close. He smelled familiar, like himself, but also faintly of baby powder. I inhaled as if I hadn't in ages, and I sunk into him. He put his hand on my chin and tipped my face toward his. He looked at me for a moment, taking me in with his sparkly blue eyes, and then he kissed me, firm and slow, pulling me closer to him, as close as I could get. His mouth opened against mine, pressing deeper, reacquainting, and reuniting after so much time away.

My hands threaded through his hair, and he squeezed my thighs through the layered fabric of my skirt. I was struck with a powerful desperation. I'd been so afraid that I'd never be with him like this again, this close. But now here we were. After so long, kissing him was like drinking water in the desert or coming up for air after swimming under water for a long time. My whole body ignited in his arms. I groaned from the ache.

Then he broke away and said, "I don't want to be without you either."

"I'm sorry. I'm so sorry."

"It's okay." He kissed me again, quieting me. Then he pulled away and looked at me, his mouth swollen and pink. His eyes had darkened. But there was something else there too. It was hesitation. "No need to rush. And we need to talk about things. Being with me might not be so easy, as you have seen today."

"No. That's not true." I put a hand on each of his shoulders and looked him firmly in the eyes.

He looked away. "It is true. You don't want to be tied down. And I am tied down tight."

"So what are you saying?"

"I'm saying we should take it slow. We should see what happens."

I nodded and kissed him again. Another long, insistent, forgiving kiss. I could take it slow. I wanted to strip off his clothes and have him all right there. But that was worth waiting for. We kissed for a while longer, and I told him about Apolline's pictures and my missing cat. And then we parted with plans for a romantic date the following evening.

Chapter Eighteen

The next day, I was outside with my head in the neighbor's box bushes looking for the cat, when a fancy carriage pulled up and stopped in front of seventy-seven. It was lacquered and polished and emblazoned with a crest. I had no idea who could be inside until a familiar well-dressed gentleman alighted. It was Antoine de Larminet; I would recognize that aristocratic air anywhere. He turned and helped Charlotte down.

In the shuffle of pulling down luggage and getting inside, they didn't see me. But I started back toward home. The cat was probably gone, anyway. It had been over two weeks, since before I'd even come back from Cabourg. And I just had to get used to the idea that I would never know what happened to her.

I did hesitate for a moment, though, before going inside. Charlotte and I had written and made peace in our letters. But this was the first time really facing her. And standing in front of a person you'd wronged wasn't easy. Not ever. Vulnerability never was.

When I went in, everyone had gathered in the foyer to welcome Charlotte home. She looked bright and happy in an eye-catching blue plaid dress. She embraced Madame. Antoine de Larminet was smiling and dressed in a light wool suit. They were like a first breath of fall, obviously happy and in love, like the world was theirs. It was in a way. And I was happy for them.

"We meet again," I said to Monsieur de Larminet.

"Ah, Mademoiselle Marnet. It's a pleasure to see you again."

"You as well. Have you both come from Vernon?"

"No, just Charlotte. I picked her up at the train station." Nadine, Madame, and Diane were peppering Charlotte with questions. No one was paying attention to Monsieur de Larminet or me, so after acknowledging this with an awkward nod, he continued. "Thank you again for directing me back to Charlotte."

"It's not a problem. I'm glad you found her. And it was the least I could do, really. I'm sure she told you it was my story in the paper. The gossip column."

"She did."

Charlotte was next to him now, smiling. I kissed her on each cheek. "It's good to see you, Charlotte."

"It's good to see you, too. And I told Antoine everything. But all that's behind us now. I'm so tired of thinking about it."

"And everything has worked out for the best, hasn't it?" Monsieur de Larminet said to Charlotte, smiling like he wanted to eat her for lunch. Seeing them so tender and sweet to each other melted something inside me. And fine, yes, it was romantic.

We shuffled into the drawing room and they told us everything that had happened to bring them together and their plans for the future. I had seen other housemates leave to marry, but I never cared as much as I did now. Charlotte and Antoine were unlikely to start with and had overcome so much that it was remarkable. Seeing them happy together was also profound because this was the first time I ever imagined that such happiness might happen to me too.

That night, I dressed in a blue silk gown, accessorized with a colorful feathery hat that Charlotte let me borrow. Nadine curled my hair and pinned it elaborately to my head. With input from everyone in the house, we planned the evening for romance. I had to defer to Nadine's and Diane's opinions on this, but I did see the value in creating an experience that allowed for the expression of feelings. Benoit did make me feel like a good dinner, like a stunning view. And so making the plans was funner than I expected.

We even discussed—and argued about—who would answer the door when he knocked. They said it heightened anticipation if I made a delayed entrance. Nadine and Diane insisted it might be more romantic for me to wait upstairs. But if Benoit Levin was going to knock on the door, there was no way I was going to let someone else be the first to see him standing there. In the end, I won. And so we were all ready and waiting in the drawing room for him to arrive. When the knock came, I smiled at Madame, and went down to answer it. His familiar shadow darkened the window. I smoothed my skirt one last time, and then pulled the door open.

There was Benoit, handsome as ever. But it was the most remarkable thing: he had the cat tucked under his arm the way one might carry a sack of potatoes or a bundle of sticks. His hand was buried in her furry belly, and her green gaze was judgmental and unbothered.

"Bonjour, darling. Is this your cat?"

I clutched my chest and nearly screamed. "Oui. Wherever did you find her?"

"She was right outside here, on your doorstep. I didn't want her to get away, so I snagged her up in case."

"She never lets anyone hold her like that."

He looked down at the cat, still peaceably gripped in his arm. "No. She's a docile girl."

"Bring her in. She must be near dead if she's letting you hold her."

He brought the cat inside and, upon Madame's insistence, carried her straight down to the kitchen. When Benoit set her down, it was clear she'd lost weight. But her legs held. Her tail flicked back and forth a few times, and she sniffed the air.

"She was just standing there by the door, then?" Cook, as shocked as I was to see the cat after all this time, scrambled to find scraps to feed her.

"Like she was waiting to be let in," Benoit said. "Has she been missing long?"

"Since we were in Cabourg."

"Wow. And here she is."

"Here she is." I bent down next to the cat, and she lovingly rubbed against my extended hand. I scratched her shoulders, which were more prominent now, though not terribly so. She purred loudly and seemed thrilled to see me. Her hair was still fluffy and tempting, and so I took the chance to scoop her into my arms. But she immediately stiffened, wailed, and reared back to swat at me.

"No," I cried, dodging the strike and setting her right back down. "My goodness. She still won't let me pick her up."

Benoit shrugged. He was wearing a black dinner jacket and white tie, smiling as if he'd won the day. "I'm told I have a way with prickly women."

"Oh, you do not."

Back upstairs, Madame poured him a glass of whiskey. And when we all sat down together in the drawing room, Madame adopted an air of seriousness.

"So, Monsieur Levin, tell me about yourself and your family."

I'd never had a gentleman caller, but I had witnessed this same line of questioning. Madame likely had a similar talk with Antoine de Larminet earlier. But she was quite thorough and decisive in her questioning. She could have been a journalist. Benoit, face flushed, answered all her questions.

After taking her last swallow of whiskey, Madame pursed her lips for a thoughtful moment of analysis and said, "Well, I'll be honest with you, monsieur. Your home life would be a large responsibility for Vanessa or any woman to step into as a wife. If that's where your intentions lie."

"You're not wrong, Madame Tremblay. In fact, I have the same concerns." His eyes skipped to me then. The drawn look of his handsome face confirmed this had truly been weighing on his mind. He'd mentioned the same concern when I'd gone to his apartment. But it didn't matter, did it? We hadn't quite reached that point. That could all come later. We had to see what happened.

"They don't have to figure that out right now, Madame." Nadine chimed in. She and all the housemates were there because everyone liked to see a nervous suitor.

"Well, yes, but still worth mentioning in this circumstance. Something to consider. However, I won't keep you any longer." Madame rose, and so did we. "Have fun."

After all the goodbyes, we were out on the street. It was early evening; daylight was fading in earnest.

"So, mademoiselle, what's the plan?"

"If it sounds all right to you, I thought we might walk to the park. Then there's this lovely little restaurant not far from there. And if we are up for it, take a cab to the Tower and go to the top."

"The top of the Tower? Have you been?"

"Not at night. My housemate Nadine went. She said it was breathtaking and the most romantic place in the world. As long as you're not afraid of heights."

"Well, I am not. And I'm sure mademoiselle won't steer us wrong."

I took his arm, and we walked up Rue de Fortuny and down Avenue de Villiers toward Parc Monceau. The carriage traffic was still heavy with people beginning their evening outings. Music playing on phonographs carried down from apartments above us. The breeze whispered breathily through the trees. The whole city was in the mood for love.

And it really was the first time we'd walked together like that. All the other times had been as coworkers with professional boundaries fully in place. Now we were walking simply as two people who enjoyed each other's company. Two people who were falling in love. Letting themselves fall in love. Fall being the operative word, though with his firm, broad arm under my hand, I was quite sure it was worth it.

As we approached the park gate, I squeezed his arm and gazed up at him. When he looked down at me, I smiled. But there was some hesitation in his eyes as well, something that was bothering him.

"There's some truth to what Madame Tremblay was saying, you know. I have a lot of responsibilities that tie me down and could potentially weigh down a wife as well."

I put my free hand to my chest. "Are you asking me to marry you?"

"No. But I'm not taking it off the table unless you tell me to. And even then maybe not." He narrowed his eyes playfully. "You can be so indecisive."

"I suppose I can be. But let's not talk of marriage just yet. Maybe let's work up to that."

"I agree that's the best approach."

"So then why do I need to be concerned about your domestic situation?"

"Because it could potentially affect your life too. Why else?" We passed through the lacy iron gates into the park and followed the wide path. A light, high breeze rustled through the trees. At that hour, almost everyone was having dinner, and so we nearly had the place to ourselves.

"Is having a family such a burden?"

His eyes dimmed then. "Yes, honestly. It is. And I hate to draw attention to it, but it's something I know quite a bit about."

"And you don't recommend it?"

"Ha. No, it's not that. I love my family. But I want what you want for yourself. I don't want you to think of me as some misogynist looking for someone to take care of his house and home. I know you don't want that."

"I wouldn't be here if I thought you were that kind of man, would I?"

"I don't claim to know the depths of your naivety, darling."

"I can't lie to you, Benoit, it's quite deep."

"Well, I don't want to be the man to disappoint you."

"Then don't."

We left the wide promenade for a smaller path under the trees, heading toward the pond. The air was clear and the trees seemed to go on forever. It was a lovely late summer day, a hint of coolness in the air, a suggestion of the coming change in seasons. When we came to the pond, where the marble colonnade stood, we sat on a bench facing the water. The fading sun sparkled and shone red and orange on the reflective surface. A frog started singing from somewhere, then stopped again.

Benoit put his arm around my shoulders, and I leaned into his warm, comforting body. He played with an errant strand of my hair for a moment and then tipped my face up to his. When his lips met mine, I put my hands on his shoulders and pulled him closer. He was incredible. An incredible man who was doing this to me, making me these promises. His breath was sweet and his mouth was insistent. I let my hands wander his body—one up the back of his neck and through his hair, the other down his chest and around his waist, under his jacket, feeling his heat through the fabric of his vest and shirt. This was no longer the kiss of hello. It was the kiss of something more to come. Hopefully soon.

He pulled away to look me in the eyes. "I missed you terribly, Vanessa."

"Oh, my goodness! I didn't know what missing someone was until you."

He leaned back against the bench and resettled his arm on my shoulder. All I wanted was to keep kissing him. But we were in public, after all, even if we were more or less alone with the frogs. But just sitting there with him, gazing at the scene before us, was so calming and fortifying. There really was something to having someone, to being in love. The world somehow seemed less daunting, more peaceful in a way. It was silly, but it was true.

Chez Lunette was a brasserie across the street from the far edge of the park, an easy walk from our bench. While headed that way, I asked about Apolline's daughter and how things were going at home. And he told me what a tremendous help Collette had turned out to be.

"My sister said she prayed last night that she'll stay with us through the duration. And Maman absolutely loves her. They haven't quarreled yet."

"That's wonderful. Do you think it will last?"

"I'm sure there will be some difficulties. There always are when people are involved. But I'm hopeful it will all be fine."

"I am too."

I'd passed Chez Lunette on my bicycle many times, and from that fast moving view, I had noticed dim lighting and lush flowers on every table, couples cuddled together at small tables. But I'd never considered trying it, or I never had the occasion. A narrow awning shaded the door and flower boxes perched underneath the front window. Today they were filled with mums and long green vines of ivy.

The maitre d' led us to a cozy table in the front window, where the darkening park that we'd just left spread out across the street. The server brought our wine and bread and one delicious course at a time. It was simple food, familiar but dressed up just enough to feel special. And dessert was the best part. We ordered and shared a piece of chocolate cake and a slice of almond tart.

As we were finishing up, though, our conversation shifted to work. I told him about the story I sent to *La Fronde* and how Charlotte had mentioned me to her editor there. It was a woman's magazine, run by actual women.

"Do you want another staff position?"

"I don't know. Everything about work has always been so clear for me, but now it isn't clear at all. It's hard because nothing that I was working toward matters anymore. I was going to be someone. I was the first woman reporter at the *L'Entreprise*. But I quit."

"You didn't quit. You broke away from a faulty institution—I'm one of the editors now, I can say that with authority—and you're blazing your own trail."

"So you think it's a faulty institution?"

"I've never denied it. I don't like what they did to your paper. I don't like that they tend not to take women seriously. But the truth is they might never have given you what you deserve." He reached across the table and squeezed my hand; the candlelight flickered in his eyes. "You can do anything you want. You can travel to wherever you want, see whatever you want. And I want to help you do that. I want to give you assignments and let you roam around and write whatever you want about the things you see and the people you meet. I don't want to tie you down to an overwhelming domestic situation, which is all I can offer you if we continue this romantic relationship."

"So why can't it be both, then? Why can't you send me away on assignment and wait for me to get back?"

He smiled with such hopeful joy; it was a smile like I'd never seen on him before. Like I just made his day. Made his life. "I want nothing more than that. If you'll have me. I said as much before."

"That's what I want. Regardless of what I said before. I want you. I want everything you can offer. All of it. All of you."

"Well, you'll have to give me a few minutes to catch up because this is all news to me."

"I am sorry about that."

"I know. You don't have to apologize. It's all in the past. I am so happy that you're here now."

When we finished dinner, we went outside and found a cab. And on the short trip from the seventeenth to the Tower, he made quick work of getting his hand up my skirt. All the passion from those nights in the hotel returned with full force. Only now, there was no question for me that he was what I wanted. A friendship, an intimacy, having him—all of him—in my life, whatever it looked like, whatever job I was doing.

"I'm in love with you, you know."

"Are you? I was hoping you might be, or would be one day."

"Oh, no—it's been going on for some time. And I fought hard. But I think the moment you opened the door to your apartment, when we came to pick you up to go to Cabourg, and you were there in your home, with your family. I think I fell in love with you then."

"You did?"

"I think so yes."

"Well, as you may know, I've always liked you. Ever since I first laid eyes on you at the theater. But I went from attracted to mad with love when you tried to kick me out of your chair at the paper."

"You did not. My behavior was awful." I didn't even like thinking about how terrible I'd been.

"No, no. I knew right then."

"But I was so sure I hated you, and that you hated me."

"I've been hoping this whole time that you'd come around. And now here you are."

"Here I am."

"I've missed you, my darling. Your presence. Your company. Your hands. Your hands touching me. Your face." He kissed me again.

He was right about us, that we belonged together, that I could have everything I wanted, and he could help me get it. He'd envisioned the whole thing perfectly because I would start doing travel writing assignments for *L'Entreprise*. He would become my editor and my husband, and no matter how far away or how fascinating the experiences I had, he was my home. And although I might never have expected it to happen to the likes of me, home would tug at my heart when I wasn't there. Eventually, I would get tired of traveling too, and we would settle down properly then. But it all started with seeing what would happen, over and over again. And deciding he was the one every time.

The Tower had recently been outfitted with electric lights and updated elevators. Benoit held my hand as we took the new elevators from the bottom to the first and then second levels, where there were restaurants and shops for souvenirs. Even in the dark, sightseers crowded the platform. But as we rose from the second level to the top, the city and all the people and hustle and bustle seemed to fall away. There were people around, of course, but together Benoit and I were separate from everything else.

On the observation deck, the wind flowed all around us. And below, the lights of the city sparkled like a sky full of stars had fallen to the ground.

"I don't deny it's breath-taking," I said. "But why is it the most romantic place in the world?"

"Because we're here together. And I get to do this." He pulled me in tight against his body and kissed me until there were no more questions about romance, only the glowing, steady belief in its power.

About the Author

Melinda Copp is a writer based in Bluffton, South Carolina. Her work has been published in newspapers, magazines, and literary journals, including *HuffPost*, *The Rumpus*, *The Cleveland Review of Books*, and *The Petigru Review*.

Melinda has a bachelor's degree in journalism from West Virginia University and a master's degree in creative writing from Goucher College. She writes essays about books, culture, and life in her monthly e-mail newsletter, *Melinda's Letter*. Like a note from a friend, new essays arrive on the first Tuesday of every month. Subscribe for a free short story and other extras here: melindacopp.substack.com.

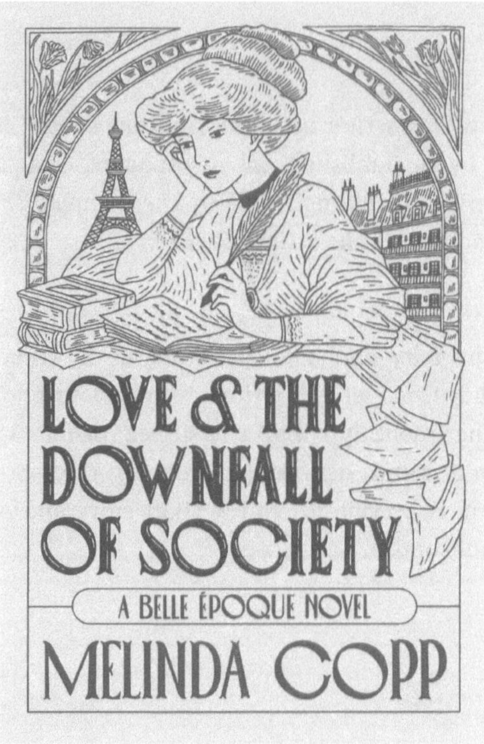

After turning society upside down with her debut story, provincial Charlotte Deveraux arrives in Paris poised for literary stardom. She's not sure where her next rent payment will come from, but she's determined to make a name for herself as a respected writer in the cultural capital of the world.

Antoine de Larminet is the last surviving son of an aristocratic family. In line to inherit a title, he has promised his parents that he'll marry a peer and carry on the centuries-old tradition. He was raised in an antiquated world where love was often found outside of arranged society marriages. Even as the French aristocracy is losing relevance to modernity, Antoine never questioned this commitment to this family legacy—until his chance meeting with clever and beautiful Charlotte.

Their attraction is immediate, and the more they bump into each other at the clubs and salons of Paris, the stronger their attachment grows. But Antoine can't marry Charlotte because she's as proletarian as they come. And Charlotte will lose all credibility as a writer and social critic if she becomes the mistress of an aristocrat.

The world around them is changing, but if love is to win, one of them will have to give up everything they stand for.

Love and the Downfall of Society is available now in bookstores.

It was supposed to be a season in France, but then she decided not to go home.

Diane Talbot is an American in Paris and desperately wants to stay that way. Instead of returning to Woollett, New York, she and her sister didn't get on the boat. Now, nearly a year later, their father's fiancée and her stepson—at Daddy's behest—have come to Paris to bring them home. When they surprise Diane in a compromising situation with French party boy Guillaume Allard, she improvises and claims they're engaged.

It's the perfect plan. As long as she can convince her family that she's getting married and has established herself in Paris, they can't take her home. The best part is that Diane won't really have to get married—not to the man her father wants or to Guillaume.

Handsome and charming Guillaume barely knows Diane. But she's fun, and he owes her a favor. He goes along with the fake engagement, but that's a decision he soon regrets.

As Diane and Guillaume spend more time together, the ruse gets harder to perpetuate, and her family gets more involved. Soon, this perfect solution is far trickier than anticipated, and their feelings for each other have grown so complicated that it can only be love. Ultimately, they're forced to face an impossible obstacle to their happily ever after: he wants a lifelong commitment, and she believes marriage is a trap best avoided.

Complications in Paris is available now in bookstores.

Louise Montmorency Finds Love...

Jilted and scandalized, Louise Montmorency retreats from Paris society to her family's isolated country home in southwestern France. For weeks, she wallows in self-pity and shame, refusing all visitors. Until her cousin and her husband arrive with a strangely compelling companion. But is falling into the arms of another man really the answer to Louise's trouble?

Against the stunning backdrop of the Loire Valley, Louise tells her side of the story as you've never heard it. And she gets another chance at happily ever after.

For a free copy of Louise's story, subscribe to *Melinda's Letter* at melindacopp.substack.com.

Let's Keep in Touch...

Follow Melinda Copp for updates about forthcoming books, new writing, and promotions!

On Substack: https://melindacopp.substack.com/
On Instagram: instagram.com/melindacopp/
On Facebook: facebook.com/melindacoppwriter/

And please consider reviewing this book on all your favorite book review sites. Your review will help new readers discover Melinda's books.

www.ingramcontent.com/pod-product-compliance
Lightning Source LLC
Chambersburg PA
CBHW031025310726
48969CB00007B/1871